Ka
Always laugh:
Tami Jo Riedeman
2007

THE GOLDEN ROAD:
French Wine or Moonshine?

Dona Bakker & Tami Riedeman

THE GOLDEN ROAD: French Wine or Moonshine?

Copyright © 2007 Pastime Publications

Pastime Publications
1370 Trancas Street, #372
Napa, CA 94558
(707) 252-4062
www.napavalleypastime.com

or

KoodB Creations
P.O. Box 614
Sandstone, MN 55072
(320) 245-6949
KoodBwriting.com

ISBN 10: 0-9760276-2-3
ISBN 13: 978-0-9760276-2-1

Cover Illustrations by Lauana Nelson, Finlayson, MN
(218) 349-1949
lauana.nelson@gmail.com

Printed and Bound by Falcon Books, San Ramon, CA

Authors:
Dona Bakker and Tami Riedeman

Dedicated to
Lasting Friendships

Tami Riedeman & Dona Bakker - January, 2007

Chapter 1

"Mabel from Missouri, what's your bid for this beautiful grandfather clock?"

"One dollar! One dollar!" yelled Bernice.

"I'll bid three thousand dollars, Bob."

"The buzzer sounded. "You have all overbid," replied Bob.

"Mabel, you big dummy, I told you to bid a dollar."

Bernice shook her head at the television set, then turned it off. While she did have an unhealthy obsession for Bob Barker, today she felt more restless, like a gas bubble perched on the edge, waiting to be released. It was easy to brood about her pathetic life, knowing that the biggest decision of her day was whether to go play a mindless game of bingo in the cafeteria or stay in her pansy purple room and watch *The Price is Right.* Her only hope of an unexpected rotation in the day's schedule would be a chance encounter with the UPS man.

Bernice mused to herself, "I could invite him to our next Jell-O social event. Maybe we could mix our different flavors together." She chuckled at her own silly joke. Deciding it could happen, the uptight and properly bred woman applied another layer of "Simply Natural" foundation and "Little Girl Pink" blush. She knew her chances of a date with the UPS man were as likely as her becoming Mrs. Bob Barker. However, Bernice surmised she not only looked pretty good for seventy-two, but believed if the rules ever changed, she could be a Barker Babe.

Pushing her dented walker towards the cafeteria, a sour mood surfaced in Bernice when she thought about her new incoming roommate. The only comment from the retirement home staff was that she is "a nice lady in a wheelchair."

"What do those nurses know anyway," Bernice huffed. "My last roommate was supposed to be 'nice' too. Angie was only 'nice' when she took her medication, which was never often enough." Bernice halted her inner tirade of negativity and for a moment felt a sliver of guilt. Her previous roommate was now covered with dirt instead of her antiseptic-scented blanket. "Maybe the new one will be different."

With pessimistic enthusiasm Bernice headed for the cafeteria. She peered in, hoping that the ratio of two men to twenty women had miraculously shifted overnight, and that she might meet someone as fine as Bob Barker. "No such luck," she muttered. The only males in the cafeteria were Nick the narcoleptic and Ed the former attorney with his oxygen tank. Deciding she was in no mood for either man, Bernice instead squeezed her ample bottom into a chair next to Trudy, a paper-thin-skinned woman who spent most of her day talking about her brief but imaginary affair with Sean Connery. Trudy slid one of her slightly filled bingo cards to Bernice. The numbers continued to rattle on.

"I-29...... .B-5...... O-65."

"Bingo!" yelled Bernice. Her reward for the simplistic time waster was a sugarless piece of candy. "Zipity-doo-da! I shoulda' stayed and watched Bob," she murmured.

After the final blackout game, the room was cleared to set up for lunch. Bernice decided to wait in the hall, rather than hobble back to her room which seemed about a mile away.

Volunteer ladies, not much younger than Bernice and dressed in flowered smocks, covered the round tables with cloths each bearing a neon smiley face design. The centerpieces consisted of child size, silk flowers stuck in baby food jars filled with marbles.

"Lovely," Bernice sighed. "Somebody needs to get Martha Stewart in here."

During lunch Bernice tried to identify the soft, gray matter on her plate by stabbing it with her fork. "Mystery meat or the contents from a bed pan," she said to no one in particular, since she was the only one at her table who could stay awake longer than five minutes at a time.

After choking down her lunch, Bernice pushed her walker slowly down the long corridor back to her ten by twelve foot "cell." The yet unseen new roommate started her thinking about another of her former roommates: her husband, Jack. They had been married fifty-two years before he died. Except for spoiling their only daughter to the point of delinquency, he had been a stupendous husband. The unhappy retirement home resident missed him terribly, but decided she was going to figure out how to spend the rest of her days doing extraordinary things. She was not going to simply exist in a building filled with men and women who had to gum their food and made trivets out of Popsicle sticks.

Bernice didn't really want to share a room, but with the high cost of everything, she was concerned about having enough money to survive. She silently prayed, "Please Lord, may what's-her-name have fully functional faculties and the personality of Mary Tyler Moore."

As Bernice arrived at the door to her room, an aged but not ancient woman in a purple wheelchair with silver painted spokes blocked the entrance. The woman's fuchsia-red hair stood out like a shrub in need of pruning.

"Excuuuse me," Bernice said a bit too loudly.

"You don't have to yell, I'm crippled, not deaf, you old bag," the woman snapped as she wheeled herself to the side of the room. She turned to face her opposition.

"Who you calling an old bag, Carrot Top!"

"Carrot Top! You color blind? This here is the exact same color of hair that Lucille Ball had." The woman's bony hands delicately touched her hair as if it were a royal crown.

Bernice was about to fire back the comment that if Lucille Ball had that color hair she would have never been on TV, but she decided she did not need to add more gasoline to the bonfire. She extended her hand and said gently, "Sorry, about the rude greeting. My name is Bernice Gibson, welcome to *Passage of Time Retirement Home.*"

"Grandy McGregor Wayland." She shook her new roommate's hand vigorously.

"You have quite a grip there, Grandy." Bernice rubbed her blue-veined hands together.

"Sorry if I was a little rough, don't know my own strength." Grandy half smiled, then began surveying her surroundings.

A slight smile found Bernice's face, and she proceeded with a cliché question one usually asks of newcomers.

"So, what brings you to our old people's oasis?"

"Ahhhh, my boy thinks I'm looney. He threw a fit when he found out I was trying to contact a scientist in Pennsylvania who specializes in UFOs. My cousin Reckon is from the star Betelgeuse and seems to have some problems adjusting to planet earth. Thought I'd help him out by taking him to see this guy. My ungrateful son told me I had a choice: a white jacket for my wardrobe or coming to live here. Dern fool kid, shoulda' left him at a bus station when he was born." Grandy exhaled a big breath and looked at Bernice with suspicious eyes, "How did you end up in here?"

If Bernice had the words to describe how she was feeling at that moment, she could have sold them for a million bucks. Instead, she found an ounce of composure and replied in the most polite tone of voice she owned. "Well, it sure wasn't because I thought I had relatives in Roswell." Bernice hesitated only a moment before continuing. "Three days after my husband broke his hip I had a small stroke. Our only daughter was not around to help out, so we had to come here. That was almost two years ago. Jack keeled over at the dinner table not long after we arrived. They said it was his heart, I say it was the food. It's going to kill us all."

Grandy said dryly, "I'm guessing the cuisine here doesn't include tender juicy steaks and chocolate cheesecake."

"No, but the macaroni and cheese isn't bad if you take out the bits of turkey wieners."

The two elderly women chuckled weakly, yet still unsure if they would be able to occupy the same room for more than a day.

3

Bernice wanted to ask Grandy if her husband was still alive, but was afraid she might be told he was the reigning king of a Sasquatch tribe. Grandy was curious as to why Bernice's daughter wasn't around, but figured the reason was probably boring and uneventful. So the new roommates just smiled and stared at each other until Bernice broke the silence, "How about I help you get settled, then give you the grand tour. It's delightful," remarked Bernice in a cynical tone.

"Does this place have a hot tub?"

"No."

"How about young male nurses?"

"Only on the calendar by my dresser."

Chapter 2

"Here's the end of our tour – the cafeteria, or as we affectionately call it, 'the slop then mop' room," Bernice said wryly.

Grandy rolled her eyes. "Sounds like my mother-in-law's cooking. Her meals were so bad even their hogs had a hard time getting fat on the leftovers."

"This is also where we meet at 9:00 for church on Sunday mornings," Bernice continued. "The service is a combination of Catholic, Lutheran, and Presbyterian." Bernice hesitated before asking, "What church do you belong to, Grandy?"

"Whatever one is handy at the time. Can't be too fussy when you travel around a lot. The Man Upstairs is supposed to be the center of every religion, isn't He?" She looked at Bernice as if it was not even a question.

"O..kay." Bernice dared not press Grandy for a detailed expose' on her philosophy. She was still trying to sort out the alien cousin story.

"Let's go watch "Oprah" in the parlor," Bernice suggested.

"That's fine, but then I need to check the update on a sighting in Rhode Island on the Internet."

* * *

As they entered the parlor, Grandy surveyed the décor. The walls were papered in a tan, black and faux gold wallpaper. Coffee-colored vinyl sofas and scratched, imitation oak end tables crowded the room. In one corner was a fake stone fireplace flickering with small, blue, gas flames. Another corner cradled a large-screen T.V., the volume loud enough to be heard down the street. Grandy felt like she was in the smoking room of a men's club.

"Sooo, where did you get the name Grandy? Sounds Irish," Bernice shouted during a commercial break.

Grandy looked with frustration at a nearly bald, shrunken woman leaning against the T.V. "Turn the sound down, Old Woman!"

"What?"

"I said, turn down the volume, it's too loud!"

The old lady put her nose to the T.V. controls and gingerly pushed on the volume button until it had reached a level of toleration.

Grandy turned her attention back to Bernice. "Well, my mother gave birth to me in the back seat of a '34 Hudson while driving through the town of Grandy, Minnesota. My father, a traveling minister, thought the last name, McGregor, sounded better than 'Krone.' And that's how I ended up with the name Grandy McGregor. Wayland, of course, is my married name which I should have dumped long ago, but the paperwork involved is too much of a hassle. Besides, the name reminds me of Waylon Jennings who is a well-respected Country Western singer, even though he's now dead. God bless his soul." Grandy briefly closed her eyes in what seemed to be a display of respect. Bernice let a moment of silence go by before asking her next question. "I see. I'm curious though, was red your natural hair color when you were younger?"

"Oh no. When I was a kid, I had hair the color of a tan towel that looked like it had wiped up a bad case of diarrhea. My friend, Lady Clairol, introduced me to this life-changing look. She helps keep it looking fine. Grandy licked her fingertips and smoothed the fly-away strands of hair around her face. "And who is that magnificent looking man sitting there in the corner?" Grandy asked sarcastically.

Bernice glanced over to Grandy's point of reference. "Him? That honey in the lime green suit and pink tinted glasses is Leisure Suit Larry. He is a constant menace to the ladies here. He thinks he's every woman's dream. Stay away from him, he probably has a disease or something."

Larry stood up and started to hobble towards the ladies.

"Sit down, Larry!" Bernice shouted, "She's not interested!"

"Let the young lady speak for herself, *Bernice*." Larry continued to inch his way across the room.

"Hey Larry, you don't mind that my sex change isn't complete, do you?" Grandy purred as she wheeled towards him. The old man, dressed like a dill pickle, made an abrupt turn and did a crippled sprint out of the room. The parlor exploded in feeble applause from sixteen weathered hands.

"Good for you, Honey," said one of the past prime residents.

It was difficult for the ladies to suppress their laughter so they let it fill the parlor like feathers bursting forth during a pillow fight.

Chapter 3

"Hello."

"Hey, Ma, it's Avis. How you doing?"

"How do you think I'm doing? You take me away from my home and stick me in a place that feels like an animal shelter. I expect somebody here to put me permanently asleep any day now. Not to mention my roommate is wound tighter than a spring and smells like a perfume factory."

"Now Mother, *Passage of Time* is one of the best retirement homes in Minnesota. And I'm sure your roommate is not as bad as you make her out to be."

"Hmmph. What would you know? You haven't visited me since I moved in. Suppose you're too busy with celebrity court cases and going to the opera with what's her name."

"Her name is Liza and we've been married fourteen years. You SHOULD know her name by now."

"I know her name, it just hurts to say it."

"Okay, Ma – we're not going to discuss my marriage right now. I just called to see if you are all right and find out if you need anything."

"Yeah, I need to sleep in my own bed. I want to eat off my own plates, use my own towels, and pee in my own toilet. I –"

"I get the idea, Mother. Look at it this way, you don't have to wash dishes, do laundry, or clean the bathroom – someone else does it for you. Besides, it couldn't have been very easy in a wheelchair."

"Avis, I've never minded doing housework and if you were that worried about it, you could have hired me a housekeeper or had my prissy daughter-in-law come over and help me out. What I *do* mind is not seeing wild turkeys and deer outside my kitchen window. Your brothers would have never done this to me, especially Dakota. Well, maybe Howard. But I could have talked him out of it given half the chance."

Silence bricked a wall between Grandy and Avis. After several moments, a small hole poked through it when Grandy's oldest son spoke.

"Ma, perhaps if your recent obsession with UFOs had not impaired your judgment, you would still be home, feeding chipmunks and dusting your ceramic elephant collection."

"My interest in flying saucers is not an obsession – it's a new hobby I find more interesting than crocheting mittens or watching Jeopardy. You're just looking for an excuse to hide me away and take my money."

"I can't believe you think that about me. It's just not true."

"Avis, as a kid you were always pawing at my jewelry. As a teenager you wanted to balance my checkbook and now you want to take what I have left

7

and lock me away like some criminal. Your lawyer techniques won't work on me. I'll get out of here somehow and then you'll be sorry."

Avis sighed, "Calm down, Ma, I'm sorry. If you just –"

"Don't tell me what to do, Avis. All the money you make and all the shining crap you own don't make you smarter than me. I still can whip your behind if I need to."

The forty-nine-year-old man flinched inside as he realized his mother, well past her prime, was still occasionally capable of putting the fear of God in him.

"As soon as I finish my closing arguments on the case I'm on, we'll come over for a nice, long visit. Augusta will be glad to see her grandma. I'll have her bring her latest report card and tennis trophy."

Grandy grumbled under her breath before telling Avis, "Fine. Tell that wife of yours, though, not to bring her homemade organic cookies. They give me the runs."

A small chuckle escaped from Avis, "Okay, Ma, I'll tell her. Talk to you soon. Be good."

Grandy hung up the phone before she heard his last comments.

* * *

"Gin Rummy" were the only words that could tear Bernice away from the television during the long evenings at the home. Grandy's quest for the competitive edge in a card game was her therapy in dealing with her seemingly uncaring family. Their exchanges during these sessions about their life experiences sparked in each woman a curiosity to know more about each other.

"Bernie, we could make this game a lot more interesting if we up the ante."

"What do you mean? Like real money?"

"No, not real money, food."

"Food? What do you mean, food?"

"You know, like you give me your dessert if I win and I give my dessert to you if you win."

"But most of the time neither one of us likes the dessert."

"Okay then. If I win, you have to buy me the latest UFO magazines and if you win, I have to buy you bottles of nail polish.

Bernice's lips twisted as she thought about Grandy's proposal.

"Well, that sounds fair only if you buy me the higher quality nail polish and not the stuff at the dollar store. *And* you could let me win once in a while if you're gonna do that. I don't want to be the one losing all the time."

"Well, pay more attention to the game then."

Grandy shuffled the cards and dealt a most unbelievable hand to Bernice. Without warning the lights went out in the retirement home.

"Did you do that?"

"Did I do what?"

"You saw my hand, didn't you, Grandy. Turn the light back on."

"I've been sitting right here, Numbskull. I did not turn off the light!"

Shrieks from the other residents could be heard down the hall as the entire building was in total darkness.

"Dang it," Grandy grumbled.

"What?"

"I can't find it."

"Find what?"

"Just a minute, ... I know it's in here somewhere?" Grandy mumbled.

"What?"

"Ah, here it is." Grandy turned towards Bernice wearing an old minor's lamp on her forehead, its light directly pointed at Bernice's face.

"You're blinding me! Turn that thing another direction."

As Grandy turned her head the lights came back on.

"Thank goodness," said Bernice, "now you can turn off the light on your head."

Grandy switched the power off but left the unit on her head. She then dug around in her dresser drawer again and produced one for Bernice.

"Here. Just in case it happens again."

"This thing looks silly, besides it will mess up my hair."

"You're right Bernice," Grandy said cynically, "it's much better to bump around in the dark and mess your face up when you hit a wall."

The grey-haired roommate reluctantly put the headlamp on her head.

"There, you happy now?"

"Come on let's finish the - oh no, look, the cards got all mixed up."

"It's okay, we can put them back the way they were. I had a great hand."

"You can't do that. They're all messed up."

"Well, that's not fair, I don't wanna play anymore. And I don't want to wear this silly piece of head gear."

"Fine, but don't ask for my help if the lights go out again."

Small murmuring escaped from Bernice's mouth.

"What did you say, Bernie?"

"If you must know, I said your lights are always out, Grandy."

As if on cue, the lights diminished once again and Bernice's feeble voice rose in pitch as she searched for her roommate.

" Grandy? Where are you Grandy? What did you do with my headlamp? Grandy?"

Chapter 4

"One dollar! One dollar!" yelled Bernice.

"I'll bid two thousand dollars, Bob."

Again, the contestants all overbid.

"These people don't know how to play the game. I should be on this show. I could teach them all a thing or two."

"Bernie, quit your squawking. You sound like the only rooster in a hen house."

When the show went to a commercial, Bernice watched Grandy henpeck away on a black rectangular box. What is that contraption of yours?"

"This here 'contraption' is my connection to this world and the ones far above us. I paid good money for my HP wireless notebook. Using the World Wide Web, I can find or buy anything."

"Can you get me tickets to *the Price is Right* show ?"

"Why would you want to go on that show? It's dumb."

"No it isn't! I really want to go. Can you look it up?"

"When I'm done researching crop circles in New Mexico I will. I also need to send an e-mail. Then I'll look up your dang ticket."

Bernice gave Grandy an impatient glance before pushing her silver rimmed glasses up the bridge of her nose. "What is e-mail and who are you doing it to?"

"An electronic note to my son, Avis. He just called me yesterday while you were in the shower. I forgot to tell him I want to change my will."

Bernice turned down the T.V. volume and stared at Grandy. "Avis? Like the car rental Avis?"

"Yup." Grandy kept her eyes fixated on the notebook screen as she explained the history of her son's name to Bernice. "I was in an Avis Rent-A-Car on my way to visit my grandma in Idaho when the little turd decided to make a four-week-early entrance. So I drove to the nearest hospital and popped him out right there in the parking lot. Little fellow had to stay a week in the hospital 'cause he needed to gain an extra pound or two before he could go home."

"Where did you stay while Avis was in the hospital?"

"My grandma's house was only about twelve miles from the hospital. I'd stay there at night."

"What about your husband, where was he when all this was happening?"

"That son-of-a-hyena's butt was off in Arizona, supposedly earning a big bonus from Jackson Fence Post Company. I'm pretty sure the posts he was pounding had nothing to do with keeping livestock corralled."

"You mean he was having an affair?" Bernice's faded white eyebrows arched in mock surprise. Although she was undeniably against adultery, she imagined being married to Grandy was no easy task.

"You betcha. Lester was constantly having some young bimbo polishing his 'family jewels.'"

"Oh, sorry to hear that." Bernice didn't want to hear anymore about Lester so she quickly blurted out the next question. "Do you have any other kids?"

"Yeah. Two more boys—"

"Let me guess, Hertz and Alamo," Bernice snickered.

Grandy shot Bernice a nasty look and snapped, "No! Their names are Dakota and Howard."

The broad bottomed roommate was about to crack a joke about states and hotels, then decided it was better to hold her tongue. There had to be a reason why Grandy had never mentioned her sons in the two months they had known each other, but she wasn't in the mood for another story about weird relatives. She smoothed the sea blue and white afghan on her lap and turned the volume back up on the T.V.

Twenty minutes later, as the *Price is Right* grand prize winner was jumping into the arms of her husband or boyfriend or whomever, Grandy looked up and said, "They're gonna be taping some shows in April. Do you want the phone number?"

"Of course I want the phone number!" Bernice stood up too quick, became entangled in the afghan and nearly fell on her face as she grabbed the phone. "Oh, I can hardly wait to see Bobby!" By now she was nearly hyperventilating.

"Calm down, Bernie, you'll give yourself an aneurysm."

"Okay, okay." As Bernice dialed the number, she said softly to Grandy, "You're going with me, right?"

"I don't wanna go see that old coot. Besides, I hate flying."

"Bite your tongue, Grandy! Bob Barker is the finest gentleman alive."

Bernice listened to the long, taped recording as she scribbled down some notes.

"They talked too fast," she started to whine, "I have to call again."

"Give me the phone," Grandy growled."

Grandy dialed and listened intently with pen in hand while Bernice stood over her, panting.

"Did you get it?"

"Yes, Bernie, I got it. Now quit drooling on my shoulder. You can either call in your request, or get the ticket online."

"You mean tickets, don't you?"

"Ooooh, no, I'm not goin.' I told you, I hate flying."

"But you have to. I need someone to cheer for me when I get called down to place my bid."

"What makes you think you will get called down to be a contestant?"

"'Cause I'm gonna get a T-shirt that Bob just won't be able to resist."

Grandy knew she shouldn't ask, but the question popped out of her mouth faster than the taste of sour milk. "And what kind of T-shirt would that be?"

"A hot pink T-shirt with the words imprinted, 'Minnesota Mama Hot for Bob Barker!'"

Grandy closed her eyelids over her feisty, blue eyes and grunted. "Bernice, I swear that if your crinkled, old body wasn't in front of me, I would think I was listening to a sixteen-year-old girl in heat."

"Just order the tickets. You and I need to get out of this half-star Hilton and go have some fun. You never know who we'll meet. Maybe Bob has some unattached buddies."

"In that case, I really don't wanna go. I need a seventy-year-old, sun-ripened, West Coast man like I need prohibition to make a comeback."

Grandy returned her attention back to the computer. Bernice stooped down and stared at her friend over the screen.

"Grandy?" she said in a little girl's voice.

"What."

"Please, please go with me."

Old Red examined the disappointed face and said in a deflated tone, "Fine, I'll go to L.A. with you under two conditions: one, you shut up about Bob, and two, you buy me enough drinks before we board the plane so that I don't know if I'm flying the friendly skies or going Greyhound."

"You're so cool, Grandy."

"What did you say?"

"Cool."

"That word ain't in style no more."

"Yes it is. I hear it on T.V. all the time."

"You watch too much T.V., Bernie."

Chapter 5

"Where do you old biddies think you're goin'?" asked Larry, still a bit unnerved about his first encounter with the redhead in a bizarre looking wheelchair.

"Just never you mind," Bernice replied sharply, as she shook her new, aluminum cane at him.

"Where's your walker?"

"This here is all that's left of my walker after I wrapped it around the last smarty marty who asked me a none-of-your-business question."

Larry slowly sat down at the opposite end of the parlor, his eyes cautiously glued on the two women.

Grandy spun her wheelchair towards Larry, giving him a dispassionate smile. "We're goin' shopping for some new threads. Hey, Lare, would you be interested in some of my old leisure suits? I won't need them anymore."

"No thanks," Larry said in disgust.

With a bit of sourness, Bernice announced, "If you must know, Larry, we need some new clothes for our trip to Los Angeles. We're going to meet Bob Barker."

"Yeah, right. You crazy, old battleaxe."

"She might be old and she might be a battleaxe, but I'm the crazy one." Grandy raised her arms, widened her eyes at Larry, and shouted at him, "BOO!"

Bernice touched Grandy on the shoulder, "Let's get out of here, our cab is waiting."

As they entered the cab, Grandy turned and blew Larry a kiss through the window.

"Where to, Ladies?" asked Habib, the young cabbie, after loading up the wheelchair.

"The Mall of America," they both chimed in unison.

Habib remained silent through the entire trip. His command of the English language couldn't keep up with the chatter from the ladies.

"Aren't you going to call your daughter to see if it's okay to stay with her in L.A.?"

Bernice laughed cunningly, "I love a good surprise, as long as it's not on me. Besides, it'll serve her right for never coming to see me. We ought to stay for a month. That'd really cook her goose, wouldn't it."

"I'm not staying a month with somebody I don't know."

"It's not the length of stay, it's the point of the matter."

"Well, point your pointer somewhere else."

"Joyce has had a bean up her butt since puberty. It's about time she was inconvenienced, the spoiled little brat."

"I know what you mean. My youngest son, Howard, believes his neurotic tics are my fault."

"How so?"

"I had a rather strong craving for green beans in pineapple juice, unsweetened of course, while I was pregnant with Howard, and the male contribution to his genes told him about it."

Bernice was totally speechless for about ten seconds. She stared at the Randy Moss bobble-head glued to Habib's dash. For a moment she forgot about Grandy and wondered if the cab driver knew Randy no longer wore the Vikings' uniform.

"I can see where Howard might think you messed with his physical well being," Bernice tried to say in all seriousness.

"Don't be daft, Old Woman. Those dern beans had nothing to do with Howard's problems. The man he calls 'Daddy' is more likely the source of all his problems. If I – "

Habib interrupted Grandy's loud complaints about her ex. "Here we are, Ladies, The Mall of America. Are you going to need a ride back?"

"Of course, we're gonna need a ride back. You think this old lady next to me can push my wheelchair ten miles down the freeway? Be at this entrance at exactly 4:00 p.m." Grandy said curtly.

"Don't mind her," Bernice whispered to Habib, "she never gets enough fiber." Bernice pulled a plastic bag full of change from her purse and counted out her share of the fare as Habib removed the wheelchair from the trunk. Grandy removed a wad of dollar bills housed in her blouse and also paid the embarrassed cab driver.

* * *

The immensity of the mall fascinated the ladies with over 500 stores, 24 restroom facilities, and scores of displays and entertainment of all genres. They chatted about the rides as well as the displays at Lego Imagination Center. The vast choices at the food courts caused them to play eeny meeny miny moe so they could finally eat and get on with shopping.

"Slow down, I can't wheel that fast."

"I gotta pee," whined Bernice.

"Swell. Aren't ya wearing your Depends?"

"They're not meant to be an actual diaper. Besides, having too big of an accident in them gives me a rash."

"Okay, okay. Let's find an outhouse for ya. Should be one right around the corner."

14

Half an hour later, Bernice finally finished wrestling with her pantyhose while Grandy maneuvered the wheelchair out of the bathroom stall.

"Now I'm ready for some serious shopping!" chirped Bernice. "Let's go in here. I need some Bermuda shorts."

"You ain't gonna find Bermuda shorts in Minnesota this time of year."

"What do you mean, it's almost spring," Bernice replied.

After visiting four stores, pawing through piles of new summer arrivals and attacking rows of separates on hangers, Grandy held up a pair of pink shorts with giant watermelons on them. Her voice thick with sarcasm, she said to Bernice, "My, aren't these just the envy of the fashion world."

"I love 'em!" Bernice exclaimed and snatched them out of Grandy's grip.

"That figures, I was only kidding."

"They'll go with my hot pink T-shirt."

"I thought you were kidding about the T-shirt."

"How else will I be able to get Bobby's attention?"

"Well, then I'm not sitting next to you." Grandy rolled her eyes as Bernice held the shorts up in front of her.

"Don't they look great, Grandy?"

"Yeah, swell. You look like a failed scientific fruit experiment."

Bernice dumped a pile of change on the counter and twenty minutes later, the transaction was finally complete.

Past a Krispy Kreme Donut Shop, Bernice found what she was searching for. "Look, a T-shirt shop! We have to find our hot pink T-shirts for the show," Bernice announced.

"Hold it right there. You don't expect me to wear any dumb T-shirt on national television?"

"Ah, come on, Grandy, don't be a party pooper. We can have the letters spelled out in sequins if you want."

"Like that will help. People will think we belong on the corner of Hollywood Boulevard."

"Okay, I'll let you pick out the lettering. But you've seen the show. If you DON'T wear a T-shirt with something flashy written on it, you're gonna stand out like a sore thumb. Besides, maybe one of your ET buddies will see you and transport you back to the Milky Way or something."

Grandy thought for a moment then stiffly responded to Bernice's comment, "All right, I'll get the dang T-shirt. And just for your information, my buddies would never take me to the Milky Way, it's too dangerous."

After the T-shirts were purchased, Grandy pulled hers out of the bag and eyed it over. MINNESOTA MAMA HOT FOR BOB BARKER. "I can't believe I let you talk me into this," she said with discontentment.

15

"Grandy, I guarantee you'll not be sorry you bought this shirt. Who knows, we might both get called to the contestant podiums. Wouldn't that be fun?"

"Yeah, fun, like chiseling a twelve-page letter out of stone. Enough about Bobby or Booby or whoever. We've got shopping to do."

After six more trips around the mall, Grandy's lap was full of packages. Bernice tried to hold her cane in one hand and her purchases in the other.

"I'm tired, these packages are too heavy, and I gotta pee again," Bernice complained.

Much to Bernie's amazement, Grandy jumped from her chair and barked, "Here, just put the packages in the chair."

There was a moment of shock and silence before Bernice was able to say in a squeaky voice, "You can walk?"

"It's called selective walking. I use it to my advantage. In this case, it is more advantageous to walk than to ride. Now put your stuff in the wheelchair and stop sounding like a two year old locked out of a toy box."

Fearing even more of the unexpected from Grandy, Bernice obeyed and started from scratch on her assessment of her roommate.

Chapter 6

Bernice, dressed in an orange and yellow floral shirt, orange shorts and new white tennis shoes, huffed at Grandy for taking so long to get ready for the airport.

"Honestly, Grandy, your hair is just fine. You keep fussing with it and it will all fall out. You'll be left with a red, bald head."

Grandy shot Bernice an evil look and snipped at her, "You old fool, my hair is red, not my scalp." She scrutinized herself one more time in the mirror and decided her new shade of red hair dye and mint green pant suit matched quite well. A frown darkened her face, though, as she noticed her shoes. "These red high tops don't match my outfit. I need my white ones."

"For heaven's sakes, Grandy, if you don't quit primping we'll miss our plane. And if I don't get to see Bob Barker, you will cease to be a resident of this home and find yourself living at Stonecrest Cemetery!" Bernice sighed deeply as she fought to regain her composure.

"Okay, okay, just let me change my shoes and I'll be ready to go. You shouldn't get so worked up, Bernie, you'll burst an artery or something."

Bernice attempted to stomp out of the room, but her cane prevented the action from being much more than an imitation of a wobbling toddler.

"Crazy, old broad," Grandy muttered to herself.

Fifteen minutes later, the California-bound biddies were waiting by the front door of the retirement home. A cab pulled up and stopped just inches from their bodies. Habib exited the cab, his eyes widened in surprise when he noticed who his passengers were. He nodded his head in a slight greeting, then began loading their heavy suitcases and Grandy's wheelchair.

"Surely Allah is angry with me," Habib lamented to himself as he tried to figure out which terrible deed he committed that would result in the misfortune of having to transport these two women in his cab again.

Once Bernice and Grandy were comfortably situated in the back seat of the cab, Habib asked in his most polite Middle Eastern voice, "In front of what airline would you like to be dropped off?"

"Northwest, and hurry! We don't want to miss our flight!" Bernice answered gleefully. She had not slept in days, anticipating their trip to L.A. Grandy, on the other hand, could not believe her roommate had talked her into riding in a flying sardine can.

Less than a mile down the road, Bernice tapped Habib on the shoulder and shouted into his ear, "Stop right here!"

Habib slammed on the brakes, with panic and worry in his voice he asked, "What's wrong!"

"Nothing, I just want to stop at Lucky's Discount Liquors. My friend here needs a little 'encouragement' before she gets on the airplane."

The flustered cab driver was swearing softly in Arabic as he pulled into the liquor store parking lot.

A few choice words flowed from Grandy's mouth as well, as she touched her face where it impacted with the beaded seat cover on the headrest in front of her. "Dang it, Bernice! You trying to kill me before we even get to the terminal? There's a bar at the airport you know?"

"But I need you really, really relaxed before you board the plane. Besides, I can get a whole bottle of 100 proof whiskey here for less than two shots at the airport."

"Make sure you buy the good stuff. Moonshine from Kentucky is the best."

"Don't worry. By the time we arrive in L.A., you won't even know we left Minnesota. I'll be back in a flash."

Habib, was still muttering in Arabic as he watched Bernice hobble into the store. He took some comfort in the fact that her slowness was to his advantage as the cab meter continued to run.

"I hope she can figure out how to use her new ATM card," Grandy thought. "If I hadn't insisted she get one, we'd be here all day while she counts her change. And this extra stop is already going to cost me my first born. Although that might catch his attention if the local law enforcement showed up at his gilded house and told him that his mother sold him to pay off some debts." The thought tickled Grandy and she smiled to herself.

Inside the liquor store, Bernice was finding it difficult to pick out the right booze. There were so many choices and her experience was not on the same level as Grandy's. In fact, one sip of communion wine produced a slight buzz in her head. So Bernice opted to pick out the bottle that had the most visual appeal. In her eyes it was Captain Morgan's spiced rum.

About the time Grandy thought she would have to go inside the store to find Bernice, the old lady appeared with a brown paper bag in her hand and a smile so big on her face that Grandy was sure she had been sipping on the purchase herself.

"What have you been doing in there, Bernie? Distilling the stuff yourself?"

"Hush up. There were more selections than I realized. Now, drink up, we have a plane to catch."

"Excuse me, Madam, illegal to drink in cab," Habib said in a nervous voice. "I could lose license and go to jail. Maybe you, too."

"Habib, that is the least of your problems if you don't get us to the airport on time," Bernice said tersely.

18

There was no doubt Bernice meant what she said, and Habib knew it. As he pushed the gas pedal as fast as he dared, Grandy flashed a skeptical look at Bernice. She hesitated a moment before taking a long swallow of the mystery medicine, then sputtered a bit before wiping her mouth with her sleeve.

"What the -?"

"It's Captain Morgan's spiced rum. I liked the picture of the pirate on the label."

"For crying out loud, Bernice, I asked for moonshine, not this stuff." Grandy realized she would have to deal with what she had, took another swig, then belched.

"'Scuse me."

"You're excused, Grandy. Habib, get this piece of blue and white tin moving faster. My Bob Barker is waiting for me."

"Yes, Madam." Habib was not about to argue with this old, grey-haired mouth, no telling what she might do.

Grandy continued to sip her alcoholic soda, while Bernice switched gears and started rambling on about Bob Barker. By the time they reached the terminal Grandy's demeanor had become more playful than passive.

As they waited for their plane, all eyes were on Grandy as she tried to do wheelies in her wheelchair. Most people averted their attention back to laptops, books, or cell phone conversations. One 4-year-old boy asked Grandy if he could have a ride on her lap.

"Sure!" Grandy said with an unnatural glee in her voice.

"Sorry, Little Guy," Bernice said in a syrupy, sweet voice, "my friend here is having a reaction to her medication, it's not a good idea to ride on her lap right now. You'd better go back to your parents."

"I wanna ride! She said I could."

"Well, I say if you don't go back to your mother right now, I'll tell Santa Claus you were a very bad boy. Bernice squinted her dusty, grey eyes at the obstinate preschooler. He opened his mouth to protest but Bernice leaned into his face so close she could smell candy on his breath. "Go," she said in a menacing whisper.

Like prey fleeing from a predator, the little boy turned and ran back to his family. "Mommy!"

The frustrated Bernice heard his cry and prayed she wouldn't get sued for harassment of a minor.

"Hey, where's he goin'?" Grandy slurred. "He didn't get his ride yet."

"He's not getting a ride," retorted Bernice. "Besides, you're supposed to be quiet and demure, not carrying on like a one-man circus act."

"Woman."

"What?"

19

"One-woman circus act. I'm a woman."

"Shut up, Grandy, before I check you in as baggage."

"Now, – "

Grandy's attempted retort was interrupted when the first announcement for pre-boarding was made over the loudspeaker. Bernice immediately grabbed onto Grandy's wheelchair handles and pushed her to the gate entrance. After she showed the flight attendant their tickets, she was almost dragged to her death when Grandy's wheelchair accelerated on the steep decline of the boarding ramp. It was ten minutes of fidgeting and fighting with overhead bins, wheelchair storage, and about who was going to sit near the window, before Bernice finally had them both buckled into their seats. Bob Barker's devoted fan took several deep breaths, then checked to make sure her cherry red, acrylic nails had survived the first leg of the trip. She dug around in her white, vinyl purse looking for the lipstick that matched her nail polish, all the while muttering to herself, "Here I come, Bobby. I'm looking fine today, can't wait to give you that big kiss."

"Wha'd you say?" Grandy's words tumbled out like an over-stuffed dryer.

"Nothing."

"I heard you say *something*, Bernie, what was it?"

"I said I'm never traveling with you again, Grandy." And with that comment, Bernice closed her eyes and began daydreaming about meeting *The Price is Right* host.

Chapter 7

The flight attendant's voice going over airplane safety regulations jerked Bernice out of her delusional dream. She looked at Grandy, seated next to her, who was becoming more and more agitated, demanding that someone let her oxygen mask be down for the entire trip. When her request was ignored, Grandy turned her frustration on the middle-aged, male passenger sitting on her other side. She pushed his arm off the armrest then stared at him in a manner daring him to say anything.

"How come you get the aisle seat? My friend, Bernie should have the aisle seat. She always has to go pee."

"If your friend has to use the restroom I'll be happy to move out of the way while she gets out of her seat. I prefer the aisle seat myself because I like being one of the first ones out of the plane when it lands. " The man's demeanor was polite but stiff. He went back to reading his book, refusing to engage in anymore conversation with this crabby, old lady.

Grandy's blue eyes became small slits and she was about to make a rude comment when Bernice lightly tapped her on the shoulder and said, "Grandy, how about I buy you a drink? They have all kinds of liquor in those cute, little bottles."

"Can I have more than one?"

"Maybe. But you have to promise to behave yourself. You don't want to get kicked off the plane, do you?"

Grandy thought a moment. "If I do get booted off the plane, will they give me a parachute?"

"Not if I can help it," Bernice remarked in a low-toned voice. She bought two little bottles of vodka and gave them both to Grandy to mix with orange juice.

Within an hour Grandy was back to being silly and a bit too friendly. She murmured in Bernie's ear," I like your outfit. It reminds me of a lawn chair I used to have." There was a slight dent before Grandy continued the one-sided conversation. "I wonder what ever happened to that chair? I bet Lester is using it in his formal dining room. My ex never did have good taste."

A loud agreement filled Bernice's head but she thought it best not to say so.

"I have to go pee, Grandy. I'll be back in a little bit."

Before the male passenger had a chance to get up, Bernice crawled over him and Grandy to get out. Her purse hit several heads as she tried to maintain balance while walking down the narrow aisle. After relieving herself and applying a fresh coat of makeup, Bernie's excitement about seeing Bob Barker was renewed and she told everyone she passed about her upcoming visit to see him.

"I get to see Bob Barker in person," she giggled. "I just know I'm going to win. I feel so lucky! Bobby is so handsome, I plan to give him a kiss when I'm on stage."

Bernice noticed the male passenger who sat next to Grandy was no longer there. "Where's the young man that was sitting next to you, Grandy?"

"He went to the back of the plane."

"Why?"

Because I told him to." It was now obvious Grandy was starting to become her usual cantankerous self, despite the liquor. "He was swearing at me. So I said that if he was going to cuss in front of a lady, he needed to go sit somewhere else." Grandy gulped the last of her screwdriver.

"What did you do to make him swear at you, Grandy?"

"Nothing. All I did was try to save him time by telling him that the book he was reading had a lousy ending, that the two main characters in story both die. He started saying bad words and calling you and me crazy, ol' biddies. So I told him to leave or I would file a report that he was sexually harassing me."

"Oh Grandy, if you don't watch yourself, the pilot might fly to a small airport in Utah and leave us there. Then how would I get to see Bob Barker!" Bernice wrung her wrinkled hands and moaned.

"Sit down, Bernie, and quit auditioning for a pity party. We need to figure out our plans once this flying closet finally lands on the ground. How far is your daughter's place from the airport?"

"Not too far."

"What's not too far? Two miles? Ten miles?"

"I don't know, I've never been there. The map shows a quarter of an inch."

"Oh, that's a big help, Bernie. Will Joyce come pick us up?"

"I don't know, probably. But I really wanted to surprise her."

"Okay. We'll rent a car and drive there. Besides, we need a way to escape if her latest boyfriend turns out to be weird or something. Do you think we can find her house?"

"I think so, but who's going to drive the car?"

"Who do you think?"

"How long has it been since you've driven a car?"

"It doesn't matter. I practice all the time in my wheelchair, it's almost the same thing."

"Do you have a driver's license?"

"Of course I have a driver's license."

"Is it valid?"

Instead of answering the question, Grandy gave Bernie a nasty look.

"I'm guessing you didn't tell the Motor Vehicles Department about the wheelchair."

"Would you?"

"By the way, where did you get that psychedelic looking wheelchair? And please don't tell me that it was a birthday present from your alien friends."

"I got it at a garage sale."

A short time later, in the most serious tone of voice she could muster, Bernice asked Grandy if they would be going to Avis car rental.

Grandy answered, "Definitely. Their full size cars have nice, large trunks and I figure by the end of this trip that's where you'll be riding."

The two were quiet for a moment before breaking out in a cackling laughter.

"Speaking of Avis. You haven't said much about him or his brothers in the last few weeks."

"My sons were the cutest children to crawl on this planet when they were young. Now, it seems like they –"

"Left their brains at the playground?"

"Yeah." A pause hung in the air. "Avis, my oldest, is a lawyer. He has a law practice in St. Paul. His wife, Liza, works in a hoity toity hair salon. They have one eleven-year-old daughter, Augusta, who believes God created the world just for her. Avis used to be my down-to-earth, animal-loving, dependable son. After marrying Liza, he became a stuck-up, flush-the-goldfish-down-the-toilet, absent son. Howard, my youngest, drives truck for Ice House Beer and is somewhat of a fence sitter. His wife has a tattoo of a black widow spider on her butt. And Dakota, my middle offspring, he's a lot like me. Never get to see enough of him, though."

"Please fasten your seat belts, we are beginning our descent to Los Angeles International Airport and should be arriving at the gate in fifteen minutes. Please remain in your seat until we come to a complete stop," a flight attendant purred over the intercom.

Bernice clapped her hands and began hyperventilating. "We're almost there, Grandy! I'm actually going to see Bob Barker. I can hardly wait! I think you're going to like Bob Barker. He is really a nice guy."

"You know, it's a shame, Bernie that you are more excited to see an old, game show fart than you are to see your own daughter."

"There are two reasons for that Grandy. One, Bob gets my dried up libido going with just a smile, and two, Bob never told me he wished he'd been born to another mother."

"Joyce, told you that?"

23

"Yeah, she did."

Grandy paused, witnessing a normally optimistic Bernice become dejected and quiet.

"Howard once told me pretty much the same thing. I told him that if he had been born to another mother she would have traded him for chocolate and nylons."

Bernie chuckled, "You didn't really tell him that, did you?"

"You bet I did, I would have, too, except the drug store didn't have the kind of chocolate I like."

Chapter 8

With little effort, Grandy grabbed Bernice's floral suitcase off the luggage carousal and tossed it at her friend's feet.

"Be careful! I have valuables in there!"

"Like what? K-Mart jewelry."

"None of your business. I'm going to get a cart for our luggage."

Grandy rolled her eyes and then spotted her own 1970s, dark brown suitcase. It easily stood out among the other baggage as the grey duct tape had been wrapped around it like a Christmas present.

The ladies loaded their luggage onto the cart. Bernice pushed it while her redheaded roommate returned to her wheelchair. The pair then made their way to the Avis-Rent-A-Car counter.

"May I help you," asked the clerk whose name tag read "Sue Lin."

"Yeah, we need a car that has room for a wheelchair, four suitcases, and two old broads," Grandy grumbled.

"I have a black Crown Victoria available."

"A cop car?" Bernice asked.

"Not a cop car, Bernie. Now pipe down while I handle this. The Vic will work just fine. Give me full insurance and a map."

"I'll need to see your driver's license and a credit card," Sue Lin said to Bernice.

"She's not the one driving, I am," said Grandy.

"But you're in a wheelchair."

"Only when I wanna be. Sometimes I get tired and just need to sit down." Grandy stood up and handed Sue Lin her driver's license and credit card. She stared at the confused girl who decided there wasn't much she could do, so she quickly and efficiently provided the old biddies with the car and a map. As Bernice and Grandy were leaving the counter Bernice blurted out, "Hey, Sue Lin, did I tell you my friend here has a son named Avis?"

"Hush up, Bernie, and get in the car."

A few miles down the road, Grandy muttered to herself as she tried to figure out how to make a lane change on a freeway that was a solid ribbon of cars. Her red hair, looking like it had gone through a bad spin cycle, could barely be seen above the steering wheel. Bernice, squirming in her seat from excitement and having to pee, was babbling once again about seeing Bob Barker, *The Price is Right*, and feeling very lucky.

"Do you feel lucky enough to find your daughter's place?" growled Grandy.

Bernice fumbled with the map. She raised her eyeglasses and squinted at the tiny lines and numbers. "I think, Grandy, you should have taken the last off ramp. You know, it's so hard to read this thing, there are too many lines."

Grandy ignored Bernice and shot across a couple of lanes, ignoring the honking cars and single-finger gestures of the Los Angeles commuters. She took an exit and parked in a BP Gas Station.

"Lock your door, Bernice, this does not look like a good neighborhood."

"How do you know it's not a good neighborhood?"

"Maybe because that car across the street is having its doors and tires removed by four kids who look to be eight years old."

Grabbing the map from Bernice, Grandy strained to find the street where Joyce lived.

"As long as we are at a gas station, I'm going to use their restroom," announced Bernice.

"I wouldn't if I was you. What if someone is waiting to mug you or there's a disease on the toilet seat?"

"I'll take my chances."

"Stay in the car, Bernie, it's only another four miles to Joyce's."

"But that's four L.A. miles. It could take us an hour to get there!"

"Quit whining, it won't take an hour."

It didn't take an hour to get to Westlake Condominiums but it did take forty minutes.

"There it is, number 2025!" Bernice announced. "Finally, I can pee. I think the whites of my eyes have turned yellow."

"I wonder if she's home, there's no lights on."

"She said she works in public relations, so she'll probably be home soon, if she has to get up early to go to work."

Grandy parked the Crown Victoria about three feet from the curb.

"Nice park job," Bernice remarked.

"Let's see you do better."

The two ladies waddled up the dark stairs and knocked on the door.

"She's not home. I knew you should have called first."

"Oh, don't get all riled up, she'll be home soon. I do have to pee really bad though. I think I'll go knock on a neighbor's door and see if I can use their restroom."

"Just go behind that bush."

"I can't do that!"

"Well, go ahead and bang on stranger's doors in L.A. I'm sure you'll be welcomed with open arms, especially when you tell them you want to use their toilet."

Bernice scowled at her aggravating friend and, although she realized Grandy may be right, her pride would not back down.

After knocking on several adjunct doors, Bernice returned to Joyce's porch. She humbly asked Grandy, "Do you think anybody will see me if I go behind Joyce's bush?"

"Just turn your butt towards the street, if someone sees it, they'll think it's a wrinkled, paper bag caught in the branches."

A vicious look was thrown Grandy's direction before Bernice smuggled her expansive bottom into the shrub. When she finished her duty, Bernie went and sat next to Grandy on Joyce's porch swing.

"Everything come out okay?"

"Shut up, Grandy. You aren't very nice."

"Never claimed to be, Bernie."

The Los Angeles air and light pink skyline soon smoothed the ladies' moods. They began sharing family stories to pass the time.

"You know, Joyce was such a sweet little girl, until she learned to talk. She was so spoiled by her father. Every time he went on a sales trip, he'd bring her a surprise. When she had every toy manufactured, he started giving her money. Then she hit puberty and things really turned bad. She went from Cinderella to one of the wicked stepsisters. During one of her dad's absences, she met a bum named Eddie while she was still in high school. What a loser he was! I went looking for those two one night when Joyce missed her curfew. I had Eddie arrested for contributing to the delinquency of a minor. That caused a few fireworks. Joyce told me to quit interfering in her love life. Love life! What does a sixteen-year-old know about love? I just couldn't control her. I refused to give her money to bribe her to be good, like her father did. So I tried grounding her. That was a joke. She'd just wait until I was asleep, then sneak out her window. Some other loser would be waiting down the street for her. When her dad came home, she'd whine to him about how mean I was."

"What did he do?"

"I'll tell you what he did. He would give her a big hug and a lot of money. Can you believe that?"

Grandy fidgeted with her tomato paste colored hair, then muttered to Bernice, "Sounds like your daughter *and* husband needed a willow branch whipping."

"Yeah," Bernice breathed out a long sigh. "Wonder what kind of loser Joyce is hanging around now? She's been married three times and all of them went by the name of Bill. Bill #1 stole just about everything she owned, which wasn't much to begin with. Bill #2 was a musician who played around with Joyce's best friend more than his guitar. And after three years of marriage to William #3, Joyce caught him wearing her clothes."

"I didn't know there were that many screwed up Bills in this world. Joyce must have been married to them all."

27

"Knowing Joyce, if there is another one left in this world, she'll find him."

"Don't feel bad, Bernie. My boys weren't exactly valedictorians of their classes, either. My middle child, Dakota, was arrested twice, once for painting images on train cars and once for jay walking in downtown Boston."

"Jaywalking isn't *that* serious," Bernice retorted.

"My son was naked."

"Well, painting pictures on train cars isn't that serious either."

"It is if the image of the lady is the local mayor, and she's naked."

Chapter 9

About the time Bernice and Grandy began contemplating finding a motel, a tall man, dressed like a cowboy from a 1940s Western movie, approached Joyce's front door. He didn't notice the two women sitting in the dark as he fumbled with his keys.

"Who are you?" Bernice asked wryly. She thumped her cane on the deteriorating wooden porch.

The man jumped, knocking his pristine, felt, cowboy hat off as it hit the unlit porch light. "Son-of-a-steer's butt!" he exclaimed. Eying the two old broads with annoyance, he asked in a strong ,Texas drawl, "Who are you?"

Grandy piped in, "Good one, Bernie, you had us sittin' in the dark for three hours and Joyce doesn't even live here."

"Shut up, Grandy... Who are you anyway? And how come you all are lookin' for Joyce? " the cowboy asked suspiciously.

"I'm her mother! Who are you?"

"I'm Buck Arbuckle, her fiancé."

"She didn't tell me that she had a fiancé."

"She told me her mother was dead."

"Well, won't she be surprised, her mother has risen from the grave." Bernice held up both arms towards the sky.

Six-foot-three-inch tall Buck was developing a sincere fear of the two old ladies standing on his porch, but deep rooted manners overruled and he opened the door inviting them inside. "Mrs. Gibson, you and your friend just make yourselves comfortable. Joyce should be home from work in the next half hour."

The visitors ignored the sign near the entrance coat closet that read *Please Remove Shoes* and waltzed inside the condo like they owned it.

"Where's your bathroom?" Bernice asked.

"Down the hallway, second door on the right. The bathroom floor is a bit uneven so be careful when you sit down, the toilet tends to rock back and forth sometimes. I'm planning to fix it this weekend," an embarrassed Buck said. He turned his attention to Grandy, "Can I get you something to eat or drink?"

"No thanks. Do you have another toilet in this place?"

"Sorry. You'll have to wait until Mrs. Gibson is done."

"Great," huffed Grandy.

Once Bernice returned from the bathroom, she settled herself on the couch. Giving Buck a strained smile, she patted the cushion, indicating he should sit next to her. The future son-in-law eased himself reluctantly next to Bernice.

"Buck, Joyce told me she has a public relations position in the food industry. She wouldn't give me exact details about what she does or where she works," Bernice offered a sardonic grin.

"Well, you see, Mrs. Gibson, Joyce does work with the public and she does work in the food industry, sort of. She's a bartender at *The Gin and Tin*. But they do serve food there." Buck closed his hazel eyes after hurrying through his little explanation.

"I see." Bernice remained quiet a moment, digesting this most recent information.

Neither she nor Buck had noticed Grandy was in the room listening to the last piece of conversation between them. Of course, Grandy just had to find a way to get back at her friend for causing her butt to get numb on some stranger's porch swing. So she asked in a faked surprise voice, "I thought you said she had a four-year degree from the University of Minnesota? How come she's working at a bar?"

"Shut up, Grandy," was all Bernice could say.

"But –"

"I said, shut up."

"Hmmph." Grandy gave Bernice a vexing look, then turned her attention to one of the living room walls where several photos of Buck and Joyce were displayed. There was also a photo of Joyce and an older man who Grandy figured was either her father or one of her ex husbands, a picture of a young Joyce and a cat, and one faded black and white print of Joyce and a middle-aged woman. Grandy smiled to herself as she recognized the familiar broad bottom and silver-rimmed glasses of Bernice. "Bet Bernie was born that way," she thought to herself.

"Mrs. Gibson, how about I go out to your car and bring in your luggage?"

"That would be nice, Buck, thank you." Bernice's tone of voice had receded to a more mellow level.

"The luggage is in the backseat. Just leave the wheelchair in the trunk, I won't be needing it tonight," Grandy chimed in.

"Yes, Ma'am."

As Bernice and Grandy explored the home, Buck hurried to the Crown Vic and began unloading the suitcases. Just as he was lifting the last one out of the car, Joyce pulled into the driveway.

"What's up, Honey? Whose suitcases are those?"

"It's a miracle, Darling. Your mother isn't dead."

Joyce stared at Buck then squeaked, "My mother's here?"

"Yup, her and some redhead."

"Redhead? Man or woman?"

"Woman."

Joyce headed for the house while Buck struggled with the heavy suitcases and mumbled to himself, "This is gonna be interesting."

Bernice met Joyce at the door. "Surprise!"

"Who let you out?"

"Very funny, Joyce. You sure have gained a lot of weight since I last saw you."

"I'm not fat, Mother, I'm pregnant." Joyce put both her hands protectively on her protruding stomach.

"Oh. When are you due?"

"In six weeks."

"Well, hurry up and come inside and sit down. You shouldn't be up and working this late anyway."

"Mom, don't start on me. You just got here and already you're beginning to annoy me."

"I'm trying to watch out for my grandchild. You didn't even tell me you were pregnant. What am I supposed to do?"

"For starters, introduce me to your friend."

"Grandy, this is Joyce, my pregnant daughter. Joyce, this is my friend, Grandy. We met at the retirement home."

"Nice to meet you, Grandy." Joyce extended her hand.

"It's a pleasure, Joyce. Your mother has told me a lot about you."

Bernice shot Grandy a "don't-you-dare" look. Grandy shook Joyce's hand and gave Bernie a sly wink.

"So Joyce, Honey, when were you planning on telling me about the baby, the job, and Buck?"

"I was planning on calling you next week, Mom, really. I've just been so busy with the job and getting the nursery together, time has just flown by."

"How come you and Buck aren't married yet?"

"Like I said, Mom, we've been busy."

"Do you know if the baby's a boy or a girl?"

"It's a girl. We've decided to name her Jackie, after Dad."

"Ah, it's a girl. Hope she brings you as much happiness as you've brought me."

"Thanks, Mother." Joyce said sarcastically.

"I'm gonna let you two continue your reunion without me. Where can my tired bones lay down for the night?" Grandy asked.

"Buck, Honey, will you please show Grandy where the guest bedroom is?"

"You bet, Sugar. Follow me Grandy."

"The bed won't shake like the toilet does, will it?"

"Don't worry, Grandy, only our bed does that."

"Buck!" Joyce shouted in a mortified tone.

"Calm down, Joyce. I'm just kidding."

Grandy smirked all the way down the hall, while Bernice and Joyce looked at each other with scarlet colored patches on their cheeks.

31

When voices and doors from the back section of the condo were quiet, Joyce broke the awkward silence, "Soooo, Mom, what brings you to California? I doubt you came just to see me."

"We got tickets to be on *The Price is Right* show."

"Bob Barker, that figures."

"You're an adult, Joyce. You could have come to visit me and your father."

"The way you and I have always fought, I didn't want to be responsible for putting any more stress on Dad."

"Well, you could have come to his funeral."

"I know. I feel really bad about that."

Bernice wasn't sure how to respond so she sat silently, staring at her chipped red nail polish. finally she said, "Where did you meet Buck?"

"He owns the used car lot where I bought my car. And yes, he is a very decent guy."

Bernice's voice was packed with judgment, "Oh yeah, real decent...sells you a car and then hops into bed with you. And then he doesn't even bother to marry you."

"For your information Mother, I'm the one that's been backing the marriage issue in the corner. Buck wanted to tie the knot a long time ago."

"I suppose you're afraid of another failed marriage?"

"Something like that."

"I guess I can understand that but why did you tell him I was dead?"

Joyce looked down, her long, blonde hair becoming a soft shield to hide her embarrassment. "I don't know, Mom. Guess I figured it was easier to say you were dead than try to explain all the problems we've had."

"Maybe if you had come to your father's funeral we could have worked through some of our problems." Tears rolled down Bernice's face as continued, "You cannot imagine what I went through when your father died."

Joyce stared at her mother then placed her hand gently on top of hers. She swallowed hard as pools of tears formed in her eyes also. "I'm really sorry about that, but I honestly didn't think you wanted me there. Last time I saw you, you called me a tramp and told me I wasn't welcome in your home."

"I never said any such thing."

"Yes you did, Mom."

"Well, if I did say it, I didn't mean it."

There was an uncomfortable pause in speech between mother and daughter. They both reached for the tissue box and smiled when their hands touched a tissue at the same time. Bernice knew that Joyce would have understood her mother better had she known about the two miscarriages and the stillbirth. Now was not the time to bring it up. Bernice spoke in a soft but determined voice,

"Perhaps it's time we put aside all our differences and concentrate on welcoming my granddaughter into this world."

"Sounds good to me. How 'bout I drive you two to the studio tomorrow?"

"That'd be great and I'm sure Grandy won't mind."

Chapter 10

"I think maybe Joyce and I are going to be okay, Grandy." Bernice had a dreamlike look in her eyes as she attempted to tease her hair into an unnatural position. "I think it's the baby."

Grandy mumbled, "Good for you and Joyce." She turned her attention back to a full length mirror and grimaced at herself. "I can't decide whether to tuck my shirt in or leave it hang out. Either way looks stupid. I can't believe you talked me into spending money on this outfit. I could've bought something much more practical for the UFO Crash Retrieval Conference in Las Vegas."

"Like what, Grandy? An aluminum foil hat? Quit your bellyaching. If you'd bought a pair of watermelon shorts like me, you'd see how nice the outfit looks. Besides, you won't be going to that conference, you hate to fly, remember?"

"Bernie, them there watermelon shorts look like a creation by Norman Rockwell on acid. UFO's are real, someday you'll be thanking me for all my knowledge about them. Now, quit primping and let's get some breakfast before we have to go to the studio."

The two bickering friends hobbled down the hall as the aroma of bacon and freshly brewed coffee permeated the kitchen. Buck stood over the stove, wearing a red-checkered apron, frying eggs in a generous layer of bacon grease. A platter of brittle bacon and another of buttered toast beckoned Bernice and Grandy from the kitchen table. Tall glasses of orange juice were positioned next to three settings of plates and silverware.

"Good morning, Ladies! Did y'all sleep okay last night?"

"Would have slept a lot better if Grandy didn't snore like a dump truck without a muffler."

"You shouldn't talk, Bernie. Your snoring brought the U.S. Marines to our room – they thought we were under siege."

Buck waved a spatula at the two old broads, hoping it would act as a magic wand and calm them down. "Why don't you sit down and have yourselves a hearty breakfast before your big day. How do you like your eggs, runny or hard?"

"Hard, please," Grandy said as she helped herself to a cup of coffee.

"Need milk or sugar for your coffee?"

"No thanks, Grandy yawned, "Got any Peppermint Schnapps?"

"Sorry, Grandy, fresh out."

"Dang."

"How about you, Ma'am?" Buck addressed Bernice with a large Texas smile.

"I'm just going to have some coffee Buck, I'm too excited to eat."

"Yes, Ma'am."

"Please call me Bernice or Mom, if you really are going to marry my daughter. You know, the proper thing to have done would have been to get married first and *then* get pregnant."

"Yes, Ma'am, I mean Mom. But just for the record, I've been trying to talk her into getting married for a long time. "

"That's what she said. But you certainly could have used more common sense when it came to the pregnancy thing. It's not that I'm not thrilled about a grandchild, it just-"

"Let it go, Bernie. You're preaching is getting old," Grandy's words could barely be understood as her mouth was stuffed with toast.

"Stay out of the conversation, Red, this doesn't concern you. And Buck, hope you continue to have a lot patience with Joyce, you're going to need it. By the way, where is she? I only see three place settings." Bernice's voice contained a hint of concern. "She said she would give us a ride to the studio today."

"Not to worry, Mom. She's just a little extra tired this morning, so I'm letting her sleep in. I'll be goin' that direction, I can drop y'all off and you can call me when you're all done."

"Thanks. You don't feed her this kind of breakfast every day though, do you?"

"No, Mom. This here kind of breakfast I only whip up when we have company or when Joyce is going to be gone all day."

"Got any ketchup, Buck? I can't eat my eggs without ketchup on them."

"Sure do, Grandy. I eat mine with Tabasco sauce. I enjoy that extra little kick."

Bernice watched in amazement as Buck swallowed his four eggs in very few bites and made three bacon sandwiches with the toast, eating those in only two bites each. Never mind his eating habits, she appreciated how his dark-lashed eyes seemed to smile every time he looked at her, and Bernice hoped this relationship would be the last one her daughter had to deal with.

"So, Buck, tell me a little about yourself. Your family and such," a curious Bernice requested.

"Well, I grew up in a little town outside of Dallas called Gunter. My mama stays home and takes care of my brother and sister. Daddy's a full-time rancher and part time-large equipment mechanic. I have an older sister living in Houston working as a nurse at a hospital and an older brother following the rodeo circuit around the country. I ended up in L.A. when my uncle needed some help at the car dealership. He died about a year ago and left the business to me. It provides a pretty decent income, but someday I hope me and Joyce can move to Texas. I sure miss being in the country. My family would love Joyce and there would always be a babysitter around."

35

"Not that my vote counts, Buck, but if I were you, I'd sell that jalopy junkyard as soon as the kid pops out and the three of you head for Minnesota. The smog here in California will kill you or, at the very least, make you goofy in the head," Grandy managed to say with her mouth full of toast.

Bernice gave Grandy a disgusted look. "Grandy might have first-hand knowledge about being goofy in the head, Buck, but you should go where it's best for you."

"Thanks, Mom. Don't worry about Joyce, I promise to do whatever it takes to make her happy. Now, it's time you two finish getting ready. I'll throw the dishes in the dishwasher."

There was a near mixup of liquids when Bernice and Grandy were splashing mouthwash in their mouths and Jean Nate' on all their exposed body parts. Bernice began to hyperventilate as thoughts of Bob Barker consumed her.

"Oh, Grandy, just think, in a few hours I will be kissing Bobby on the cheek. What a fantasy come true."

Grandy rolled her jet-lagged eyes and shook her head. "Bernie, there is no guarantee that you will get that close to the old man. You'll probably be arrested for stalking him before we even get in the door of the studio."

"No way, Grandy, I'm feeling lucky today."

Before leaving for their big adventure, Bernice quietly peeked in on her daughter. A confused memory and slightly poor eyesight played a three-second trick on her, though. She was about to tip-toe in the room and pull the covers snug around her six-year old daughter when Buck whispered to Bernice, "It's time to go, we still have traffic to deal with. She'll be fine, Mom."

As Buck drove his two house guests to the studio, he handed Bernice Joyce's cell phone and a slip of paper. "Here's my cell number. Call me when you're ready to be picked up."

"How do you work this thing?" Bernice asked.

"I'll show you, Bernie. We've taken enough of Buck's time. He needs to get to work."

"Good luck, Mom and Grandy. Hope y'all win big!"

As the old women watched Buck drive away, Bernice asked Grandy, "How do you know how to work a cell phone? You don't have one."

"Yes, I do, Bernie. I keep it out of sight, it's an important transmitting device, don't need to waste my minutes on frivolous, earthly conversations."

Bernice ignored Grandy's last comment, put the cell phone in her pocket and began walking briskly towards *The Price is Right* studio, her cane barely touching the ground.

"Slow down, you old bag," snapped Grandy, "you don't wanna get all sweaty for Bob."

"Yeah, you're right," Bernice replied. "Besides, look at the line. We're going to be here a while."

The two ladies took their place in line and waited for the doors to open. Every audience member waiting to get in was scrutinized by Bernice's nervous grey eyes.

"Do you think that lady's green shirt with the dollar signs on it is better than ours, Grandy?"

"Everybody's shirt is better than ours," Grandy said dryly. "Hey look, Bernie, there's a man wearing a pair of pants with pineapples on them. He a friend of yours?"

"If I didn't know you better, Grandy, I'd say you were trying to belittle me."

"Heck yeah, Bernie, I'm trying to belittle you. No friend would insist her friend be seen by millions on T.V. dressed in an outfit like this."

It was always a mystery to Bernice whether Grandy was sincere in her comments or displaying a form of less than obvious humor. Just when Bernice was about to interrogate Grandy further, the loudspeaker began spilling forth instructions. The doors were opened and potential contestants filed in one by one, through the security check and into the studio.

"I haven't had that much fun, Bernie, since I was in labor thirty-six hours with my third born." Grandy gave her friend a cutting stare. "You've redeemed yourself though, because your cane has given us front row seating. Not that I care."

The room was filled with men and women of all ages, dressed in imprinted T-shirts or sweatshirts. Bernice and Grandy sat in their seats and spent the first half-hour reading some of them. "Barker for President," "Bob, Ask Me What My Price Is," "My Dog and I Both Bark for Barker," "Want to Plunk My Plinko?"

"Bernie, I didn't think anyone could have a more idiotic saying on their T-shirt than ours. Boy, was I wrong."

"Try to be nice, Grandy. You know how important this is to me," pouted Bernice.

"Yeah, yeah."

A gentleman entered the stage. The crowd roared but quickly quieted when they realized it wasn't Bob.

"Good afternoon, Ladies and Gentlemen." The man proceeded to give instructions to the audience. There were lighted signs telling the groupies when to sit, when to stand, when to clap, and when to be quiet. He explained the procession down to the front when their names were called and expounded on on-stage etiquette. "And please turn all cell phones off until you are out of the building."

Bernice whispered to Grandy, "I'm gonna plant a big, juicy kiss on Bob Barker. He didn't say I couldn't do that, did he?"

"Shhh," Grandy scolded.

When the "all quiet" sign was lit, the audience became silent. Bernice took a quick look around, wondering if anyone else could hear her beating heart.

"Did you turn off the cell phone, Bernie?"

"It's off, I checked."

All eyes were on the stage as the theme music began. The enthusiastic voice of the announcer, Rich Fields, filled the room.

Chapter 11

"Milly Maxwell, come on down!" From the middle of the room an immense woman scurried to the bidding podium, screaming loudly enough to damage ear drums. She wore a bright yellow T-shirt imprinted with the words, "I Love Bob Barker."

"Wendy Simpson, come on down!" Wendy showed just a pinch more reservation in her approach towards the podium. She also sported a T-shirt expressing her devotion to the game show host.

"Patty Redman, come on down!" Doing a jive dance down the aisle towards the podium, Patty continued her dance exhibition while waiting for the fourth and final contestant to be called.

"Phil Wilson, come on down!" Phil, a slim but muscular, 20-year-old college student pranced his way next to the three female contestants. Not wanting to be out of place, he also wore a T-shirt, which read, "I Love the Barker Beauties."

The noise level had reached its peak when Rich announced, "And here's your host, Bob Bar-ker!"

Bernice heaved her big bottom off the seat and began shouting, "I love you, Bob!" Her body allowed short bursts of jumping. Grandy snickered to herself as she noticed Bernice's ample boobs keeping rhythm with her waving hands.

The first item up for bid was a bag containing exclusive golf clubs. That was a no-brainer bid for Phil as he was as passionate about golf as he was about girls. When he was told he could win a trip to the Caribbean Islands, Phil was so excited, he did a handstand on stage. After a nerve wracking game of Cliff Hangers, Phil won the trip. In response to this thrilling event, he did a cartwheel. He and two more contestants won the chance to spin the big wheel in the first half of the game show. Phil was as lucky as he was agile, and the first one to win a place in the Showcase Show Down.

The second half of the game was about to begin and Bernice squirmed in her seat, anticipating that the next name to be called was hers. She envisioned being a big winner and maybe even kissing Bobby on the lips.

"Grandy McGregor, come on down!"

The two friends looked at each other in disbelief. Bernice almost peed her pants. Grandy turned to her friend and said in a whisper tinged with panic, "Pretend to be me, you go up there."

"We can't do that, Grandy. Hurry up and go, they're waiting on you."

Grandy stood up and made an attempt at excitement by waving her white, blue-veined arms. She silently cursed to herself because a) she didn't want to go up there, and b) she knew as much about the game as a copy machine repairman does about milking a cow. A disillusioned Bernice made an attempt at rallying for her friend, but a tear rolled down her face as she watched her opportunity to kiss Bob Barker wither away.

"Now Ladies, here's your next item up for bid…. An elegant crystal chandelier!"

A massive, opulent light fixture appeared from the ceiling and settled at eye level. While the audience used utterances of admiration during the description of the prize, Grandy rolled her eyes and shook her head.

"Grandy, what's your bid for the chandelier."

She stared a moment at the hanging piece of impractical home furnishing and reluctantly mumbled, "$50."

Bob arched his eyebrows and asked, "Are you sure?"

"Of course I'm sure."

Bernice was perched at the edge of her seat, sure that her loony friend would make some comment about not wanting that ridiculous item. Much to her amazement, nothing else proceeded from Grandy's mouth.

It was no surprise that Grandy did not win and Bernice crossed her fingers when the second round of bidding began. It was an entertainment package including an iPod, computer software and hardware. Grandy didn't know what the heck an iPod was, but she knew a little bit about the computer software. She didn't even bother to look at Bernice for a bid number as she figured the old biddy knew as much about computers as she did about welding.

When Grandy's turn came to bid, she said "$1.00," knowing she was safe with that number. It was the one bit of information she finally remembered Bernie telling her about bidding, because most contestants usually bid too high.

"The retail price for the entertainment package is $875!"

Everybody except Grandy knew what had happened, she just stood there waiting impatiently for the next bidding war to start.

Bob exclaimed, "Grandy you're our winner!"

"Yeah, Grandy!" Bernice shouted. For a moment though, she wished Grandy would die of a heart attack.

On stage, Grandy stood passively next to Bob Barker. He looked over at her with mild interest.

"Where you from, Grandy?"

"What does my T-shirt say, Bob?" Grandy pointed to her chest.

Bob professionally ignored the sarcasm and asked, "What city in Minnesota are you from?"

"Grandy."

Bob thought it wise not to pursue any further his geographical questions, so he asked a less complicated question, "Anyone you want to say hi to?"

"Just my friend sitting in the audience. Hi, Bernie," she said in a monotone voice. Grandy displayed a wimpy wave to her friend.

"Okay, Grandy, let's get started. Do you know how to play Plinko?"

"No. But Bernice does."

"Here's how it works. I'm going to give you one Plinko coin. But first, Rachel here is going to show you several items with two corresponding numbers. If you can tell me which number is included in the price of that item, you will not only win that item, but I will give you one more Plinko coin for each correct answer. Are you ready to play?"

"I guess so."

The first item was a Sunbeam electric can opener. The two numbers were 9 and 5.

"5…9…5…9" The audience hollered.

Grandy didn't know the answer so she looked at Bernice, who was holding up five fingers.

"Five," said Grandy.

Grandy was able to get all three correct, thanks to Bernice, which gave her a total of four Plinko coins.

"Now, Grandy, up you go. Let's see if you can hit the $10,000 slot."

Grandy shuffled up the Plinko steps and began, one by one, to drop her Plinko coins into the slots.

"Five hundred dollars!"

The crowd cheered.

"Zero."

"Aaaah," sympathized the audience.

"One hundred dollars!"

The audience raised the volume of their enthusiasm.

Grandy's shaking fingers plunked the Plinko one more time and won $10,000. She wasn't exactly sure what had happened, but guessed it must be something big because the crowd was going crazy and Bernie was jumping up and down like a kangaroo with one lame foot. When Bob explained what had occurred, she turned to him and held out her hand and asked, "Where's my money?"

Bob paused only a second before explaining to her that she would get it after the show. One of the Barker Beauties stepped in and quickly ushered Grandy off the stage.

"It was bad enough Grandy got to go on stage, now she's making a fool out of herself on national TV," Bernice mumbled to herself. She tried to hide by slouching in her chair.

Next thing Grandy knew, she was sitting next to Phil and the other contestants in the front row to the left of the stage. Not fully aware of what was going on, she became annoyed and started firing questions at Phil.

"How come we have to sit here? When am I going to get my money? This is such a dumb show. Did you know Mr. Barker wears makeup? Old men shouldn't wear make-up, it makes them look like they're getting ready for their own funeral."

Poor Phil wasn't quite sure how to pacify this red-haired grandmother, so he tried to give her some tips about spinning the big wheel. "Remember to stand firmly, hang on to the wheel tight, and pull real hard."

"Sounds like putting on a girdle."

It wasn't too long before Grandy was back on stage ready for her turn at the big wheel. Then the most incredulous event occurred. Grandy spun $1.00 on her first try and since nobody else did the same, she was destined to join Phil in the big showcase.

Chapter 12

"Okay, Grandy, you are our big winner. You'll go first. Rich, tell us what we have in our first showcase."

First up, a Sony digital camera!" The audience cheered on cue. Grandy was mildly interested and didn't look at Bernice.

Rich continued, "You will have plenty of opportunity to use your new camera when you take it with you on your trip to France!"

The audience whooped and hollered. As Rich described the vacation accommodations, Grandy tried to picture in her mind what a trip to France would be like – sitting on a tiny café chair, next to rude people with body odor, eating buttered snails, and looking at an over-sized ornamental piece of metal. "Yeah, sounds like fun," she thought sarcastically.

Rich's booming voice broke her pessimistic mental wanderings.

And when you get home from France, you can take another vacation in this red Pontiac Sunbird!"

Grandy had not looked at Bernice during the showcase announcements. She did not want to feel pressure to bid or pass on what Bernice might say was the wrong prize. So when Bob asked her if she was going to bid or pass on the showcase, her decision was based on a "heads or tails" game she played out in her mind.

"I'll pass."

"No!" screeched Bernice. She began waving a paper napkin taken from her purse, trying frantically to catch Grandy's attention. "Bid on France, Grandy, bid on France!"

Grandy shrugged her shoulders at Bernie and gave her an "Oh well" look. Bernice plopped back down in her seat, deflated as a popped, blood-swollen wood tick. And Bob had already moved over by Phil, asking him his bid price for the European Showcase.

"I'll bid $35,000.00, Bob."

"Okay, Rich, what do we have in Showcase Number Two?"

"First up, a pair of Schwinn, 28-speed mountain bikes. You and a friend can travel many miles on the comfort and durability of these bikes. And when your legs become tired from pedaling, continue to enjoy the great outdoors on this set of Mongoose Electric Scooters!"

Cheers from the audience increased in volume while Bernice sat still, silently praying Grandy would bid too high on this showcase of recreational suicide. Panic blistered in her stomach as she noticed the beginnings of a smile on Grandy's face while she listened to Rich's description of the scooters. Bernice tried to envision herself and her crotchety, old roommate riding something not much bigger than a skateboard on the two-lane roads of Minnesota. All she could imagine was the two of them having deadly reunions with four-legged creatures.

The visions from Grandy's slightly demented mind followed a different course. She imagined herself and Bernie in leather jackets, custom-painted helmets, and goggles, the fresh countryside air encouraging them down roads of adventure. She wondered if Dakota could paint flames somewhere on the scooters. Maybe she could trade them in for a slightly larger scooter with a sidecar? Since Bernice didn't have a driver's license, Grandy was going to have to chauffeur her around. Old Red's reflections were interrupted by Rich's announcement of the final prize of the showcase.

"And finally, when you feel the need for more comfort and convenience, this beautiful Fleetwood Terra 26Q Motor Home!"

If Grandy had been wearing bloomers, she was sure she would have split them. "A motor home!"she almost screamed out loud. As Rich rattled on about the specifications of the motor home, Old Red unpacked a memory from her youth - her mother, father, her brother, Dale, and herself, laughing as they tried to set up an old, canvas tent near the Mille Lacs Lake. It was the family's first attempt at camping, but not their last. Grandy loved camping. It was like having a permanent home compared to the life of a traveling preacher's daughter.

The wary host looked over at Grandy and hoped she would not do anything unusual like ask to see the inside of the motor home first. He cautiously asked her, "And Grandy, what's your bid for the Cross-Country Showcase?"

The red-haired grandma scowled as she noticed her friend gesturing the zero sign with her hands.

"I bid $1.00."

Bob raised his eyebrows at her and the audience politely applauded while letting loose a mixture of verbal expressions.

"We'll be back after these messages to see who our Showcase winner will be," said Bob.

During the commercial break, Grandy looked at Bernie but received only a freezer cold stare. "Figures," mumbled Grandy. "She wanted the trip to France. The old lady doesn't even realize what a waste of time that would be. Why would anybody want to travel thousands of miles to drink old wine and visit even older broken down buildings, when right here in the United States you can visit the landmarks of famous UFO sightings."

Bob said to Phil after the break, "Phil, you bid $35,000 on your showcase. The actual retail price is $22,875. You have over-bid by $12,125. Phil slapped his forehead while moaning and groaning along with the audience. Bob turned to Grandy and in sincere delight, "Grandy, that makes you our Showcase Winner!"

The theme music echoed through the studio. Bernice took her fake smile and joined Grandy on stage. They hobbled over to the bicycles, scooters, and motor home.

"Don't even begin to entertain the idea that we are going anywhere in that small, metal box," Bernice hissed at Grandy. "And for sure those bicycles and motorbikes are going to be sold so we can – "

Bernice stopped her muffled tirade as Bob approached the ladies to congratulate Grandy. She immediately changed her demeanor and scuttled close enough to the game show host to plant a kiss on his cheek.

"Oh, Bob, I've been a fan of yours since the 70s! I just – "

Once again, Bernice was interrupted in her attempts to convey sentiment. This time it was the William Tell Overture resounding from her shorts. Bob looked at her with a quizzed expression.

"I thought you said the phone was turned off," Grandy said with mild disgust.

"It was, I mean, I didn't hear any dial tone."

"Oh, for crying out loud, Bernie, hurry up and answer the phone."

"I don't know how!" The scared senior thrust the cell phone at Grandy and said, "help me!"

Old Red hit the on button and handed it back to Bernice.

"Hello."

"Mom, its Buck. We're on our way to L.A. General. Joyce is in labor!"

"Oh my gosh, Buck! What happened? It's too early? Is Joyce okay? Oh my gosh! We'll be right there!"

Hyperventilation had kicked into code red for Bernice. She hung up the phone and grabbed Grandy by the arm.

"We have to get to L.A. General fast, Joyce is in labor! How are we going to get there? We need a taxi or bus or something!"

"Relax, Old Lady, we'll take the motor home. All we need to do is find a way to drive off it the stage."

"We can't take that thing now."

"Why not? It's mine. I won it fair and square."

Fortunately for Bernice and Grandy, Bob had overheard the cell phone conversation. He felt sorry for the two old ladies whose matches didn't seem to fit in the box.

"Your friend is right, Grandy. You can't take your prizes home today, but I have to make an appearance at a fund raiser for my foundation tonight. I could have my driver drop you off at the hospital, if you like."

"Oh, Mr. Barker, that would be wonderful. Thank you a million times," Bernice said in an anguished gush.

"Go fill out the required paperwork for your prizes, Grandy, and I'll meet you and Bernice at the studio back door."

After completing necessary formalities concerning the game show prizes, the concerned grandmas climbed into Bob's long, white limousine. While Bernice tried to deal with conflicting emotions – fear for her daughter and unborn grandchild, and the thrill of sitting next to her unsuspecting heartthrob – Grandy surveyed the interior of the ornate car.

"You got a bar in this here fancy car?" Grandy asked.

"Grandy! How rude of you to be asking questions like that! Mr. Barker has been kind enough to give us a ride to the hospital. Don't be treating him like some redneck relative of yours!"

"Mr. Barker is a host, isn't he? And a good host always offers his guests refreshments." Grandy gave her roommate a look of "I-can't-believe-you-didn't-know-this."

Bob chuckled and patted Bernice's knee, "It's okay, Bernice, it's been a long day for all of us and I'm sure your friend just wants to celebrate her big winnings. Look in the compartment next to you, Grandy. I'm sure you'll find something to satisfy your thirst."

"Thanks, Bob, you're all right."

While Grandy poured herself a glass of brandy, Bernice spoke to her in frustration. "Speaking of winnings, *Grandy,* how come you passed on that trip to France? What are we going to do with bicycles and a metal coffin on wheels?"

"We're going camping, Bernie. You always said you wanted more adventure in your life."

"Well, I'm not going anywhere with you, especially in a mechanical nightmare like that. Besides, all I care about right now is Joyce and the baby. Are we almost to the hospital, Mr. Barker?"

"Not much farther, Bernice."

"Hey Bob, what's this foundation you're raising money for?" asked Grandy in a not-really-that-interested tone of voice.

"DJ&T. It's a foundation I started to obtain grants to encourage more mobile units for the spaying and neutering of pets. I love dogs and cats, but, just like people, they all need a happy home."

"Hmmmm, a mobile unit to neuter my ex would have come in handy. God knows he's been way too generous with his sperm. Maybe you could start a foundation for spaying husbands and boyfriends," Grandy said in a casual but serious voice.

Bob wasn't sure if Grandy was kidding, but based on the little knowledge he had of her, he thought she was probably quite sincere. He breathed a big sigh of relief as they pulled into the hospital emergency parking lot.

"Well, here we are Ladies, L.A. General. I hope your daughter and grandchild will be okay, Bernice. I wish you both the best of luck."

"Thanks again, Mr. Barker," Bernice said. She gave him another kiss on the cheek. She then hurriedly exited the limo and headed for the hospital entrance.

Grandy was a little slower in getting out but she also thanked Bob for the ride.

"Sorry, no kisses from me, Bob. I appreciate the camper and all, but to tell you the truth, I think "*The Price is Right*" is a dumb show. No offense."

"No offense taken, Grandy," he said with a whimsical smile.

Chapter 13

Bernice leaned over the nurses' station, panting loudly.

"I'm here.... to see ... my daughter... Joyce Gibson."

"Are you okay, Ma'am?" asked the nurse, trying not to stare at the inscription on Bernice's T-shirt.

"Yes, just... tell me where ... my daughter..." For fifty years Bernice had successfully repressed her pain and grief of having two miscarriages and a stillbirth. Now she was gripped with fear that her daughter had inherited her baby making difficulties.

"She's in room 322, on the third floor. Turn left after you get off the elevator. Can I get you a wheelchair? Are you going to be okay?"

"I'm fine, thanks."

Grandy raised her index finger, "I'll take that wheelchair."

For a moment, the nurse experienced double vision, as there appeared another old woman with a hot pink shirt bearing the same inscription.

"Do you need – "

"No, she doesn't need a wheelchair!" Bernice said in a blaze of temper. "Come on, Grandy, quit screwing around."

Bernice ignored her frustrating friend on the elevator. She was too worried about Joyce to deal with her anger over Grandy's good fortune, and how she frittered away a trip to France for a stupid motor home.

"Hi, Mom... Grandy ... nice outfits," Joyce rolled her eyes.

"Are you okay? You had me worried to death." Bernice stroked Joyce's seriously bleached blonde hair with one hand while her other hand rested gently on Joyce's arm.

"False alarm, Mom. Not to worry."

"Doc says she's been on her feet too much. No more bartending for this little mama," Buck added.

"I'll say not! You are going to put your feet up when you get home and leave them up," Bernice said emphatically.

"Amen to that," Buck said with kind firmness.

In an exasperated voice, Joyce said, "Great, now I've got two mothers."

"Now, Joycie, quit your whining. We're only trying to do what's best for you."

"Please don't call me 'Joycie' Mother, I hate that name."

"It does sound kind of stupid, Bernie," Grandy chimed in.

"No one asked you," Bernice spit out at her friend. Switching gears, she cooed at Joyce, "When are they going to release you from the hospital, Honey?"

"Sometime tomorrow morning."

"See, I knew you didn't have anything to worry about, Bernie," Grandy stated.

"Yeah, you just know everything, don't you," Bernice retorted.

Grandy rambled on. "I thought you might have that baby on the way to the hospital. I'm the authority on that subject, since I was born in the backseat of a car, all three of my boys were born in the backseat of a car, and come to think of it, my oldest was even conceived in the backseat of a car."

Everyone chuckled as Grandy tried to take the center of attention away from the mother-to-be, everyone, that is, except Bernice.

"Shut up, Grandy. Our only concern here is Joyce – not how many times your feet rested on the inside roof of a car."

Grandy gave Bernice the evil eye.

"Minnesota Mama Hot for Bob Barker," Joyce read out loud. "So, did you finally meet your heart throb, Mom?"

"Oh, I met him," Bernice pouted. "But this crazy old broad next to me got called as a contestant instead of me. I should have been the one on stage, but they made a mistake."

Buck and Joyce looked at each other with an "Oh no, hear we go" expression. "Did you win, Grandy?"

Grandy pushed her chest out a size or two, "Sure did! I won a motor home!"

"Yeah, can you believe that? She passed up a trip to France for a stupid hotel on wheels. What is she going to do with an over-sized metal breadbox?"

"Oh, Mom, you should be happy for her." Joyce touched her big belly as little Jackie began doing back flips. "Calm down, Girl, let's try to hold on for a few more weeks."

A circle of grins appeared on the faces of Buck and the ladies as they watched Joyce's stomach expand and contract from the baby's premature effort to escape her mother's womb.

Grandy barely skipped a beat, and continued on her boasting spree. "Yup and I also won bicycles, motorcycles, computer stuff, and CASH!"

Bernice winced as she watched her friend being in rare form. Not in the few short months that she'd known Grandy had she been quite so *cheery*. It made Bernice stew even more seeing her roommate revel in her lucky streak, because that's all it was, pure luck. Grandy didn't win based on knowing anything. In fact, if it wasn't for her guidance during Plinko, Grandy would never have made it to the showcase.

"Yeah, your mother and I are going on a trip."

"Hush up Grandy, you traitor," Bernice snipped. "I'm not going anywhere with you."

"Maybe we'll see the Mother Ship if we get far enough out in the desert. Besides, you owe me for dragging my butt on an airplane then embarrassing myself in this ridiculous T-shirt."

"Yeah, and if I'm lucky, the extra-terrestrials will take you with them," a miffed Bernice said.

"Yeah, you mock me now, but just wait."

Buck tried to maintain a serious composure. "Okay, Ladies, that's enough bantering for today. Joyce needs her rest."

"You can't be serious, Grandy. Wouldn't you rather sell it and take the cash?" asked Joyce.

"Hey, I can probably dump that thing for ya down at my place," added Buck.

"No way, Buck. It's being delivered in a few short weeks and we'll be on our way."

Bernice rolled her eyes.

"Okay, but if you change your mind, I can give you the names of a couple of reputable RV dealers in Minnesota."

"Nope. Some Tupperware and a trip to Sam's Club and we're good to go."

Bernice decided it wasn't worth debating the issue with Grandy. She was sure that by the time this whole thing was over, her psycho traveling companion would make the Clampetts look like refined royalty.

"If you're done yapping, I'd like to tell my daughter the rest of the story."

"Oh, you mean the limo ride with Bob Barker?"

"You old hag. Don't you ever shut up?"

A venomous stare from Bernice made Grandy think twice about a verbal comeback.

"No way! You really got to ride with Bob Barker?" Joyce asked.

"I sure did. I even got to kiss him on the cheek, twice!" Bernice's demeanor had quickly changed from an angry, old lady into an imitation of a star-struck teenager. She clasped her dried hands together and closed her eyes to relive the event. "He is soooo handsome," she said in a feather-soft voice.

"Mom!"

"Hmmph! I was just as close to him as your mother and I didn't think he was worth writing down in my little black book," Grandy huffed.

"Your idea of handsome, Grandy, is anything four feet tall, green, with bulging eyes," Bernice quipped.

Joyce gave Buck a "please-make-them-stop" look as she once again rubbed her moving stomach. Her future husband adjusted his cowboy hat and interrupted the bickering, "You two ladies hungry?"

"You buyin'?" asked Grandy.

"Sure I'll buy y'all supper."

"You two run along, I'll sit here with Joyce," Bernice answered, "I'm not really hungry."

"You sure? Can I bring you back something?" offered Buck.

"Maybe a cup of strong coffee, if it's not too much trouble."

"You got it, Mom, no trouble at all."

"Well, I could eat a horse. Let's go, Buck," Grandy demanded, grabbing his arm.

Buck kissed Joyce on the forehead and rolled his eyes at Bernice, as if to say *thanks for leaving me alone with your lunatic friend.*

Grandy kept Buck entertained in the cafeteria by revealing the more unusual activities of her childhood. As the old lady downed a chicken fried steak dinner and a piece of banana cream pie, she talked anytime her mouth was not too full. Buck tried not to choke on his supper as he listened to her descriptions of making hogshead cheese and trying to squeeze eggs out of a chicken by using her daddy's vise. His interest in her ramblings peaked though when she started talking about the trip across the country in a motor home with his future mother-in-law.

"You think you two are up to traveling cross country by yourselves?" Buck's voice projected concern, even though he was sure Grandy could probably take care of herself.

"Of course we are. We're old, not dead. If your wimpy future mother-in-law won't go with me, I'll go by myself. She can be such a fuddy-duddy sometimes. Besides, Bernie is always complaining about the hole we live in and how she's too young to give up on life."

Buck observed the red-haired grandmother with amusement. She was crabby, bizarre, and rude, but always projected a manner that led one to believe she was a true friend. Despite the bickering between her and Bernice, Buck knew Grandy was probably the best friend Bernice had or ever would have. And lucky? Boy, was this senior citizen lucky. And everybody needs luck.

"Ahh, Grandy, she'll go with you. She's just a little bent out of shape because her dream to participate in *The Price is Right* game didn't come true. Give her some time to calm down."

"She better get her knickers out of a knot because I'm tired of her whining," Grandy's voice was woven with threads of frustration and disappointment.

"Like I said, give her a little time and maybe lay off the talk about aliens and Mother Ships. That might be scaring her a bit."

Grandy's lips twisted as she gave Buck a look of guarded surrender.

"Let's get your friend her coffee."

* * *

Meanwhile, Joyce further queried her mother about Grandy. "Doesn't she seem just a bit *off* to you, Mom?"

"All I know is, she looked pretty ridiculous up on stage. She kept staring at me for the right answers. Then I tell her what to do, and she does just the opposite. I am so angry right now. I can't believe it. I could be on my way to Paris."

"I don't know, Mom. This traveling around the country, just you and Grandy, doesn't sound like a good idea."

"It probably isn't, but staying in that retirement home isn't a good idea either. Maybe I don't want to ride around in an over-sized sardine can and eat off paper plates, but somebody's got to watch out for Grandy. That old fool will end up getting lost on the top of some mountain because she thought she heard ET calling her home."

Joyce reflected a moment before meekly suggesting to her mother that she come live with her and Buck. Now that their relationship was on the mend, having her around might not be so bad.

"So, what do you think? You want to come stay with us?"

A thousand yeses wanted to come out of Bernice's mouth. She imagined playing with Jackie and going shopping with her daughter. The Minnesota winters would no longer attack her weak bones and dealing with Grandy's intense personality would be two thousand miles away. But oh how her infuriating roommate made her laugh, which was something she hadn't done a lot of since Jack died. After all, she and Joyce never got along before. Could a baby really have the power to change all that?

"Mom? What do you say?"

"I'd love to live with you, Jackie, and Buck, but I can't. Grandy needs me even more than you do. The three of you can take care of each other. Grandy doesn't have anyone who really cares about her except me. I know she's a little different but she means well. I'm sorry, Joyce."

Bernice's daughter smiled at her mother and wrapped her firm, tanned arms around her. "It's okay, Mom. You promise to visit often though, right? And stay away from people who say, 'Beam me up, Scotty.'"

"Don't worry, Honey, we'll be fine."

Buck and Grandy entered Joyce's room, chuckling over the two-inch scar Grandy was pointing to on her left forearm.

"What's so funny?" Joyce inquired.

"Grandy was telling me how she got that scar on her arm. She said tipping over outhouses can be a dangerous profession at times. Make sure you watch for barbed wire hidden in the bushes around it."

"Yeah, I'll remember that next time I have the urge to examine someone else's poop," muttered Bernice.

Buck stood next to Joyce's hospital bed, gently touched her on the shoulder, and whispered into her ear. Both their eyes lit up and Joyce nodded her head in agreement.

"What?" Bernice and Grandy said in unison.

"We decided that if Joyce feels up to it tomorrow, we're going take a trip to the courthouse."

"The courthouse?" asked Bernice.

"Yeah, now that Joyce is off work, we'll have time to get married. And I know she'd love to have you there, Mom."

"I love weddings!" exclaimed Grandy, oblivious to the fact that she wasn't directly invited.

"Oh kids, I don't know what to say. I'm so happy for you!" Bernice's face suddenly registered panic, "I didn't bring any clothes for a wedding."

"We'll figure it out, very informal. I don't really care what you wear, as long as it's not that T-shirt and those ugly shorts," Joyce replied.

"Amen to that!" Grandy proclaimed. "I'll buy the rice and decorate the car."

"That won't be necessary, Grandy, this is going to be a quiet, private ceremony," Joyce said in a firm but kind voice.

Comprehension slowly spread over Grandy's face. "Gotcha. Guess you don't need a white dress or veil, either?"

Chapter 14

"Well, that was the shortest wedding ever," commented Bernice. Noticing emotional injury in Joyce's green eyes, her mother quickly added, "It was a beautiful ceremony, though, Honey. Really it was."

"Yeah, fancy bouquets and throwing rice are way overrated," Grandy managed to say while gulping down a glass of apple juice. "When me and Lester got married, he wore the overalls that he just finished milking cows in and I yanked a handful of tulips from my neighbor's yard. Heck, we were two kids in love, didn't give a whip about swanky decorations or big diamond rings."

Joyce and Bernice looked at each other, acknowledging the same thought, "please don't let this woman talk about her honeymoon."

The wedding party of four was seated in a booth at Denny's Restaurant for their post-wedding feast. The ladies from Minnesota were dressed in the clothes they had planned to wear on the trip home, a paisley print dress for Bernice and a navy blue, seer sucker pant suit and red high tops for Grandy. The bride wore black slacks and a white maternity blouse. The groom opted for faded blue jeans, dusty cowboy boots, and tan corduroy jacket with dark brown felt patches on the elbows.

"All I know is, this one was a lot cheaper than your first wedding," Bernice said while reviewing the menu.

"Thanks for the reminder, Mom." Joyce shifted uncomfortably, placed her small, delicate hand on Buck's, and gave him a reassuring squeeze. The new husband gave his wife an empathic smile.

"Your real name is Bill Arbuckle? Hmm, did you know Joyce's first three husbands – "

"Zip it, Grandy," hissed Bernice.

Buck chuckled within at the two old women sitting across from him and Joyce. Despite their juvenile bantering, he found them to be like a pair of worn, flannel pajamas – thin but hard to part with.

"I know about Joyce's ex-husbands and I know their names were Bill. Don't worry, Mom and Grandy, I'm not a cheater, shyster, or cross dresser. I promise to love, honor, and obey Joyce forever." Buck's handsome smile radiated sincerity and warmth as he looked first at his new bride, then at Grandy and Bernice.

"Oh, I know you'll be a good husband, Buck, it's just that I'm worried –"

"Bernie, leave the newlyweds alone, let them be happy and quit hen-pecking your daughter. You sound like an irritating creak in a car door."

Looks of annoyance passed between Bernice and Grandy. Finally, the new mother-in-law spoke in a more festive voice. "I'm buying since I didn't have time to get you a wedding present."

"I didn't get you anything, either, but I won a can opener you can have."

"Thanks, Mom. And that's okay, Grandy, we have everything we need," Joyce looked at Buck with amusement.

A college-age waitress appeared at the table, ready to take their orders. Joyce and Bernice each ordered turkey club sandwiches, while Buck chose the Grand Slam Breakfast. Grandy decided to challenge the patience of the waitress by requesting each item of her meal be cooked in a special manner.

The waitress remained calm, repeating back the instructions, all the while thinking that this old broad would probably leave her something weird as a tip, like a pamphlet on how to make bird feeders out of ketchup bottles or a roll of crushed breath mints.

"Give it a break, Grandy, just eat what shows up." Bernice was clearly irritated with her friend's particular demands. She then turned her attention back to Joyce.

"We didn't get any pictures of the wedding."

"Oh, that's okay. I don't really want any photos of me looking like a blimp."

"Darling, you don't look like a blimp, you look beautiful," Buck assured Joyce.

"Yeah, you look – glowing, like most pregnant brides," replied Grandy.

Bernice gave Grandy a daggered stare and again turned to her daughter. "So Joyce, when's your exact due date?"

"Memorial Day, but I doubt I'll make it that long. I don't think I can get any bigger."

"Well, soon as you get home today, you stay there until little Jackie says it's time to go back to the hospital. I'll try and get back in a few weeks to see you, and my new granddaughter, of course."

"That would be wonderful, Mom."

"Hey you newlyweds, is it okay if we park the motor home in your driveway when we come?" Grandy's eagerness was quite apparent.

"Ignore her," replied Bernice, "She won't be driving any over-sized metal shoe box across the country."

"You just watch me – "

Bernice rolled over the rest of Grandy's sentence by asking Joyce questions about baby accessories.

* * *

Thanks again for lunch, Mom."

The foursome stood outside the restaurant, absorbing the comforting rays of the April sun.

"Yeah, thanks, Mom," Buck added.

Grandy elbowed Bernie and chimed in, "Yeah, thanks, *Mom*."

"You're very welcome, Joyce and Buck. We better get going though, it's time to get Grandy out of the public eye." She glanced over at her friend, giving her a "gotcha back" look.

Mr. and Mrs. Arbuckle tried not to laugh, but Grandy's pouting expression was comical.

"Our plane leaves at 4:00 and we still have to return the rental car," said Bernice.

* * *

Back at the condo, an exhausted Joyce collapsed on the sofa while Grandy and Bernice gathered their belongings for the trip home. Rather than try and explain directions back to the airport, Buck offered to drive to the airport and let the ladies follow him.

"I'm going, too."

"No, Joycie, you stay here and rest," insisted Bernice.

"Only if you promise to never call me Joycie again."

"Sorry, Honey."

"At least let me walk you to the car."

Buck grabbed the larger suitcases while Grandy and Bernice handled their carry-ons.

"Why don't you put them in the trunk?" asked Joyce with a puzzled look, as they began piling everything into the backseat.

"My wheelchair's in the trunk," Grandy exclaimed in a matter-of-fact tone.

"Wheelchair?"

"I'll explain later," Bernice whispered to Joyce.

The new mother-in-law then hugged her daughter tightly and touched her stomach with the greatest of tenderness. "See you soon, little Jackie. And you," pointing her index finger gently into Joyce's chest, "get some rest. Call me when she gets here."

"I will, Mom. I promise. You have a safe trip." Then leaning in a little closer to her mother, she said softly, "Remember, the offer is still good."

Joyce extended her hand to Grandy, who shook it with the force of a woman much younger. "Nice meeting you, Joyce. And thanks again for having us."

"You are quite welcome, Grandy. It was nice meeting you too. Come back and visit again." Joyce silently prayed God would forgive her for telling that little white lie.

Once the two vehicles were traveling towards the airport, Grandy asked her roommate, "What offer?"

"What do you mean?"

"I heard Joyce mention an offer to you."

"Never mind, nosy, just make sure you keep Buck in your sight."

"I'm not about to lose him and make a wrong turn, I know how well you read maps."

"Very funny, *Red*."

Buck stopped in front of the Avis drop-off as Grandy skidded in behind him.

"Told ya, so." Bernice yelped.

"Told me what?"

"That you were following too close."

"Hey, your air bag didn't go off, did it?"

Bernice got out, looked at the quarter-of-an-inch clearance between the two bumpers and shook her head in disbelief. "For crying out loud Grandy, you drive better after a visit with Captain Morgan."

The red-haired senior citizen fidgeted in her wheelchair as the three of them waited for the bus to the terminal. Buck extended his large hand to Grandy, "It was a pleasure meetin' you, Miss Grandy."

"Yeah, you too, Buck," Grandy said as she shook his hand. He was surprised at the strength of the old lady and at that moment realized, that she and Bernice would probably be just fine traveling the United States highways.

Bernice and Buck gave each other a parting hug.

"I'm glad my daughter married you, Buck. I think she made one of the smartest decisions of her life. Now, you take good care of my girls."

"Yes, Mom."

* * *

Once through the security check at the airport, Bernice let loose a big sigh.

"You had me scared to death, Grandy, the security people rummaging through your carry-on and asking all kinds of questions. Next time, take the batteries out of your electric toothbrush."

"You'd think those morons would have seen an electric toothbrush a thousand times before. They acted like it was a machine of mass destruction."

"I'm sure they have seen electric toothbrushes. But the sound of yours turned on, accident or not, must have sounded like some kind of activated weapon."

"Dern fools, I'm going to have a drink. You comin'?"

"No. You're on your own this trip. Just try to stay out of trouble and don't miss our flight."

Remembering Buck's advice to give Bernie time to cool off, Grandy turned her wheelchair around and headed to the bar, leaving her roommate to sulk by herself.

After two very expensive shots of whiskey, Grandy slept all the way to Minneapolis while Bernice wrestled with her conscience. She thought maybe if she stopped her resentment towards Grandy, God would answer her prayer for a healthy granddaughter. She knew in her heart that holding a grudge was a sin,

57

and it really wasn't Grandy's fault they called her name as a *Price is Right* contestant. But no matter how much she rationalized it, she couldn't get rid of the knot in her stomach.

* * *

The weary travelers arrived home at around midnight. The eery silence of the lobby was broken as Larry approached the ladies, dressed in floral, synthetic-silk pajamas and matching robe.

"Nice outfit, Lare," Grandy said dryly.

"You two old broads are full of it. You weren't on *The Price is Right*."

"Yes we were! Grandy was the big winner on Tuesday."

"Dream on. I watched every day and you were not on T.V."

"It's taped, you big dummy," Bernice snipped.

"Yeah, sure," the old man spit back.

"Let's go, Bernie. Don't waste your time with a man who dresses like a Barbie Doll reject."

"Hmmph, look who's talking," Larry mumbled as he shuffled back to his room.

Chapter 15

Returning to the home was quite a letdown after their whirlwind adventure in Los Angeles. Bernice and Grandy displayed their disappointment by tossing their carry-ons in the corner of their room. The disillusioned future grandma remained silent as she slipped into her teal-colored, silk nightgown. She lay in bed reevaluating her daughter's proposition.

After putting on her Tweety Bird pajamas, Grandy tossed and turned in her bed, mentally going through a detailed list of supplies she would need for the motor home.

The sound of Grandy's mumbling and keyboard tapping woke Bernice at 6:00 the next morning.

"What on earth are you doing at this hour of the morning?"

"I'm planning our trip. We need to make a list of supplies for the motor home plus maps and directions to some of the places we plan to visit."

"You don't even have the motor home yet. What if you can't drive it?"

"I'll be able to drive it. You're the one who should learn how to drive."

Bernice rubbed her eyes, yawned, and responded, "At my age there's no reason to learn to drive. And when I was younger, Jack always took me where I needed to go. Besides, we lived in town, and most of the businesses I frequented were within walking distance."

Grandy brushed strands of deep red hair away from her face, then continued her searches on the laptop.

With a quick yank of the sheet, Bernice pulled it over her head, trying to muffle any noises from her roommate.

"Hey Bernie, check this out. A two-story outhouse."

"Keep it down. Can't you see I'm sleeping?" Bernice tried to sound irritated, but under the starched sheet there was a tremendous effort to suppress a giggle, as she imagined Grandy trying to tip over a two-story outhouse.

"You don't sound like you're asleep."

"Well, I was."

"Well, now you're not."

A sharp comment was about to fly from Bernice's mouth when she was interrupted by the pitiful moans of Pauline, a woman in the room next to theirs. "Somebody please help me. Hello, could somebody please help me?"

"You want to listen to *that* the rest of your life, Bernie? I've heard that old woman piss and moan every day since I arrived here. If I don't leave this place soon, I'll have to feed that woman a late night snack of pillow feathers."

Bernice peeked over the covers. "A two-story outhouse doesn't exactly sound a whole lot more exciting."

"Fine. Look here at these pictures of Yellowstone Park. You like pretty flowers and all. There's tons of them there."

At the mention of flowers, Bernice crawled out of bed and put her glasses on. She slowly made her way next to Grandy's side and peered over her shoulder as Grandy scrolled through breathtaking mountain scenes, fields of flowers, and wildlife. A few seconds later the screen displayed huge, deep blue and white waves headed for an empty beach.

"Just think, Bernie, you can visit places like these, or, you can spend your evenings playing bingo with Loser Larry – maybe win a piece of candy and hope to keep your slacks clean after Larry tries to put his hands on them." There was only the briefest of a pause before Grandy threw in her biggest poker chip. "We can stop in L.A. to visit Joyce and Jackie."

Bernice's ears perked up at the mention of her family. A smile spread across her face as she demurely replied, "I *do* want to see my daughter and granddaughter."

"Well, then, let's get started on planning our trip."

"But I can always fly to California –"

By now Grandy's patience level was about depleted and she retorted, "What in tar nation are you afraid of, Bernie?"

Embarrassment spread across the grey-haired lady's face as she remembered it was only just last night that she was pouting because she didn't want to be in the retirement home anymore. What was she afraid of? Everything. Fear of chipping a nail in the middle of nowhere, running out of Depends, Gas X, and Imodium, and of course, the big one – having to sleep in the same bed with her snoring friend. On a smaller scale were the fears of running out of gas, breaking down alongside the highway, or getting mugged in a rest area. Bernice dared not mention *all* her concerns to Grandy though, as she might ridicule her, or even worse, leave her at the retirement home to eat mystery meat the rest of her life. No, it was time, Bernice thought to herself, to act upon that wild spirit she felt just a few short weeks ago.

"Okay, Grandy, I'll go with you on the road, but I have a few questions for you."

"All righty. What are they?"

"How do I get my medication?"

"There's a Wal-Mart in almost every town. You're on their main computer already."

"What about my money? How do I get that?"

"Our checks are automatically deposited. You can use the ATM card we got for you a couple of months ago. And, instead of writing a huge check to this place, we can use the money for gas, food, and other necessities."

"I have to have my nails done once a month. How do I find a decent manicurist?"

"We'll ask around, Bernie. And if worst comes to worst, you can buy a set of press-on nails at Wal-Mart."

A disgusted look from Bernice was thrown at Grandy. But she decided it was better not to make a scene over painted fingernails.

"I suppose you're going to say the same thing about my hair."

"No, you can't buy press on hair at Wal-Mart, Old Woman. I'll do your hair for you."

"Oh, no, I'll find a real beauty shop. You'll be trying to match my hair with my red nail polish and I'll end up looking like you."

"And what's wrong with that?" Irritation clearly projected from Grandy's voice.

"It's just that I prefer my grey hair to red, that's all."

"Grey? The last time you had your hair dyed, the beautician put so much blue tint in it that you look like a Smurf."

An awkward silence took over the room as the two biddies mulled over their next comments to each other. Finally, Bernice said, "If this doesn't work out, I can always take Joyce up on her offer."

"What offer was that? You never did tell me."

"She said I could move in with them if I want to."

Grandy chuckled a deep, throaty laugh, "Sounds like Joyce was on too many hospital drugs when she made that offer."

Bernice honestly wanted to hurt her pencil-thin roommate, but was afraid Grandy might substitute her fiber for moon rocks.

"I'll have you know that I seriously considered her offer on the way home. I could move in tomorrow, if I wanted to." Bernice crossed her loose skin arms and glared at Grandy.

"Fine. Go ahead. I'm sure smelling like spoiled milk and baby poop will be much more fun than enjoying the experience of being near majestic South Dakota buffalo or seeing the Grand Canyon." Grandy winced as she bit her tongue. She had almost let slip her excitement to visit UFO landing stations.

Bernice squared her shoulders and announced in a firm, squeaky voice, "Let's get working on those lists. I am now ready to hit the road."

"Yeah!" Grandy clapped her hands, her blue eyes twinkled as she replied, "We are going to need kitchen, bath, and bedroom items for the motor home. Maybe my brother, Dog Face Dale can help. He works at the local flea market. Oh, and I have lots of neat stuff in a storage unit."

"Dog Face? I'm afraid to ask, but where'd he get that name?"

"You'll see."

Chapter 16

"Hello."

"Hello, Grandma."

"She's here? Oh my gosh!" Meeting Bob Barker and now this. How much more excitement could Bernice handle in such a short amount of time. She hollered at Grandy while banging on the bathroom door. "She's here!"

"Well, whoever she is, she'll just have to wait her turn," Grandy grumbled.

"She's here!" Bernice yelled even louder.

Joyce covered the telephone mouthpiece and smiled at Buck. "My mother is just a little excited."

"Oh, I can hear her," Buck laughed.

"Joyce. You've made me the happiest mother, I mean grandmother ... How are you? How did it go? Are you okay? Is Jackie okay? It is a girl, right? They didn't make a mistake? And only one, right?"

"Yes, Mom, they were right. She was big enough to be two, but only one, thank God."

"How big is she? And who does she look like?"

"She weighs eight pounds, ten ounces and she looks just like Daddy – bald." Joyce giggled.

Bernice laughed and dabbed her tears of joy with a hanky as Grandy exited the bathroom.

"Who's here? And what you cryin' about?"

"Shhh, it's Joyce. I'm a grandma."

"Oh, well I hope you see more of her than I see of my granddaughter. Spoiled little brat."

"Can we have some privacy, here?"

Grandy wheeled herself to the other side of room and put her computer on her lap.

"How was your labor?" asked Bernice.

"Well, I woke up about 2:00 this morning with some pains, and by the time we got to the hospital, I was dilated to 10. Poor nurse said she almost had to deliver the baby herself, but not to worry, she was a veteran, delivered a lot of babies. It was exciting. Wish you'd been here. Buck did get it on video so you can watch it when you come."

"Oh, I don't know. That's kinda personal. Maybe I'd better not."

"Oh, Mom, we're all family."

"So when do you get to go home?"

"Probably day after tomorrow. They wanted me to stay an extra day because I was running a little bit of a fever. Nothing to worry about."

"Well, you stay as long as you can, because once you get home, you won't get much rest. I remember when you were born, your dad was on the road. I came home and had to take care of you all by myself. Your Aunt Char came out for a week, but she wasn't much help. She never had kids, probably because she got stuck babysitting me all the time."

"I almost forgot about Aunt Charlotte, how is she anyway?"

"She's still in San Francisco, been in a rest home since your Uncle Frank died. I guess her Alzheimer's is getting pretty bad. I call every now and then and talk to the staff. Maybe I can get Grandy to stop by there on the way to L.A. Not that she'd even know I was there, but I'd sure like to see how she's doing."

"I remember the time when I was 11 or 12 and the three of us went to Pier 39. I thought you would die of embarrassment when Aunt Char and I pretended to be a mime act and held her straw sun hat out for donations. "

"Yes, and I remember you two received a stern lecture from the local law enforcement about panhandling." There was a brief pause before Bernice continued, "she and I had sure had some good times. When she moved to San Francisco, I got to go spend weekends with her by myself, without the folks. We went to Playland and the beach. Oh, how we'd spin around on the rides until we both got sick."

"Remember when I was 5 years old? You and Char took me to the Fun House. All I can recall is the laughing lady in the box. I had nightmares about her."

"Oh, Laughing Sal. I heard she was in a museum in San Francisco somewhere."

"Why didn't Aunt Char have any kids?"

"I'm really not sure. It could have been a medical problem. Your Grandma Gert said it was because she was so vain and didn't want to get fat. I thought that was kind of a mean thing to say, but it may be true. I guess we'll never know."

"Mom, how come you waited so long to have me? You were 32, weren't you?"

"Well, Honey, I never liked talking about it, and I swore your dad to secrecy because I just wanted to forget, but I guess its okay to tell you now. I had two miscarriages right after we got married. And a couple years later I had a little boy that was stillborn." Bernice sniffled and wiped her eyes. "By the time you came along, we had all but given up trying again. You were a little bit of a surprise, since your dad was 47 years old."

"Oh, Mom, I'm so sorry. I had no idea. I wish I had known."

"Yeah, in hindsight, I think I wish you had known, too. If I hadn't suppressed it, if I had talked about it, you and I might have gotten along a little better than we did."

"I think you're probably right, or at least I might have had a better understanding of why you acted the way you did sometimes."

"I know, and I am so very, very sorry. Can you ever forgive me for the time I wasted being an angry, old woman?"

"Oh, Mom, you know I love you. I'm so glad we're getting closer now. I need to thank Grandy for bringing you to see me."

"Speaking of Grandy, if you want a good laugh tomorrow, she'll be on *The Price is Right*."

"Really, tomorrow? Buck, tomorrow, *Price is Right*, Grandy's going to be on the show."

Buck smiled and nodded his head.

"We wouldn't miss it. You're not still thinking about traveling around the country in that motor home, are you? Have you reconsidered my offer?"

"We'll be leaving in a few days. Grandy said she'd bring me to see you. And yes, your offer is still on the back burner. If things don't work out, I may just take you up on it later."

"Well, they're bringing the baby in to nurse in a couple of minutes, so I'd better be going. By the way, if you get Grandy's e-mail address to me, I'll send you a couple of photos of Jackie."

"How wonderful! I'll ask her about that."

It was sure nice talking with you, Mom. Can't wait to see you."

"And I can't wait to see you and Jackie, and Buck, of course. I'll call you from the road and let you know when we'll be there."

"Okay, I love you, Mom."

"I love you, too.

"Bye."

"Bye, Honey."

Chapter 17

"Move over, you saggy senior citizens!" Grandy's patience was wearing thin as several residents horned in with their wheelchairs, blocking Grandy and Bernice's view.

"My eyes are bad, *Red*, I need to be closer to the television," whined a plump, 85-year-old woman wearing a synthetic, black wig.

"Me, too," said Betty, a woman so thin that she would have fit into a high school locker with room to spare.

"Well, that doesn't mean you can park your carcasses in front of us. Move somewhere else."

The retired hairdresser knew she'd never win a battle with Grandy, so she squeezed her chair next to Leisure Suit Larry. Several other complainers were forced to sit in a far corner of the room.

Ignoring the fussing and feuding around her, Bernice sat calmly in her chair, waiting for *The Price is Right* to appear on the screen. She still held a grudge against her roommate for being on the show instead of her, but seeing Bob Barker reminded her of the ride in his limo, the kisses she gave him, and the kind words he spoke to her. Today the occupants of the retirement home would see that she and her roommate were not making up stories about being on the show or winning prizes.

"It's about to start, so everyone pipe down!" Grandy snapped.

There were lots of questions for the two retirement home celebrities as each minute ticked by and the only television shots of them were while they sat in the front row.

Exasperated, Bernice tried to explain that Grandy was called on stage during the second half of the show. A couple of times, snide comments were projected about the ridiculous T-shirts the two friends wore or how silly Bernice looked waving and smiling at the camera, while Grandy sat emotionless. An aide and the daughter of one of the residents did remark about how television made the former contestants look younger.

Grandy and Bernice occasionally glanced at each other with small smiles. While watching themselves on television was exciting, it paled in comparison to their anticipated arrival of the new motor home, which was the only thing holding up their departure.

Just as Grandy made her Plinko debut on national television, a nurse entered the room and announced, "Grandy, you have a phone call."

"Take a message, I'm busy."

"It's Wild Wheels RV. They said it's important."

Grandy spun her wheelchair around, crushing toes as she attempted to remove herself from the sea of senior citizens. Bernice quickly hobbled behind her as bodies were pushed aside by the wheelchair.

"Get out of the way!" The two old friends chanted in unison. Eyes, elbows, and heads became bruised targets as Grandy and Bernice made a determined dash for the phone.

"Hello!" Squealed Grandy in a rusty voice.

"Is this Ms. Grandy McGregor?"

"Yes, yes it is."

"This is Bailey from Wild Wheels RV, we have your Fleetwood Terra motor home in our lot ready to be picked up. We –"

"I'll be there in an hour." Grandy hung up on Bailey, then immediately began dialing the phone."

"Who you calling?"

"Hush, Bernie, I'm getting our ride to the RV center." Bernice fidgeted with the zipper on her lavender sweater as she watched Grandy's red eyebrows arch, then scowl.

"Answer the phone, Dog Face," she said in a low gruff voice.

"Ah, the famous Dog Face."

"Shut up, Bernie, I'm on the phone!"

"Hello?"

"Dog Face, it's Grandy and I need a favor."

"What you need, Sis?"

"Pick me up at the retirement home, now! The motor home I won on *The Price is Right* is ready to be picked up at Wild Wheels RV."

"You were on *The Price is Right*? When did that happen?"

"A few weeks ago. Come pick me up."

"Sure. When?"

"Now."

"Now?"

"Yeah, now. I wanna get out of this smelly joint."

"Okay, Sis. I'll be there in fifteen minutes."

"I'll be waiting by the front door."

"Okay. Bye."

Grandy hung up without saying good-bye and headed for their room. Loud cheers could be heard from the parlor, as Grandy continued her winning streak on television.

"Come on, Bernie, we need our purses and you have to put on another layer of makeup."

"Is what I have on smeared already?"

"No, you just never go out in public without two or three layers, and that takes you awhile to put on, so hurry up!"

While Grandy lacquered the fly away strands of her hair to her head, Bernice applied layer after layer of a purplish-red lipstick. She thought she would pass out from all the recent developments happening. First, she became a grandmother, now she was on her way to pick up her new "home." What next? A boyfriend? Becoming a lotto winner? Her mind reeled with all kinds of possibilities. Perhaps, -

"Ouch!" A small punch on her arm brought Bernice out of her dream world.

"Pay attention to what you're doing, Old Woman, you put enough of that ugly lipstick on to coat the lips of all the show girls in Vegas. Let's go. Dog Face is probably waiting for us."

Grandy's brother had not yet arrived, so Bernice took the opportunity to ask about him.

"What's his real name?"

"Who?"

"Dog Face."

"Dog Face Dale."

"That's the name he was born with?"

"Oh, you betcha, Bernie, that's his birth name," Grandy retorted as she rolled her pasty blue eyes. "His first name is Dale, and his middle name is Evans."

"You're kidding, right?"

"No, I'm not kidding. My folks were big fans of Dale Evans and decided that, no matter what gender their first born was, he or she would have the name Dale Evans."

Just when Bernice thought the story about Grandy's cousin Reckon was the most bizarre tale imaginable, she was jolted by another lightning bolt of Grandy's unbelievable family history. She didn't dare ask how Dale got the nickname Dog Face. It was probably way more information than she wanted to know. While processing the most recent information concerning Grandy's brother, Bernice heard a peculiar sound in the distance. It seemed to be a mixture of industrial coughing and an engine not married to its muffler.

"I hear Dog Face coming, he should be here any minute," Grandy commented in a nonchalant manner.

"What's he driving? It sounds sick, or broken, or dying."

"Nah, it works better than it sounds."

A rusty green, 1970s Dodge pickup creaked to a halt and a short, stout, greasy-haired man appeared to roll out of the truck. Red-veined jowls seemed to keep rhythm with an abdomen that lapped over a barely visible peace sign belt buckle. Dog Face bent over Grandy and deposited a sloppy kiss on her cheek.

"Hey, Little Sister! You lookin' as gorgeous as ever! If we weren't related –"

"Knock it off, Dog Face," the fiery redhead snapped as she smacked her brother. "We don't have time for your lewd shenanigans. Me and Bernice need to get our RV so we can load up and hit the road."

Dog Face examined Bernice with his bulging, midnight blue eyes. She felt the creepy crawlies slide down her spine as this man who resembled a bulldog grabbed her hand and planted a juicy kiss on it. A small trickle of brown chewing tobacco saliva ran between her fingers. Mortified by this horror, Bernice just stood there, unable to move or speak.

"Sorry about that, Miss Bernice," Dog Face pulled a dirty, red handkerchief from his pocket and wiped her hand, removing the saliva but leaving behind streaks of black grease.

"Oh, my gosh, I'm –."

Bernice yanked her hand from his and stammered, "Iiiittt'ss – okay, I'll take care of it." She dug into her handbag and ripped open a moist towelette and furiously wiped her hand.

"You moron, Dog Face, just load up my wheelchair and get us to Wild Wheels," Grandy said as she punched him in the arm.

"Yes, Ma'am." Dog Face leaned over and tried to whisper another apology to Bernice, "I'm sor –"

"Don't worry about it, Dog Face, let's just help Grandy, okay?" Bernice found the smile used for insincere occasions and shared it with him.

Much to Bernice's dismay, she ended up in the middle of the two red necks, hitting her head on the gun rack every time they went over a bump and Dog Face's expanded thigh touching hers. After several silent but desperate prayers, Bernice was determined that the next time Grandy suggested one of her relatives to help out, Bernice would ship her to the South Pole.

Chapter 18

"Sooo, Sissy," Dog Face drawled as he spit a tobacco wad out of the truck window, "how is it you got to go to California and get on that crazy game show?"

Bernice butted in and replied in an acid tone of voice, "Pure luck."

"Sounds like you're not happy about my sister being on the show."

"Hmmph! I should've been the one on stage winning a trip to France."

"Grandy, you won a trip to France, too?"

"No, you moron, I won the motor home and a bunch of other stuff. Old sour puss here still has her undies in a twist because I didn't bid on a trip to Paris. You need to get over it, Bernie. We'll see a lot more interesting things once we're on the road." She elbowed her friend in the side trying to get her to concentrate on something else.

"Ouch! You ancient redheaded bag, I'll – "

Dog Face slammed on the brakes, creating a mild whiplash for the bickering broads. "Here we are Ladies, Wild Wheels RV. Do ya need me to come in and keep these guys in line?"

Bernice gave Dog Face a look of mild disbelief. "You really think your sister is going to let anyone take advantage of us?"

Dog Face's chubby cheeks turned pink and he meekly said, "No, Miss Bernice, I guess we don't have to worry about that."

"See ya Dog," Grandy was already out of the pickup and six steps away when she mumbled her goodbye.

"Grandy! Your wheelchair!" Dale hollered.

Grandy made an abrupt turn around and retrieved her purple transportation. "Can't afford to forget my wheels, they sure come in handy. Remember Dog Face, don't tell Avis about the wheelchair. He'll really give birth to a cow if he finds out."

"Don't worry, I haven't talked to him in years. 'Fraid it will cost me money just to say hello. Besides, he always did seem a little different." Dog Face turned his attention to Bernice who was deep in thought as she attempted to exit the pickup.

"Different. That's too mild a word to describe Grandy and her relatives," Bernice thought to herself. She couldn't wait to meet Avis, thinking he might turn out to be the most normal one of the bunch.

Bernice politely thanked Dog Face as she quickly slid her behind along the bench seat of the truck and away from his groping hand.

"Sure made my day meeting you, Miss Bernice. Maybe someday we can get together for a beer."

"Maybe. Bye, Dog Face."

"Bye, Good Lookin'."

Dog Face watched the attractive senior citizen hobble in record speed as she attempted to catch up with his sister.

"Bye, Bernice!" Dog Face shouted, not the least bit conscious of his yellow-tooth grin.

Once she caught up with Grandy, Bernice hissed at her, "You could have sat next to your brother instead of making me do it. That man's hygiene is atrocious! He should be riding in the back of the pickup, not driving it."

"Did he kiss you on the lips?"

"Heavens no!"

"Did he ask you to marry him?"

"Of course not!"

"Then what in tar nation are you all uptight about? He gave us a ride, didn't he?"

"The man drooled on my hand. There isn't enough bleach in the world to sanitize it."

Grandy stopped and stared at Bernice, "You are the most uptight, worrisome, old fool I know. Bernice, relax. Don't spend the last few years of your life wound tighter than the foot of a Geisha."

Old Red continued at record pace to the office of the RV dealership. Bernice decided to remain silent until she was able to think of a comeback that would put her crusty friend in her place.

"I'm Grandy McGregor. Somebody called and said my RV was ready." The feisty, old lady parked her wheelchair next to the customer service desk, staring up at the two men behind it.

"Do you remember who called you, Ma'am?"

"Of course I don't remember who called me. Don't all you guys know what's going on around here?" Grandy's impatience was already beginning to show. Bernice just weakly smiled at the men and shrugged her shoulders.

"Let me check with Bailey, Ms. McGregor. He's in charge of new sales."

* * *

It was two hours of major frustration for both Grandy and the Wild Wheels staff, but all the technical details involving license, tax, and insurance were eventually worked out. The biggest hurdle was convincing Bailey that the wheelchair was not a necessary medical requirement for Grandy. After she threatened to dance on Bailey's head, he eagerly handed her the keys and wished her happy travels. In great anticipation, the ladies climbed into their new motor home and prepared to leave the lot.

Surprised at the luxury of the motor home, Bernice's hands gently touched the lush, aquamarine textures of the sofa, curtains, and bedspread. She opened every cupboard door, taking delight in the many hidden cubby holes. Top-of-the-line appliances brought a subdued smile to her face.

"Pretty nice, isn't it, Bernie?"

"Yeah, it's not bad, Grandy." The grey-haired skeptic's voice was soft and humble.

"Not bad! Can't you just admit you were wrong?"

"What do you mean, 'wrong?' I never said it wouldn't be nice."

"You called my motor home a traveling tin can."

"I never said any such thing!"

"Dang near. Anyway, we gotta make a stop before we pack up our stuff at the home."

"And where would that be?"

"My storage unit. We need a few items for our trip."

Grandy ordered Bernice to sit down and buckle up. She then started up the Fleetwood and squealed the tires as she left the parking lot. Five minutes down the road a timid voice said, "Grandy?"

"What?"

"I have to pee."

"Use the toilet in the bathroom."

Alarm saturated Bernice's voice, "In here? While we're driving?"

Of course, in here and while we're driving. I'm not gonna stop just because you have to pee. Besides, that's why they put a bathroom in this unit."

"Well, I don't know. I won't fall through the toilet onto the freeway, will I?" Bernice was genuinely concerned about the possibility of her derriere scraping the asphalt.

"Only if you're too heavy for the commode and you break through the steel floor of the motor home."

Bernice displayed a nasty scowl that she somehow hoped Grandy would see. "Not funny, Red." She then made her way cautiously towards the back of the motor home, hanging onto whatever was available. Opening the bathroom door, she burst into laughter at the minute size of the shower/tub, sink, and toilet. There was no way, she or Grandy would ever be able to use any of it.

"Grandy!"

"What!"

"You or I will never be able to use this bathroom, it's too small."

"Bernie, your butt may be big, but it's also doughy enough to squeeze through that door and sit on the toilet."

The terrified traveler forced her expanding figure in front of the toilet and sat down for her business. She left the bathroom door open giving her enough space for her knees. As the motor home bounced and swerved down the road, Bernice hung on for dear life. One particularly rough bump, though, caused one-half of the frightened senior citizen's bottom to slide off the toilet seat and become wedged between the toilet and miniature bathtub.

"Help!"

"Now what's your problem?"

"I'm stuck!"

"What do ya mean you're stuck?"

"I fell off the toilet and I'm stuck between the toilet and bathtub."

Hysterical laughter filled the motor home.

"It's not funny, I need help!"

"Okay, okay, I'll pull off at the next exit." Grandy was still chuckling as she pulled into the parking lot of a Target Discount Store. She stood staring at her trapped friend, thinking of the best way to get her out.

"Oh, Lordy, I wish I had a camera at this very moment."

"Shut up and help me."

Grandy grabbed her large, neon orange, canvas handbag and dug around inside of it until she pulled out a small jar of petroleum jelly.

"Here Bernie, smear this on you, then you can hang onto one of the handles of my purse and I'll pull you up."

"I don't want that goop all over me, can't you think of something else?" Bernice whined.

"It's just Vaseline."

"I don't know."

"Oh, for crying out loud, I don't have all day. Here, I'm going to put this on you whether you like or not." Grandy coated Bernice's right butt cheeks with the yellow jelly, had her take a hold of a purse handle, then gave a big yank. The action caused Bernice to tilt forward so her hands hit the floor and her butt faced the ceiling. From there, the grey-haired grandma was able to pry herself loose and stand up.

Mad as a cat being given a bubble bath, Bernice quickly pulled up her pants and gave Grandy the most murderous look she could muster. Her words leaked through her teeth slowly, hard and angrily, "If this is what being on the road with you is going to be like, I'd rather room with Leisure Suit Larry."

"Honestly, Bernie, you just have to learn to use balance and common sense while traveling in a motor home. We need to get to the storage unit. Now try to stay out of trouble!"

Chapter 19

It was a few more miles before the ladies drove into the driveway of Store-More storage units. Grandy maneuvered their future home next to the large, roll-up door of her unit.

"Number 13. Here we are, Bernie. You are going to be amazed at all the nifty treasures I have."

"Can't wait," came the mumble from her still fuming traveling companion.

Grandy opened the door, turned on a dimmed light bulb, and started working her way around the dozens of cardboard boxes stacked seven feet high.

"For goodness sakes, Grandy, I've heard of packrats, but this is ridiculous. Have you ever thrown anything away in your life?"

"Hey, I always save everything because I never know when I might be needing it."

"Like this? What is it, anyway?" Bernice asked hesitantly, as she thought it might be paraphernalia for some illegal substance.

"It's a spice grinder. See, it hangs on the wall," Grandy demonstrated. "Where'd ya store all your stuff?"

"We had an estate sale and kept only what would fit in our room at the retirement home."

"You'll be sorry someday, Bernie, that you didn't keep all your goodies."

The overwhelmed friend said softly, "I doubt it, Grandy, I doubt it."

"We can sure use this," Grandy announced, as she held up an antique toaster.

"Yeah, if you wanna blow up your new motor home. Look at the cord. It's frayed and it doesn't even have a plug."

"Aw, Dale can fix that. He can fix anything."

"Grandy, for fifteen dollars you can buy a brand new one."

"But why waste the money when Dale will fix mine for free… Hey, I know I'm taking this on the road." Grandy pulled out an old, rusty sawed-off shotgun.

"Oh, no. I hate guns!"

"Oh, Bernie, it doesn't even work, it's just for intimidation. It'll scare the crap out of someone if they try to attack us."

"How do you know it doesn't work? Wait a minute, what am I saying?"

"It's broke, see," Grandy replied as she pointed the gun at Bernie's head and jiggled the trigger.

"Knock it off, that's not funny," Bernice pushed the gun away from her face.

Grandy started a pile of items she wanted to take including a dusty ball of twine, a red plastic milk crate, half a bag of cat litter, cribbage board minus the markers. As Grandy continued to add odds and ends to the pile, Bernice worked her way through the maze of magazines and books. Grandy had a collection of how-to books and magazines on everything from crocheting to zoology. Just about every book ever written on paranormal phenomenon sat in cardboard boxes.

"You are not taking any of these UFO books, Grandy."

"Don't touch those! I know exactly which ones I AM taking."

In Bernice's opinion, trying to salvage useable items from this junk shed was a waste of time. Cracked Tupperware bowls without lids and a broken toaster and shotgun were not necessary items for their trip. Just as Bernice was about to remove herself from the storage unit, she stumbled over a tricycle, knocking over an old wooden crate. A blood-curdling scream escaped from her gut.

"What's wrong now?" Grandy peeked around a stack of mismatched kitchen chairs to see Bernice pointing to the object of her distress. "Oh, that's Pepe Le Pew. I read a book on taxidermy and he was my first attempt at stuffing animals. I ran him over on my way back from my Cousin Reckin's place one night. It was so dark outside, I didn't realize I left his tail on the highway. When I went back the next day, I couldn't even scrape it off the road."

"And what is this?" Bernice scrunched her face up in a disgusted gesture as she pointed to another example of road kill.

"Oh, that's Felix, my pet ferret, God rest his soul. Come here, little fella, we're takin' you along for good luck."

Bernice wiped her hands on her lavender, polyester pants and announced, "That's it, Grandy, we don't have room for anymore of your useless junk."

"Ah, come on, Bernie. We want it to be like home, don't we?"

"Grandy, I have never seen a home decorated with the kind of garbage you've got in this storage unit. No wonder your boys put you in a retirement home. If this stuff was in the house you lived in, it was probably condemned."

"Oh, yeah. And what did your house have in it? White starched sheets and army green walls?"

"As a matter of fact, I had beautiful antiques and artwork. Jack wined and dined me, treated me like a queen."

"And now all Queen Bernie does is whine."

"Come on, Grandy, we're going to Wal-Mart for a new toaster."

Chapter 20

A large, pink bubble gum bubble burst and covered half the pimpled face of Howard's wife, Blackie. She peeled it from her shiny cheeks and stuffed it back into her mouth. Her eyes squinted at the TV as she studied the contestants of *The Price is Right* show. Although Blackie had met Howard's mother only once, she was pretty sure that it was Grandy she was witnessing on TV. Blackie quickly dialed Howard's cell phone number.

"Hey, Baby, it's me. I just saw your ma on T.V."

"What?"

"Your ma's on *The Price is Right* show, right now!"

"Are you sure?"

"Of course I'm sure. There's an old, redheaded broad with a name tag that says *Grandy from Minnesota* on it and she's just won a motor home."

"Holy cow, Blackie. I thought Ma was in a retirement home crocheting pot holders. Guess I'd better call Avis and find out what's going on. Thanks for the call, Babe. I'll see ya tonight."

"Bye, Baby."

Howard cursed under his breath as he drove the last few miles on Interstate 43 towards Grafton, Wisconsin. His mother on TV! What was going on? Why didn't she tell anyone about being on the show? How did she get to the show? Ma would never fly in an airplane. Many other questions circled like small stray satellites in Howard's head. Maybe Avis would know the answers.

Reflections of his childhood soon covered the curiosity about his mom being on TV. "She sure was something else," Howard mused to himself, "keeping everyone on edge with her bizarre ideas and unpredictable plans." He remembered the time when he was eight years old and his mother decided that Howard and his two brothers needed to help her make homemade tomato sauce. Her blender was broken so she had the boys stand on the roof of the barn and throw the tomatoes into an old bathtub below it. Saved her the elbow grease needed to otherwise smash them by hand. Avis almost fell off the roof and Dakota decided to aim and fire tomatoes at the rooster walking next to an old set of harrows. Needless to say, the tomato sauce supply was rather sparse that year.

Howard pulled into the parking lot of the liquor store to make a delivery. He dialed Avis' cell phone and waited. Cell service wasn't the best, so he listened to static while waiting for Avis to answer.

"This is Avis Wayland, I'm unable to answer your call at the moment. Please leave your name, number, and a brief message and I will return your call as soon as possible."

"Hey, Avis. This is Howard. Blackie just saw Ma on TV. She won a motor home on *The Price is Right* show. Call me."

About four hours later, Howard received a call back from his older brother.

"Hey, Howard. Avis. What's this about Ma being on TV?"

"That's what Blackie said."

"Is she sure? She hasn't been smoking bathroom chemicals, has she?"

Tersely Howard responded, "No, Avis, she hasn't. And Blackie is not a druggie. You assume just because she has a tattoo that she does drugs."

"Sorry. I just can't imagine why anyone would want a black widow tattoo on their butt."

"Forget Blackie's butt. What's the deal with Ma?"

"I don't know anymore than what you just told me. I'm in New York right now working on a big case and I can't leave for another two days. I'll just have to call the retirement home and find out what's going on. I bet Ma's roommate has something to do with this. She's probably trying to get Ma's money."

"Yeah, like you aren't, Avis."

"Hey, I'm looking after Ma's best interest. If somebody doesn't take care of her assets, she would blow them all on UFO paraphernalia."

"Leave Ma alone. She's not hurting anyone or anything with her fascination in the supernatural. You know she's always been a sugar cube short of a full bowl. Just let me know what's going on, I gotta deliver this beer."

"When I find something out, I'll let you know, Howard."

"Bye."

Avis took his round-framed, tortoise shell-colored eyeglasses off his face and rubbed his eyes. "Oh Ma, what have you done now?" he mumbled. When she didn't answer her cell phone, he called her retirement home room number and left an urgent message for his mother to call him back.

Chapter 21

The ladies arrived at the retirement home exhausted but brimming over with exhilaration. The anticipation of future adventures was only on a slightly higher level than their excitement of knowing this would be their last supper at *Passage of Time*. As they pulled into the parking lot, the dining room window was adorned with residents and aides, wide-eyed with mouths hanging open at the site of Grandy's prize on wheels.

An explosion of applause and compliments blasted the roommates as they entered the building. "You looked great on TV!" "Yeah, you must be really smart to win all those prizes!" "Look at the motor home, it's so big!"

Grandy, sporting rhinestone sunglasses and a straw hat adorned with silk daisies threw back her shoulders and walked proudly into the room with an arrogant confidence. In her excitement, she had left the wheelchair in the motor home. Bernice, holding her cane tightly, hobbled behind with a half-smile, trying to disguise her lingering jealousy over Grandy's good fortune.

Lillian, one of the aides, noticed Grandy's strut. "Say, Grandy, where's your wheelchair?" she asked in a suspicious tone of voice.

"It's a miracle!" Grandy shouted while waving her wrinkled, white arms above her head.

"Come to think of it, you weren't in the wheelchair on the show, either, were you?" Lillian continued.

"Hallelujah, it's a miracle." Bernice agreed, as she and Grandy hurried past the crowd into the dining room. Grandy subtly elbowed Bernice and whispered between her teeth, "Why didn't you remind me to get the chair out of the motor home?"

Bernice tried to ignore Grandy as she, too, imitated someone famous with her posture. "I was on TV, too, at the end. Didn't you see me?"

"I saw ya and all I can say is, where on earth did you get those shorts?" asked Larry.

"At a boutique at the Mall of America, of course," not that it was any of his business, but Bernice knew one thing – famous people always shopped at boutiques.

Larry didn't share what he really thought about the shorts because he was about to ask Grandy for a peek inside her new motor home. Before he could make his request known, several other residents and staff had swarmed around Grandy.

"Can I have a ride?"

"Yeah, me too, I've never been in a motor home."

While most were envious of their two fellow residents, others were a bit skeptical. Larry began taking bets on how long before they'd return, begging for their old room back. At the same time, he tried to think of a plan in which he could convince the old broads to take him along on their travels. Maybe he, too, could escape his confines and see the world.

Caught up in the fanfare of being near famous, Grandy announced "Free rides after supper."

Everyone cheered, as if they had all won something really grand. During the meal, the grateful residents offered Grandy and Bernice their cups of rice pudding and dry dinner rolls. After supper, Grandy went back to her room to use the bathroom before the ride. She noticed the light blinking on the answering machine. Her face made a corkscrew expression as she listened to the message from Avis. "Better call him back before he and whatever army he hires comes to check on me," she thought with disgust.

"Hello."

"What'ya want now?"

"Ma, what is going on? Blackie saw you on TV. What's this about a motor home?"

"Yep, I won a motor home. So what. It's mine. You can't have it."

"What are you going to do with it?"

"I sold it and spent the money already. So there." Grandy hung up the phone. She returned to the cafeteria where Larry, Trudy, Betty, Loretta, and Nick, along with Lillian were headed to the front door. Bernice was shocked at her roommate's kind gesture, but when Grandy began barking out orders, Bernice realized it was more gloating than generosity.

"Put out that cigar, Larry, and keep your hands to yourself. You, too, Nick. And Loretta, don't be drooling on the furniture."

"And she says I'm wound tight," Bernice thought to herself.

Larry mumbled under his breath as he looked around for a place to extinguish his cigar. Pretending to admire the appliances, he opened the freezer door and threw it inside.

"I'm ridin' shotgun," announced Betty, as she plopped her bottom into the front passenger seat. "What's this?" She asked.

"Don't touch anything."

Not able to hear Grandy's response, Betty pushed a button that shook the motor home with the loud volume from the radio. Grandy scuttled into her new unit, turned off the radio, and cursed at Betty.

"I told you not to touch anything!"

Betty shrank into the seat and whimpered an apology. "I'm sorry, Grandy."

Meanwhile, another small commotion was taking place back in the bedroom.

"Oh, my God, get an exterminator in here, you've got rats," Loretta screamed as she noticed Felix sitting on the bed. She plummeted him several times in the head with her purse.

"What's going on back there?" Grandy hollered.

Bernice clasped her hand over Loretta's mouth. "Shhhhh. Nothing, Grandy. Everything's fine. I just stepped on Loretta's foot."

Bernice removed her hand from Loretta's mouth and whispered, "I think you killed it. Let's keep this to ourselves. We wouldn't want to upset Grandy, now would we?"

"No, I guess not." Loretta was shaken from the double assault, first an unknown creature laying on the bed, then her breathing cut off by a crazed, old woman. She slid into the dining booth, shrinking into the corner as far as she could.

Grandy settled into the driver's seat and buckled her seatbelt. "Everybody ready back there?"

"Can we watch TV?" asked Trudy.

"No! You wanted a ride and that's what you're gonna get. You can go inside and watch your own TV. Everybody just sit down." Grandy started the engine as the seniors began to clap and holler like a bunch of teenagers taking their first limo ride to the prom.

Grandy shifted into drive and lurched into the parking lot. After one 15 mph loop around, the passengers hollered, "more, more!" so she increased the speed, squealing the tires, and running over the curb. Everyone screamed and grabbed onto anything that seemed to be strong enough to keep them from falling onto the floor.

"Had enough?" Grandy yelled. Fortunately for the others, they did not notice how her fly-away hair and mischievous grin made her look like a psycho patient from a horror movie.

"Yes! Yes! Stop! Stop!"

The motor home came to an abrupt halt and the residents' weakened grips dissolved, sending them into a pile on the floor. Silence was present for only a short time before a small, squeaky voice said, "Can we go get some ice cream?"

"No food allowed," Grandy said in her not so subtle tone of voice.

"I think I'm gonna be sick," whined Trudy, as she staggered towards the back of the coach.

"Oh, no ya don't!" Grandy hollered as she spotted Trudy heading for the toilet room.

"Ride's over. Everybody out. Trudy first."

Lillian assisted Trudy down the steps.

"Thanks, *Red*. Nice ride. First time you ever drove anything except your wheelchair?"

"Shut up, Larry. I was hoping you would knock your head against the cupboard and pass out so I could dump your body in a ravine somewhere."

"No such luck, Grandy. But you could take me along with you and Bernice. I'd make a great navigator."

"Dream on. The only navigating you're going to do is right back to your small, dirty room."

"Ten bucks says you'll be back in less than a week, crying to have *your* small, dirty room back."

"You're on, fashion disaster. Put your money where your mouth is." Grandy held out her hand. "You might as well pay me now, 'cause I'll put a gun to my head before I'll ever come back to a place where you live."

Larry exited the motor home, complaining, swearing and snickering as he remembered that he left his cigar in the freezer. "Ha! What a nice going away present I left them," he mused to himself. "Nice goin', Trudy." Larry held his nose as he stepped over the regurgitated mixture of mystery meat and boiled carrots on the walkway.

Following the exodus of elders, Grandy took inventory. "I can't believe I let them all in here. What was I thinking?" Upon entering the bedroom she noticed Nick asleep on the bed.

"Hey Narco, ride's over." There was no response. She gave him a little shake, still no response. She slapped him in the face and shook him violently. Then she leaned over to check his breathing.

"Bernie, I think Nick's dead." Grandy shook Nick again. "Wake up, you old fart. I don't have time for your stupid jokes."

"Maybe he's just asleep. That's all he does, you know." Bernice placed her hand over Nick's mouth. Her face displayed an expression of complete panic. "Oh my gosh, Grandy, I don't feel any breath coming from his mouth!"

"This is just great. My new motor home is cursed." Grandy looked at Nick with disgust and then at Bernice with determination. "Okay, Bernie, let's just drag him to his room after everyone has gone to bed tonight. When he's discovered dead tomorrow, everybody will just think he died during the night."

Bernice could not believe what she was hearing. "Grandy, we can't do that! We need to call 9-1-1 right now, maybe he can still be saved!"

"Nick can't get much stiffer and colder than he is right now. Besides, if anyone calls for an investigation, we won't be able to leave tomorrow on our trip. Do you want to stay here for another week?"

Bernice's eyes welled up with tears as she stared at Nick's lifeless body. The scene was all too familiar to her as she remembered the night Jack died.

"Well?" Grandy's stern voice brought Bernice back to the current dilemma.

"Are you sure we should be doing this? I don't want to end up in jail."

"Don't worry. We'll just sneak him back to his room late tonight."

"Won't anyone miss him before then?"

"We'll just tell Lillian that we're letting Nick take a little nap in the motor home. She won't care."

Uncertainty still plagued Bernice, but she definitely did not want to spend one more minute than she had to at the retirement home. So the ladies began laying out the complete plan on how to cover up the death of Nick the Narcoleptic.

Chapter 22

"Hey, Dog Face."

"Who is this?" The voice answered in an irritated and gruff tone.

"It's Grandy. I need you to...."

"I'm kinda busy right now, Grandy, call me back later."

"This is a matter of life or death, Dog Face, whatever you're doing can wait."
Grandy tried to decipher through Dog Face's loud sigh the indistinguishable
sounds in the background.

"Okay, Grandy, what do you need?"

"Meet me at the retirement home at midnight and bring a blue tarp and duct
tape. And turn the engine off half way down the block and coast into the parking
lot. I don't want you waking anyone up."

"What are you up to?"

"You'll see when you get here."

"Is Miss Bernice going to be there?"

"Never mind Bernice. Just don't forget a blue tarp and some duct tape."
Grandy hung up the phone and turned to Bernie. "Dale can't wait to see you."

Bernice felt a shiver down her spine as she rummaged through her clothes
for something unflattering to wear. "He gives me the creeps."

"Oh, Bernie, relax. He's the only one who can help us. You do want to leave
in the morning, don't you?"

"Yeah, I guess. But what's the duct tape for?"

"Oh, I thought we'd put some over Nick's mouth in case he wakes up,"
Grandy answered in a sarcastic tone. "I don't know, Bernie, it's just always good
to have some on hand at times like this."

"Times like this? You mean you've done this before?" Visions of unmarked
graves throughout the United States assaulted Bernice's mind.

"No, I haven't done this before, but I may do it again if you don't shut up.
Now let's just get packed while we're waiting for Dale. That way we can leave
at sun-up and get out of this dump."

"I knew we should have called 9-1-1," Bernice thought to herself as she
finished packing her things, mostly clothes and small keepsakes, along with ten
boxes of Depends.

"We don't have room for ten boxes of diapers. Take two or three and we'll
stop along the way and buy more."

The silver-haired lady wanted to argue, but was too shaken by all that had
transpired in the last few hours. In the back of her mind she decided that in an
emergency she could use Grandy's UFO magazines.

At the stroke of midnight the ladies crept down the hall.

"Grab that chair over there. We gotta prop the door open or we'll get locked out."

Dog Face Dale met them at the door, hair slicked down, and an overdose of pungent aftershave creating a cloud around them.

"Hi Gals!"

"Shhhhh! You big dope, you'll bring attention to us," Grandy scolded as she whacked him on the arm.

Dale absently rubbed his arm as he turned and grinned at Bernice. In a sickly sweet voice he asked, "What can I do for you young ladies?"

"We've got a small dilemma. Nick the Narcoleptic is dead in my motor home and we gotta get him back to his room so we don't get investigated. We're trying to get out of here by morning."

Grandy said this so nonchalantly that Bernice and Dog Face were convinced she had encountered this situation many times before. Sweat began to form miniature pools on Dale's face.

"You killed a guy?"

"No, you idiot, he croaked on his own. We just don't want to delay our trip because of some bureaucratic nonsense. Another meal in this place and I'll have to have my stomach pumped."

Dale stared at his sister before his choked response fell out. "Okay, Grandy, if you're sure this won't get you in trouble." Grandy only stared back at him, so he grabbed Nick's legs and yanked him off the bed,. He then dragged the body into the small living room, and studied the body. He gingerly lifted up his hand, and then dropped it.

"He's still warm, Grandy. Are you sure he's dead?"

"Just help me get him out of here."

"Get your wheelchair, Sis. We'll stick him in that then park him in the parlor and turn on the TV."

"Dale, sometimes you can be pretty smart."

Bernice could have debated that statement, but kept quiet, praying this would all be over soon.

Once Nick was placed in the wheelchair, Dale pushed him up the ramp to the building as Bernice held the door open.

"Someone's coming," Bernice whispered frantically, as she began to hyperventilate.

Dale torqued up his waddle a few notches and managed to park the wheelchair, get the TV turned on, and hide himself behind a bush outside the retirement home.

Lillian spotted the two women coming in from outside. "Everything okay, Ladies?"

"Yeah, just loading a few things in the motor home. Hey, if we don't see you before we go, it's been nice knowin' ya." Bernice's voice was unusually high and seemed to quiver.

Grandy noticed Lillian's uncertain look.

"She's just excited and nervous about tomorrow. Big day you know." Grandy put her arm around Bernice and gave her a firm squeeze.

"Yeah, I can see that. Well, you two have a safe trip. And come back and see us."

"Oh, we sure will," they answered in unison.

As soon as Lillian was out of sight, Dale came out of hiding. He met the old gals outside. The nervous brother wiped feverishly at the cascades of sweat on his face and neck.

"Don't call me for no more favors, Grandy. I don't have the personality for prison."

Grandy muttered a mini curse at him and went into the motor home to make a mental list of last minute items she and Bernice would need for their trip.

Dale sidled up next to Bernice, smiling like a lotto winner. He reached for her hand but she quickly thrust it into her sweater pocket and stepped back two paces.

"Miss Bernice, you can call me anytime. I'm at your service 24/7."

Bernice choked out a polite thank you and excused herself. She hurried into the retirement home before Dog Face was able to contaminate the air she breathed.

Chapter 23

Carlos, one of the aides, had just completed his night shift. He offered to carry the last load of Grandy's and Bernice's belongings out to the motor home. Staggering under the weight of UFO books and boxes of Depends, his breathing was heavy and sporadic. "We sure are going to miss you two gals around here."

"Sure you will," replied Grandy. "Sorry to say we won't miss this place. No offense, Carlos."

"None taken, Grandy."

They walked the rest of the way through the retirement home silently so as not to wake any of the other residents. The sun, a deep brilliant maize color, had just begun to crest the horizon. As Grandy followed Carlos to the motor home, Bernice trailed behind, taking one last glance around her former home. She accelerated her gait past the parlor, determined not to look at Nick's cold body.

"Tell *Red* she forgot her wheelchair."

The hair on Bernice's neck seemed to grow six inches. She almost screamed but slapped her hand over her mouth and then hastened her cadence, nearly tripping out the door. Grandy was already in the driver's seat revving up the motor.

"What took you so long? I've already wasted a gallon of gas waitin' on ya."

Bernice planted herself in the passenger seat, buckled her seat belt tightly and stared straight ahead. Her eyes were large, her normally pale complexion faded to an almost invisible shade.

"Bernie, you okay? You look like you've seen a ghost?"

"I did. Nick spoke to me."

"What?"

"Nick spoke to me. He's alive, Grandy. I know he is. I heard him."

"Oh, you're crazy. People with rigor mortis don't talk."

"I'm not kidding, Grandy. He talked to me."

"What did he say?"

"He wanted me to tell you that you forgot your wheelchair."

"Oh, my gosh, my wheelchair. I gotta go back and get it."

Frustration now masked over Bernice's fear as she couldn't believe her friend was more concerned with a wheelchair than the uncertain condition of Nick.

"Forget the wheelchair, let's just get out of here."

An argument was about to rupture, but Grandy thought twice as visions of being sued by the old man entered her cross-wired brain, and, for once, she took Bernice's advice.

The motor home tires squealed as the ladies left the retirement home parking lot. A car slammed on its brakes and honked its horn as the coach swerved in front of it making a left turn.

"For crying out loud, you're going to get us killed before we even get out of town!"

"Hush up, Grandma, I know what I'm doing."

Once Grandy was driving down a straight stretch of highway, Bernice dug into her purse to make sure she had her blood pressure medicine. She then reached over and turned on the radio.

"You tryin' to put me to sleep with that elevator music?" Grandy quickly tuned in a Country Western music channel.

"Hey, after what you put me through, I need to relax. And I hate Country Western."

"Well, you better learn to like it, because that's what I listen to."

"Can't we take turns listening to different stations?"

"I suppose, but absolutely none of that dentist office music. Find a rap or jazz or rock station."

"Fine." Bernice pouted as she pushed buttons trying to find a mutual channel. All at once Grandy shouted, "Stop!" and slapped Bernice's hand.

"Ouch!"

"The UFO talk show. Let's listen."

"Oh, great, now you're trying to indoctrinate me into the Land of Oz. Peter Popov would be better than this."

"Who's Peter Popov?"

"He's that healing preacher."

"You believe in that poppycock, but you don't believe in UFO's?"

"I never said I believed it, but I have seen him on TV, and I have yet to see a UFO."

"Well, we got a better chance of seein' a UFO than seeing some crazy preacher performing magic tricks. You forget who yer talkin' to. Them so-called healers gave good traveling preachers like my daddy a bad name."

Bernice decided to stir the pot a bit. "Well, I saw a National Geographic special where these two guys confessed to making those crop circles themselves. What'ya think about that?"

"I saw that same documentary and there's no way they made them all. They are all over the world, and the designs are way too elaborate to be man made."

"So who made 'em, then?"

"Aliens with too much time on their hands."

Bernice gave a deep sigh and rolled her eyes. "I'm getting hungry, Grandy, let's stop and eat."

"Already? We just got started."

"I know, but I need to take food with my blood pressure medication. How about we just drive through a McDonald's or something?"

"Oh alright, I guess I'm getting a little hungry myself."

It was only another mile before Grandy found an exit advertising The Golden Arches. She pulled into the drive-thru lane behind several other vehicles.

"Are you sure we should be in this lane? Isn't this motor home a bit too big to go under the awning?"

"It'll be fine. Just watch my side mirrors so I don't hit a post or something."

The Fleetwood barely inched through and both the McDonald's employee and Bernice sighed a breath of relief. Much to their dismay though, Grandy managed to drive through a juniper bush and knock over a trash can as she left the parking lot.

The ladies ate their breakfast as they listened to the UFO show which Bernice thought was ludicrous. After finishing her meal, she propped her pillow up against the window and watched the scenery go by until her eyes became heavy and she fell asleep. Grandy listened intently as the radio commentator took calls from like-minded listeners.

"Hank from Iowa, how you doin' today?"

"Great. Just wanted to agree with that last caller. I saw those same lights last night, and it was just the way she described it."

Grandy waited to hear the location of the sighting, hoping she and Bernice could get a glimpse of the craft. A honking horn jolted her concentration and she peered in the side-view mirror.

"Go around if you don't like my speed!" Grandy tapped her brakes as the car behind her screeched its tires and swerved, just missing oncoming traffic.

"What's wrong!" Bernice was jerked out of her peaceful nap by Grandy's hollering.

"That air head behind me. Men just don't realize women are the only ones who can multitask. He was trying to talk on the phone and drive at the same time. I just had to teach him a lesson." She didn't mention that she was going 35 miles an hour in a 70 mile an hour zone.

"Well, you're right about men not being able to multitask. I remember riding in the car with Jack. He'd be trying to talk and his arms would be flying around like an Italian as his foot went up and down on the gas pedal. I nearly got carsick just riding downtown with him."

"Yeah, but I bet you could change a diaper, peel an apple and put on your makeup at the same time."

"You bet."

The ladies laughed as Grandy reached over and turned off the radio. "Isn't this a beautiful country? And this machine just purrs like a kitten. That Bob Barker, he's not such a bad guy."

Just hearing the name "Bob Barker" made Bernice's heart skip a beat.

"Hey, you ever been to the SPAM factory? It's right up the road." Grandy pointed to a billboard.

"No I haven't."

"Funny, I've lived in Minnesota my entire adult life and I've never been there either."

We aren't really going to stop there are we?"

Of course we are, I love SPAM."

Well, I don't and I'm really anxious to get to L.A. and see my grandbaby."

"You'd better not start that already. If I'm doin' all the drivin', we're gonna have to make a few stops. There's a lot of neat stuff to see. We're not just doing this for your benefit, ya know."

Bernice mustered a half-smile, not wanting to upset her chauffeur. Then it dawned on her, the more times they stopped, the less times she'd have to use that miniature bathroom.

For the next half-hour the ladies shared SPAM stories.

"When I was a kid, we had to eat it almost every day for eight months when my dad lost his job. My mother fried it for breakfast with eggs, made SPAM sandwiches for lunch, and then she'd stick it on a platter at dinner time with some potatoes and carrots and try to pass it off as a pot roast. " Bernice scrunched her mouth at the thought of eating the disgusting meat mixture.

"You are totally un-American, Bernie, SPAM not only fed our American troops during the War, but it is a high quality food."

"You're kidding, right?"

"No, I'm not. A person can create an excellent dish made with SPAM in any food category. Appetizers, salads, even desserts."

"Don't even tell me what kind of dessert you can make with SPAM. If I never eat it again that will be fine with me."

"Hey, Miss Prima Donna, we didn't have much choice. Lester was no Jack Gibson, at least in a vocational sense."

"So, what recipes did you create with the stuff?"

"Let's see, we had crepes de' SPAM, SPAM Creole, SPAM tortillas, SPAM stroganoff, Swiss SPAM. Then there was SPAMaroni, SPAM lasagna, and my all time favorite, SPAM cordon bleu."

"What did your boys say about eating all that SPAM?"

"Never said a thing. They weren't really into the dining experience. They pretty much inhaled their food without ever tasting it."

"Well then why'd you waste your time getting so creative?"

"Hey, I had to eat, too. And besides, I always loved a challenge."

Bernice didn't know what else to say so after a few moments of silence, Grandy turned the radio onto a '50s music channel. Bernice tried not to laugh as her friend sang along with Bill Haley and the Comets: *"We're gonna rock around the clock tonight, we're-."* Old Red's voice sounded like a metal bumper being dragged down the highway.

* * *

Avis hadn't slept all night. Something was telling him his mother was lying. "I bet she didn't sell that motor home," he thought as he dialed her retirement home number. This time he received a recorded message that the number was disconnected. He then called the main number for the home and asked for the manager.

"May I help you?"

"This is Avis Wayland, Grandy McGregor Wayland's son. I need to speak to her immediately."

I'm sorry, Mr. Wayland, but Ms. Wayland and Ms. Gibson left early this morning in their new motor home. I was under the impression she told you."

"Do you know where they're going?"

"No, I'm sorry. They just said they were off to see the world."

"Why didn't anyone call me?"

"Like I said, we thought you knew all about her plans."

"I'm the one who set her up in there, I should have been notified about this situation."

"I'm sorry, Mr. Wayland."

"Never mind!" Avis slammed down the phone and then looked for his mother's cell phone number. "I don't think she's ever used it. Hopefully she didn't donate it to some alien cause," he thought.

"Hi, this is Grandy. Leave a message and maybe I'll call you back, or maybe I won't."

Avis left a message for his mother to call him immediately. He then closed his green eyes and tried to formulate a new plan to locate his wacky mother.

Chapter 24

"How many cans of that stuff did you buy, anyway?" asked Bernice.

"You'll be thankin' me once you've tasted my famous SPAMaroni," Grandy answered as she stacked the cans in the cupboard of the motor home.

"Does SPAM freeze?" Bernice asked as she opened the freezer door. Grandy almost dropped a can of SPAM on her foot as Bernice let out a ear-splitting shriek.

"There's a shriveled up finger in our refrigerator!" The grey-haired sissy began to hyperventilate.

Grandy pushed Bernice out of the way and looked in the freezer. "You old dork! That's not a finger, it's Larry's cigar." She gave her friend a subdued smirk then the two of them laughed at the gross reminder of their former dreary life at the retirement home.

"Is it okay if I call Joyce?"

"If you keep it short."

"I just want to tell her when we'll be there. What shall I tell her?"

"Tell her we'll be there when we get there and you'll call her again when we get to California."

Bernice dialed Joyce's number and received a recording. "Hey, Sweetie, this is Mom. Hope you're doing okay. We left early this morning and I'll call you when we get to California. Not sure exactly when. We're doing a little sightseeing along the way. Kiss Jackie for me. Love you. Bye."

Bernice handed Grandy the phone. "It says on here you have a message."

Grandy punched in her password and listened to the message. "Ma, call me, NOW!"

"Who was it?"

"Avis, the bossy brat. Probably found out I escaped."

"You going to call him?"

"Heck, no. I imagine he's got an APB out on me by now. He already tried to get me to sign power of attorney over to him. You and I both know where I'd be if I'd given in to that. They all think I'm crazy. Truth is, they're hoping if they lock me up long enough, I *will* go crazy and then they'll get it all, and leave me with nothing."

"Ungrateful generation."

"You got that right."

"So, where to next?" Bernice inquired and the two resumed their seats in the cockpit.

"Grab that piece of paper out of the glove box. I made a list of stuff we might want to see along the way."

Bernice removed the list of sights Grandy had meticulously organized by states. "Let's see, for Iowa, you have listed the world's largest Cheeto. Cheeto? Why do you want to see a giant piece of junk food?"

"Why not?"

"Sounds disgusting."

"Sounds interesting. It's probably in the shape of a space ship or something."

"Swell. It says it's at Sister Sarah's Restaurant in Algona. At least maybe we can get a decent meal."

"This might be a good time to try out our new navigation system. It's gotta be better than you trying to read a map." Grandy plugged in the destination and the directions were displayed on the small screen.

"You sure that thing is accurate? What if it sends us to Kentucky or Alabama?"

"Bernie, you worry about the dumbest stuff. Just learn to trust technology. It's the way of the world. If you don't hop on board, you're gonna get left behind and won't know how to do anything."

"Kind of like those new fangled toilets that flush themselves."

"Now that's one piece of technology that needs some work. It always flushes before you're done wiping."

"Yeah, and then it sprays water all over your butt," Bernice added as she watched the signs for the turnoff to Algona.

"I take it back. Forget technology. This thing isn't gonna cut it. I can't even see the writing on the screen. And if I can't, you sure won't be able to, your eyes are worse than mine."

"I am older than you, remember. So you should show me more respect."

"Don't worry about respect, just make sure we take the right exit."

"Where are we going again?"

"Algona. Now watch for the turn."

"I am Grandy," Bernice tried not to sound irritated. She closed her eyes, rested her arms on her legs, her middle fingers touching her thumbs, and took some deep breaths and slowly exhaled. "In through the nose, out through the mouth."

"What are you doing?"

"It's yoga. I learned it on TV. Supposed to help me relax."

"Well it makes you look stupid."

"Hmmmph." Bernice ceased her breathing exercise, realizing she would never attain total concentration with Grandy sitting next to her.

"I told ya, you watched too much TV."

"I only watch educational stuff."

"Yeah, like *The Price is Right*."

"Yeah, like *The Price is Right*. If I hadn't taught you how to bid, we'd still be choking down mystery meat."

"Speaking of food – "

"Yeah, like that was food."

The comment produced a slight chuckle from both ladies. A short time later they pulled into the side lot of Sister Sarah's Restaurant. This was especially delightful for Bernice as Grandy wouldn't be indulging her just yet with one of her SPAM concoctions.

As they entered the restaurant, there it was displayed for all to see – the world's largest Cheeto.

"It looks kinda like a shriveled up tennis ball," Grandy said somewhat grimly.

Bernice began to read the plaque, "It says it was auctioned on eBay. The town of Algona raised $180 to bid on it. They thought it would put them on the map, then the guy who owned it donated it to the town." Bernice paused, "What's eBay, Grandy?"

"It's where people buy and sell junk, like a flea market on the Internet. I heard some lady got almost two hundred dollars for an eight-inch french fry."

"Are you serious?"

"Hey, maybe we can sell Larry's stogey and say it belonged to somebody famous."

"Or maybe we could sell some of your UFO magazines."

"Better yet, we could sell you, I could advertise you as a 17th century science experiment gone wrong."

The look Bernice gave Grandy could have melted asphalt. She stared at the orange glob. "We stopped *here* to look at *this*? I wonder how come it hasn't gone rancid and turned green since it's made of cheese?"

"Chuck full of preservatives," Grandy replied.

"Can you imagine how many chemicals they put in that stuff to keep it from going bad? Can't be good for you."

"Yeah, and I like those things. Don't think I'll eat a whole bag at a time anymore. Come on, let's order a little lunch." Grandy made a dedicated effort not to show Bernice that she, too, was disappointed in their first unusual landmark.

"I'll have the steak, well done, with french fries, make them nice and crispy, and a chocolate malt, not a milkshake." Grandy smacked her lips, closed the menu, and handed it to the acne-faced young waiter.

"Yes, Ma'am."

"What breed of cattle is the steak?"

"What?"

"What breed of cattle? Hereford? Angus? Charolais?"

"I don't know. Does it matter?"

"Yes, it does, I want to make sure it's the good stuff. You see, we just escaped, what I mean is that, where we used to live, we could never tell what kinda meat we were eating,"

A frightened look began to surface on the older teenager. Worried they wouldn't get served, Bernice quickly began talking about the meal she wanted.

"I'd like to order the chicken breast, but I want to make sure, its real chicken?"

"I think it is," squeaked the timid voice of the waiter.

"Could I have a house salad too, please?"

"Yes, Ma'am."

"And separate checks," Grandy added.

The waiter gave the ladies a weak smile as he hurried towards the kitchen.

"Great, now he's gonna think we're escaped convicts or something," Bernice whispered after he was out of ear shot.

"They can't arrest us for complaining about the retirement home food."

The waiter placed the orders and then went behind the counter to use the phone.

"He's calling the cops. Can you believe that? Nice going Grandy."

"Oh, he is not. And so what. We didn't do anything wrong."

"You better hope Nick really is alive, that's all I can say. And what about Avis. You said he'd have an APB out on you."

"For what? I haven't done anything illegal, yet. Let's just relax and enjoy our lunch and then we can get settled in over at the KOA campground.

After a filling meal the ladies paid their bills. They had agreed to pay their own ways, and take turns filling up the gas tank. On their way out, they took each other's picture in front of the large Cheeto.

"There's probably some fool out there who'd pay good money for this picture," Grandy exclaimed, as she posed with one hand behind her head and the other hand on her hip.

"Doubt it. It'll probably end up on a 'wanted' poster."

"Funny, Bernie. Hurry up and go pee so we can get going, or else I'll leave you behind with the giant Cheeto."

Chapter 25

Grandy, outwardly confident, was not about to let her buddy see how she was crumbling inside. In their highway home only a day, the UFO fan was becoming overwhelmed at the thought of being responsible for setting up camp every night by herself. Knowing Bernice lacked any knowledge concerning motor homes, traveling, or surviving outside a five-star hotel, the redhead wondered how long it would take to train her friend in the ways of the world. "Can't take any more patience and time than it did to teach my dearly departed miniature goats to pull red wagons," she thought to herself.

"Bernie, how far to the KOA campground?"

The co-pilot squinted, then lifted her glasses as she tried to make sense of the atlas sprawled across her lap.

"About half an inch from Algona."

"How far in miles, you dope?"

Exhausted from sightseeing and new emotions, Bernice gave her roommate an ugly stare before adding up the tiny mileage numbers on the atlas.

"Ten miles. You happy now?" she snapped.

"Only when you come down with a medical condition that causes you to stop being a nincompoop."

Just as the tangerine-colored sun was slipping into a dusky envelope, the ladies pulled into the campground. Grandy was feeling extremely grateful when she found out their camping space was a pull-through. She sighed as she turned off the motor home, "I'm bushed. What say we turn in early? Then we can get a fresh start in the morning."

"Don't you have to hook up hoses or something?"

"Not tonight. We'll do it when we stay more than one night somewhere."

"So how do we wash up?"

"There's water in the holding tank."

"Is it enough to take a shower?"

"You don't need a shower tonight, you took one this morning."

"I need to wash. I feel grubby."

"Then grab a wash rag and scrub your pits, there's plenty of water for that. You're not gonna die if you go one night without a shower. I swear, Bernie, you waste more time worrying about your personal hygiene. Nobody here to notice you anyway except Felix, and I don't think he cares."

Bernice stood over the kitchen sink wearing only her underwear. She wiped her face and hands with a washcloth and then ran it over the rest of her upper body and under her arms.

"Golly sakes, Bernie, put some clothes on." Grandy covered her eyes at first glance of her half-naked roommate.

"After my sponge bath."

Bernice slipped into her gown and then went through her nightly ritual of brushing, gargling and flossing. She then generously applied night cream to her face, neck, elbows and feet.

"Keep that stuff on your side of the bed."

"And you keep the noise down."

"What do you mean?"

"I mean you sound like a sawmill when you're asleep." Bernice stuffed cotton balls in her ears and pulled the covers over her head.

"I've never heard myself snore."

"Did you say something?" Bernice yelled.

"No, go to sleep."

Bernice managed to stay asleep for a couple of hours, but Grandy's snoring soon began to penetrate the cotton balls. Tired of holding her pillow over her head, Bernice shook Grandy's shoulder.

"Grandy!"

"What's wrong?" Grandy shouted as she abruptly sat up in bed.

"Awwwwh! You almost knocked me out of bed! And you snore too loud. I can't sleep."

"I swear, if you ever wake me up like that again, I'll sell you for hog feed at the next livestock mill."

"Roll over. Maybe you won't snore so loud."

"Don't tell me what to do, you old fool," Grandy grumbled as she buried herself beneath the covers. She fell back asleep and the snoring ceased just long enough for Bernice to get another hour of rest.

"Grandy. You awake?"

"No."

"I gotta pee."

"Oh for goodness sakes, Bernie. Why'd you pack a boatload of Depends if you're not gonna use them?"

"They're just for leakage. I gotta pee real bad. Is it okay to use the toilet?"

"Well, where else would you go pee, in the sink? Now be quiet."

"I can't see."

"Turn the light on."

"How do you do that?"

"The switch on the wall, Bernie. And the towel on the bar is for drying your hands."

Deciding she was the more mature one, Bernice refrained from elbowing her roommate in the side.

After using the bathroom, Bernice stared into the darkness, contemplating a place to escape from Grandy's snoring. She found her way to the sofa, wrapped up in an afghan, and fell back to sleep for the rest of the night.

Grandy had her eight hours of sleep in by dawn. She awoke to find Bernice still on the coach, head back, mouth open, drool spilling out like a minuscule stream.

"That's attractive, Bernie," she quietly mumbled.

Old Red decided to get dressed and go find a sight more soothing to her eyes. As she strolled along the gravel roads of the campground, she whistled the theme song of the *X-Files*.

"Keep it down out there, people are trying to sleep," an angry male voice spoke.

Several large dogs barked violently as she passed a hippie van covered in graffiti.

A bumper sticker with "Area 51" on an old, hail-bitten Winnebago sparked Grandy's curiosity. She knocked on the door and an elderly gentleman with white hair and white beard opened the door. He was dressed in patched overalls and a plaid, flannel shirt.

"I couldn't help noticing your Area 51 bumper sticker. Have you really been there?"

The man looked at the wild-haired woman wearing cut-off jeans and red sneakers with suspicion in his dark eyes. He was about to shut his door without a comment, but Grandy stepped closer.

"My name's Grandy McGregor. My friend and I are on our way to visit Area 51 and the crop circles. I thought maybe you could tell me if it's worth the trip there."

The trailer door opened wider for the excited senior citizen, "Come on in Grandy McGregor. I'll tell you all about it. By the way, my name's Roscoe, Roscoe Smith."

"Thanks, Roscoe." Once inside the camper, Grandy surveyed a decor consisting of miles of loose wiring, three computer set-ups, and at least a hundred boxes of Hostess Ding Dongs.

"What's all the boxes of Ding Dongs for? Does it attract extra terrestrials?"

"No, I just like them. As for Area 51, Grandy McGregor, not only have I been to Area 51, I actually saw a UFO."

Grandy sat like a star-struck teenager as she listened to Roscoe describe in great detail the UFO he saw and the experiences he encountered at Area 51.

"Where did you see the UFO?" Grandy asked.

"The first one was when me and my brother Bruce were out chukar hunting in northern Nevada. It hovered for a long time, then came almost close enough to touch down. After a few seconds it just disappeared."

"What did it look like?"

"Standard disk shape with hundreds of multi-colored lights around the base."

"Bet it was beautiful."

"Haven't seen a UFO in the last two years. Before that, I'd see one at least every couple of months."

"Well, I'd love to continue discussing extraterrestrials with you, Roscoe, but I'd better be getting back to my motor home. My friend is probably awake by now and freaking out because I'm not there."

"Is she kinda short and round with bluish-grey hair?"

"Yeah, how'd you –" Grandy looked out the window and saw Bernice wandering around in her nightgown. "Gotta go, Roscoe! Nice to meet you and thanks for all the info." Grandy hurried to Bernice's side just as she was about to start knocking on trailer doors.

"Where have you been? I've been awake for hours looking for you."

"You old fool, I've only been gone about 45 minutes. And you were sleeping when I left."

"Well, it felt like hours. I locked myself out of the motor home. I need to eat so I can take my medication."

"Nice goin', Bernie." An exasperated Grandy went back to Roscoe and asked if he could help.

Roscoe walked to the back door of the Fleetwood and turned the knob, it was unlocked.

Grandy rolled her eyes at Bernice.

"Thanks for everything, Roscoe. Grandy offered him the latest edition of her UFO magazine. "Have you seen this one?"

"No, sure haven't."

"It's yours. It's the least I can do."

"Thanks. Maybe we'll see you in Nevada or New Mexico sometime."

Bernice gave the two paranormal buddies a puzzled look and thanked Roscoe for his help. As soon as Roscoe left, Bernice lectured Grandy on the dangers of talking to strangers. "You tryin' to get us killed?"

"And how did you know the people behind the doors you were about to knock on weren't serial killers?"

"Well – "

"Bernice, I'm not a little kid. I knew right away Roscoe was one of us."

"Us! Don't put me in the same category with you bunch of weirdoes."

"Prima Donna."

"Freak."

Chapter 26

"You're going the wrong way, Grandy. California's that way." Bernice pointed as she frantically tried unfolding an Iowa map.

"Don't worry. We're taking a little detour."

"What for?"

"We're going to Riverside."

"Riverside's in California. And California is west, not east."

"No, silly, Riverside, Iowa."

Panic began a fast creep into Bernice's voice. "Why are we going to Riverside, Iowa?"

"It's the annual Trek-Fest." Grandy's excitement meter jumped up a few bars as she continued to explain the annual event.

"Can I get hurt there? Will it cost a lot of money?"

"Would I do something to raise your blood level, my blue-haired friend? Trek-Fest is the celebration of the future birth of Capt. James Kirk. You remember, Star Trek?"

Bernice gave Grandy a puzzled look.

"Captain Kirk? Starship Enterprise? Don't tell me you're not a Trekkie."

"I've heard of it, and no, I'm not a Trekkie. I had more important things to do than watch some stupid science fiction show." Bernice's eyes darkened another shade of grey as she began stewing about the abrupt travel change.

"Stupid? Are you kidding? To boldly go where no man has gone before? You call that stupid?"

"You *do* realize it was only a TV show."

"Yeah, a TV show of future events. And Captain Kirk is going to be born in Riverside, Iowa in about two hundred years from now."

"You really believe that?"

"Well, even if I don't believe it a hundred percent, it makes for a good excuse to go to Riverside."

"What else is in Riverside? Will I be able to buy something healthy there or will I be stuck eating green slime from a spaceship cup?"

"Don't be ridiculous, Bernie. Riverside is a normal, Midwestern town with normal people."

Bernice was an inch from letting a sarcastic comment exit her mouth but decided it was a waste of breath. It was Grandy's motor home and she was the passenger. If this was how the rest of the trip was going to be though, Bernice felt the crazy redhead should be driving herself to the nearest psycho ward.

"So how far is it? I'm really anxious to get to L.A. to see Joyce and my new granddaughter."

"We'll be there in a few hours. Relax. Jackie probably looks like her mom and you saw her when she was a baby, so it's not going to be any big surprise. And if she looks like her dad then you might want to wait until she's older anyway, give the poor child a chance to develop some female qualities."

"Grandy! You are mean and warped! How can you say such things about my family?"

"You'd better control the steam coming out of your ears, Bernie. It's liable to fog up your glasses."

"I don't know if I'm angrier about being hijacked to Iowa or your rude comments about my granddaughter."

Grandy sighed as if her friend was accusing her of murdering Bob Barker. "Bernice, Dear, you've got to learn to mellow a little and not take things so seriously. Enjoy the adventures, have some fun, develop some healthy and unhealthy fantasies."

"I just wished you'd discuss these things with me first," Bernice grumbled.

"Okay, let's discuss it now. We're going to Riverside, Iowa to the Trek-Fest. There. We discussed it."

"And I don't get a say in anything?"

"I told you before, Bernie. I wanna see some sights and have a little fun. I'm not just drivin' you to L.A., although if you don't quit you're whinin', I just might leave you there."

A pouting Bernice mumbled, "Okay, I'll try to enjoy being around your space aliens, but I want an apology for the comments you made about Jackie."

"Sorry, Bernie, that I insulted the fruit of your loins."

* * *

The rest of the journey to Riverside was spent in silence between the two roommates. When billboards advertising the Trek-Fest began to appear, Grandy couldn't contain herself any longer.

"See, Bernie. This is a really big deal. We're gonna have so much fun!"

Bernice continued to stare out the window, focusing her thoughts on her new granddaughter, wondering if she was ever going to meet her.

"Wake up, Bernie, we're here!"

"I'm awake. Oooh, that SPAM sandwich didn't set too well," Bernice complained, "I'm going to eat a couple of saltine crackers."

"While you do that, I'm going to change clothes."

Grandy went into the bedroom and shut the door while Bernice searched the kitchen for a box of crackers.

"Oh my God!" Bernice nearly choked on her snack as Grandy exited the bedroom dressed in a beige and black Spandex space suit and moon boots. The body suit was so tight, nearly every crease, roll, and wrinkle on Grandy's body was revealed.

"What's that on your ears?" asked Bernice.

"These are Vulcan ears."

"You're not wearing that outfit in public? You look like a one of those ugly, hairless dogs."

"Now who owes who an apology? Take a look outside."

Bernice peered out the window to see an ocean of spacemen and women, aliens and other weird looking creatures and suddenly felt underdressed.

"Let's go, Bernie. This is gonna be great! See, over there, corn dogs, hotdogs, hamburgers. Let's eat."

Bernice exited the motor home with great caution. Seeing all those extra terrestrials started her questioning about the validity of Grandy's obsession. Perhaps there might really be other life forms. And if that was the case, she silently prayed they would not single her out for experiments.

"We're just in time for the children's parade. Look! There's Mr. Spock!"

"Yeah, and there he is over there, and over there, too."

While the ladies munched on a Martian Meat special, (Bernice the whole time dying for a Cobb salad), they watched a parade of children dressed in costumes of tin foil antennas and lime green leotards. When a tangerine-orange sun began its evening descent, Grandy and Bernice headed towards their motor home. Along the way, Grandy picked up a schedule of the next day's events.

"Look, Bernie. Tomorrow's parade includes adults. Maybe we can be in it."

"You mean you're planning to spend another day here?"

"Of course! I'm looking forward to meeting a few Klingons."

"But I'm tired and bored of this weird place. Let's head for California tomorrow."

"Look here, Bernie, you might like this one. A tractor pull."

"Why in the world would you think I'd like a tractor pull? I was raised a city girl, not a redneck farmer."

"Careful, Bernie. "Don't you be disrespecting the farmer, he's the one that feeds your budding butt."

Bernice tried to pull her T-shirt farther down around her bottom. She then glanced at the schedule and pointed. "I might like this one, a swap meet. Wonder what I could get for a redheaded psychopath."

Chapter 27

Before dawn had the opportunity to yawn, Grandy decided she was going to be in the Trek-Fest parade for adults. She enhanced her space outfit by gluing bent forks to the shoulders, fashioned a hat from colored paper plates, and used a green facial mud to coat her face. Bernice tried to suppress a giggle as she observed her friend rummaging around in a drawer for something to use as a hand-held communicator.

"Say Grandy, does this parade give prizes for the best *and* worst costumes?"

"I don't know. Does it matter? Just hurry up and get ready. The line-up for the parade is 9 a.m."

"I can't believe you're doing this."

"Take your camera. Get a picture of me in the parade."

Bernice started to protest when she suddenly saw the golden gift handed to her, a picture of Grandy dressed like that. She could blackmail the old broad for the rest of her life.

Back at the festival, Grandy found a spot near the end of the parade lineup while Bernice stood in the shade of a concession stand watching the unusual festivities around her. As she was snapping a couple of pictures of Grandy, a man dressed in streets clothes stepped in front of her camera. He was flanked by people holding scraps of paper and pens, talking to him in voices that all seemed to be requesting the same thing.

"Excuse me," said Bernice, raising her cane in the air, "could you please move over a bit? I'm trying to take a picture of my friend."

"I'm sorry," said the gentleman. "I didn't realize I was blocking your view."

"It's alright."

The throng of people surrounding the man seemed to guide him farther down the sidewalk almost without his knowledge.

Grandy was towards the end of the parade, her self-styled, red hair climbing towards the sky. Bernice joined her for the last few yards of the parade route.

"Did you get my picture?"

"Yes, but some man with a lot of people following him blocked my view. At least he was polite enough to apologize."

Grandy pointed towards a group of people standing in front of one of the local stores. "Is that the man over there?"

Bernice squinted, "Yeah, that's him. Why do you think all those people are following him around?"

"Because, you moron, that's William Shatner! You know, Captain Kirk? Did you get his autograph? What did he say to you?"

"No, I didn't get his autograph. How was I supposed to know who he was?"

"We're at a Trek-Fest, how could you not see the resemblance between him and all the Star Trek posters?"

"If you want his autograph so bad, go get it. He's only half a block away."

"Fine. I will."

Trying to march off in a frustrating walk, Grandy only increased her ridiculous appearance when her angry gait looked more like an injured goose dipped in green paint.

Since Bernice had no idea how long it would take her bizarre friend to accomplish her mission, she decided to cool her hot throat and rest her swollen feet at a concession stand. She ordered a large glass of lemonade and found one of two of the last spots at the end of a long picnic table. It seemed only a few moments before a middle-aged gentleman approached her.

"Is this seat taken?" he asked, in a deep, baritone voice.

"No, go ahead."

Bernice noticed that this was the second man she'd encountered today dressed in normal clothes. Perhaps he was capable of carrying on a conversation that was not peppered with the words, "alien, ET, or flying saucer." The man noticed Bernice trying to read the name tag on his khaki shirt.

"Chet Baxter, K-TAZ Radio out of Chicago. I have a booth over there by the entrance."

"Oh, yeah, I think I saw that when we came in. My name's Bernice Gibson."

"Nice to meet you, Bernice. Are you enjoying the Trek-Fest?" His smile was infectious and warm.

"Not really. I'm here because my best friend is into this Martian stuff and since I'm the passenger in her motor home, I go where she goes."

"I see. Where is your friend right now?"

"She's off running around like a crazy woman trying to get Captain Kook's autograph."

Chet chuckled, "You mean Captain Kirk?"

"Yeah, whatever. I don't really know anything about all this science fiction stuff."

"Where you ladies from?"

"Minnesota, we just – "

Bernice's explanation was cut short by Grandy's high crackling voice, "Bernie! Bernie! I got it! I got it!"

Chet observed the incoming, elderly woman with amusement. Her skin-tight outfit seemed to restrict her movements, causing her to do a walk-waddle. Red hair of different shades formed a volcano on her head, and blue eyes sparkled through a facial expression that seemed frozen because of the dried mud. She was carrying a brightly colored, plastic shopping bag. Compared to her complacent friend (who's only absurdity was watermelon shorts), it was difficult to believe they were travel companions. As Grandy approached the picnic table, Chet stood up and extended his hand to her.

"Hi, my name is Chet."

"Name's Grandy." She abruptly turned her back to Chet and began talking to her friend. "Bernie, I got Captain Kirk's autograph, and I did a little shopping for you and Jackie."

Bernice rolled her eyes, "And what, pray tell, did you buy that is suitable for my granddaughter?"

"Bean bag aliens. Look, aren't they cute! And for you, I bought a pair of Vulcan ears. Now you won't feel so out of place."

"Grandy, if I wanted to fit in with these people, I would have made myself to look like you, without the costume."

It took all of Chet's efforts to suppress a hearty laugh. Surely, he mused to himself, this pair of old ladies couldn't be for real.

"Do the two of you come to the Trek-Fest every year?"

"Thank heavens, no!" Bernice blurted out.

"Well, we might be here next year, depending on where we are," said Grandy. "Since we have a lot of places to go and things to see, we might have to attend a Star-Trek convention somewhere else in the U.S."

"I'm just trying to get to Los Angeles to see my new granddaughter."

"Bernice said you traveled here by motor home."

Grandy's chest swelled up as she replied, "Yup! The new motor home I won on *The Price is Right* show. Now me and Bernie here, we kissed the retirement home good-bye two days ago and are exploring this great nation of ours."

Chet, Grandy, and Bernice continued talking for the next hour about the ladies' trip, their lives, and their future plans. By the end of the conversation, Chet was so intrigued with the senior citizens that he made a proposal to them.

"How would you gals like to be on my radio show?"

"What for?" asked Grandy.

"Well, I have a syndicated radio program heard around the country. Usually I cover topics in the news, but I think it's time for America to be inspired by its citizens. You girls could sort of be tour guides for the listening audience, inspiration for other people too afraid to venture out."

"How can we be on the radio if we're traveling around the country?" Bernice interjected.

"How about I provide you with a cell phone so you could call in every day? It would only take about fifteen minutes of your time Monday through Friday, and you can quit anytime it becomes too difficult for you."

The old ladies looked at each other, Grandy grinned and Bernice wrinkled her nose.

"We'll need some time to talk about it," said Bernice.

"No we won't, we'll do it, Chet!"

103

"But – "

"No buts, Bernie, it'll be fun!"

"Excellent! Now are you sure you will be able to call in everyday at the same time? That is a really important element of this deal?"

"No problem," piped Grandy.

"Okay then, why don't you meet me at my booth say about, 6:00 tonight. We'll take care of the technical mumbo jumbo, and then I'll buy you supper."

After Chet left, Bernice angrily said to Grandy, "Don't I get any say so in anything!"

"Not really, Bernie, now put your Vulcan ears on and let's join the party."

Chapter 28

"Answer the damn phone, Avis," Lester grumbled.

"Avis Wayland."

"Do you know how hard it is to get a hold of you?"

"Hello to you too, Dad."

"Your mother is touring the country in a brand new motor home. I heard her on the radio yesterday."

"I know, I listened to her this morning. As for the motor home, I've known about that for awhile, Howard called me."

"How come you didn't let me know about it?" Anger was rapidly invading Lester's voice.

"Because it really isn't any concern of yours."

"Yes, it is. We're still legally married, so that makes half that motor home mine. You need to find her and explain that to her."

"Dad," Avis' voice was tight with frustration, "you left Mom over 20 years ago for other women, so I think *you* should find her and explain the situation to her."

A long pause followed Avis' last statement. He imagined his dad, reclining in a dirty brown vinyl chair with duct tape over the rips. The chair would be located in the small apartment of his latest girlfriend, a woman probably 50 something, dressed like a 20-year-old, wearing enough makeup to supply half the women in the United States. She would probably be off working in some greasy restaurant, earning money to pay for Lester's beer. Most likely, his father still had untrimmed, thinning, gray hair in his eyes and a bulging belly. Avis was pretty sure he could hear his dad pouring beer into a bowl of Rice Krispies. He broke the silence by saying, "Dad, you still there?"

"Yeah," Lester's voice was low and tinged with fear. "I don't think it's safe for me to talk to your mother face to face, she'd probably shoot me and mount me as a hood ornament on the motor home."

"She probably would. Would you blame her?"

Another bout of silence ensued before Avis said, "I'm trying to catch up with Ma myself. I'll keep you posted, but don't expect I'll let you take advantage of her."

"Okay, but make it soon. I don't know how long I can keep hiding from the IRS." Lester hung up before Avis could get in a parting comment.

Avis stared at the phone a moment before dialing the number of Stanley "The Storm" Herrod, private investigator.

Stanley's update on Avis' mother did little to pacify his already irritated disposition.

"How can you not know where she is?"

"Because, despite the fact that we know she is headed west, it is impossible to know exactly which roads she is traveling at what time. Based on the radio broadcasts, she and her buddy are stopping at various tourist attractions off the main highway. You would need an army of P.I.'s to search for them."

"Then get an army of them." Avis hung up with the same abruptness as with father.

* * *

Two states west of Minnesota, a young man with long, black hair, turned his truck radio up several notches. He shook his head in disbelief as he listened to the familiar voice of his mother rambling on about a Trek Fest or something along those lines.

"Oh, Ma," Dakota sighed, "I sure hope Dad and Avis don't catch up with you."

"What was that, Honey?" asked Skye, his young bride.

"Nothing, Love. I think you, me and the baby need to head south for a bit. My mother may need our assistance."

"After we finish our search in Yellowstone."

"We'll give ourselves a week."

"We'll give ourselves whatever time we need, Dakota. This is important." The voice was soft but firm and seemed out of place coming from the woman who had features similar to an innocent fawn.

When the radio interview with Grandy and Bernice was over, Dakota started his rusty, red Chevy and he and his family headed towards an entrance of Yellowstone National Park. If luck was with them, they would finally find the lost treasure indicated on a map he had purchased from a Native American hitchhiker, named Akando. But unbeknownst to Dakota or Skye, the name Akando means, "ambush."

Chapter 29

A couple of days after the motor home mamas left the Trek-Fest, Grandy carefully applied a thick layer of Noxzema to the rash on her face. She finally conceded that using a Brillo pad to remove the green mask of mud was not one of the more intelligent ideas she had.

"What time is it?" asked Bernice.

"We've got about ten minutes."

"Are you sure? Remember what happened yesterday."

"A time zone difference is an honest mistake. Besides, you didn't remember, either."

"Well, the most important thing is, no matter where we are, Bob Barker is always on at 10 a.m.," Bernice's voice was thick with infatuation.

"Yeah, that's REAL important," Grandy smirked.

"Did you forget where you got this motor home?"

"Yeah, yeah."

"I think I'm going to have to use the bathroom real quick before you call."

"Well, hurry up."

A few moments later, Grandy hollered, "I'm dialing the number!"

"Wait one more minute, I'm almost done!"

The selfish redhead ignored her friend and dialed the cell phone.

"K-TAZ Radio, how may I direct your call?"

"Put me through to Chet."

"Chet Baxter?"

"How many Chets you have working there?" said a grouchy Grandy.

"One moment, please."

"Hey Grandy, how's it goin'?" Chet's voice was cheerful and kind.

"Fine."

"The commercial break will be over in about 45 seconds, and then we will start our conversation on the air. Are you both ready?"

"Well, I am. Bernice is still on the pot. She must have run into a road block." A rusty snicker erupted from Grandy's mouth.

Chet was caught off guard by this statement and was unable to produce an immediate response. It didn't take him very long, though, to regain his composure. Neither was it taking him long to understand Grandy's bizarre personality and Bernice's reserved but generous spirit.

"I wouldn't make mention of that fact on the air, Grandy, it might create a lot of embarrassment for your friend."

"So."

"Grandy, get ready, we're on the air in five seconds. Welcome back, Ladies and Gentlemen. It's the top of the second hour here and our traveling grannies, Grandy and Bernice, are on the line. Let's see what they've been up to. Ladies?"

Muffled sounds of panting and what sounded like a phone dropping resounded over the air.

"Give me the phone, Grandy!"

"Let go before I hurt you!"

Chet quickly interrupted. "Remember, I told you about that little button on the side of the phone, you'll be on speaker and you can both hear me."

"Oh, yeah, now we can hear ya," answered Grandy.

Chet tried to regain control of his show. "So Bernice, what did you do yesterday? What wonderful landmarks of the U.S. did you see? Any interesting encounters with people you would like to share?"

"We finally got to go to church. Well, we didn't actually get to go *in* the church because it was built out of straw and they didn't allow anyone inside."

"Where is this church located?"

"Arthur, Nebraska."

"Tell us more."

"There isn't much else to say about the church, but right next door is the smallest courthouse in the country, where we almost had to pay a fine because big-mouth Red here threatened to burn down the straw church."

"I did no such thing!" Grandy yelled from the background.

"Well, Grandy, let me ask you a few questions."

"Yeah, Chet, ask her about her pyro experience," injected Bernice.

"I did not threaten to burn down the church!"

"I believe you, Grandy, I'm just interested in what happened."

"Nothing happened, there was just a misunderstanding with the local officials when I asked someone for a match."

"Why did you need the match, Grandy?"

"None of your business. Besides, the whole incident is over and done with. Let's talk about something else."

"Okay, what else have you seen in your recent travels?"

"We went to a place called Carhenge."

"Oh, tell us about that."

"It's like Stonehenge, only made out of cars," answered Grandy.

"Where is this?"

"Alliance, just up the road from Oshkosh."

"We're still in Nebraska, right?"

"Of course, how fast do you think I drive?"

Chet could not help but laugh at the senior citizen on the other end of the phone line.

"I'll give you the details, Chet. Grandy's only good at describing spaceships and little green men. Carhenge is fashioned after Stonehenge, only it's made out of old cars. It was built at a family reunion back in 1987 and later they painted it all gray because it was too much of an eyesore."

"Sounds like a place everyone should see at least once. Anything else of interest?"

"Not really," said Grandy.

"Well then, onto another subject, Ladies. Do you eat most of your meals on wheels?"

"We try to eat breakfast and lunch in the motor home, and then go out for supper if we're in an interesting place," replied Bernice.

"Yeah, and we usually go early enough to get the senior discount."

"Who does most of the cooking?"

"Grandy. She's a much better cook than I am. I have to admit, she does most everything concerning the motor home. She sets up camp, fills and empties the tanks, and does all the driving. Bernice's voice was decreasing in volume with every sentence she spoke.

"I'm sure you contribute just as much as Grandy does."

Silence filled the airways as Bernice tried to think of what it was she did besides complain. Before the situation became too awkward, Grandy added, "We would be lost if it wasn't for Bernice's navigation skills and our bodies would have turned into the shapes of hogs if Bernice didn't put a stop to eating SPAM twice a day. "

"Those are important facts when it comes to traveling," empathized Chet.

"And one more thing, Bernice doesn't know how to drive so I never have to worry about ending up in a ditch."

Bernice was too angry to speak so she gave her companion an icy stare.

"We only have a couple minutes left, time for about one phone call, Ladies. Anybody out there have a question for Bernice or Grandy?"

Chet watched as the telephone console lit up like the main strip of Las Vegas. "Go ahead, caller, you're on the air."

"Hi, my name's Harry. I was just wondering if when Bernice gets to California, she would like to come to my house and see my collection of homemade hanging air fresheners? I could make one in the likeness of her and even create a unique scent for it."

Grandy snickered while Bernice's embarrassment could be felt through the airwaves.

"Wow, Harry, you've rendered Bernice speechless," said Chet.

"She's as red as the spanked cheeks of a newborn," Grandy said trying not to laugh too hard.

"Do you have an answer for Harry, Bernice?"

"Yes, I mean no. I mean yes, my answer is no."

"Well, folks, that's about all the time we have with Grandy and Bernice. Ladies, can you give us a little sneak peak of where you're headed today?"

"Now, Chet, that would spoil the surprise. We'll tell you all about it tomorrow," Grandy answered.

"So tomorrow it is. Same time, same station."

"You betcha," answered Grandy. She hung up the phone and looked at her shaken friend. "Well, that was fun. You should've got Harry's number."

"Yeah, just what I need." Bernice answered sarcastically, "another mentally unstable person in my life."

Chapter 30

While Grandy spit and polished (literally) the tarnished treasure she purchased at a garage sale, Bernice slumped glassy-eyed in front of the television. She was too deep in thought to even notice that Bob Barker was on.

"What's wrong, Bernie? You look like a deflated, 'Over the Hill,' party balloon."

A minute river of tears was making a trail through the thick layer of Bernice's makeup. "Nothing, it's just ... it's just that I'm worthless."

"What are you talking about?"

Between shoulder wrenching sobs, the old, silver-haired matron tried to explain her feelings.

"Quit crying, I can't understand a word you're saying. Did you have another stroke or something?"

"No, I'm just worthless. I know you tried to make it sound like I was contributing, but I'm not. You really DO do everything, I don't do an-y-thing," Bernice cried.

Grandy shoved a wad of tissue in Bernie's face and and grabbed her arm.

"You wanna do something? Come here. I'll show ya how to empty the grey and black tanks."

Bernice wiped her nose and eyes and followed Grandy outside where she received a detailed lesson on plumbing.

"First thing – put on these black rubber gloves – if you get sewage on you – the smell of poop won't be so bad on your hands. Then–" Old Red continued on with detailed instructions on how to empty the holding tanks.

"Are you feeling better now?" Grandy asked after their fifteen-minute lesson plan. "Maybe in a couple of days I'll teach you how to drive."

"But I don't have a license."

"Doesn't matter. Here in Wyoming, eight year olds and jackrabbits drive in the middle of this nothingness. Now let's get going or we're not gonna have anything to tell Chet tomorrow."

"Thanks, Grandy, you're a good friend." A grateful smile radiated from Bernice.

"Whatever you say. Now sit down and get your map out. There's got to be *something* to look at out here."

A herd of large, black clouds passed over the Wyoming sky, frightening Bernice with its display of bolts of lightening and loud thunder. The raindrops were powerful but brief, just enough to settle the dust. When Mother Nature was finished with her party, the ladies settled into silence, admiring the snow hats on Medicine Bow Mountains. Bernice dreamed of teaching little Jackie how to make snow angels. Grandy's wild imagination seriously considered the Wyoming

Mountains to be an ideal place to hide fleets of UFO spaceships. After an undetermined amount of time had passed, the quiet was split open by Old Red's sandpaper voice. "Bernie, check that Wyoming map and see how far it is to Saratoga."

The sound of paper folding and unfolding resonated through the RV.

"I think it's about 30 miles."

"Yeah, that's what the sign said a couple miles back."

"If you saw the sign, then way did you have me look it up?"

"Just proving that you're useful. Someday those map skills of yours will come in handy."

Bernice sighed and shook her head. "What's in Saratoga?"

"Hot springs. I thought a dip in a steamy pool might relax you, you're so uptight."

Bernice wasn't sure if she had been insulted, or if Grandy really cared. "Wait a minute. I don't have a bathing suit."

"Who needs a bathing suit?"

"Gran-dy!"

"You can wear shorts and a T-shirt –"Grandy stopped short and began to chuckle. "Did you think I meant skinny dipping?"

The shy senior citizen turned red with embarrassment as she realized her hasty jump to conclusion.

"I, I, I just thought…."

Grandy's laughter increased as she attempted to pull her friend out of an awkward moment. "Of course I meant swimming naked! We were born in the buff, why not proudly display what God gave us?"

Total confusion entered Bernice's mind and she tried to determine what Grandy said. She just knew she would not be seen soaking naked in public.

* * *

The parking lot next to the hot springs was nearly full and it took longer than expected to maneuver the RV into a parking spot. There was a bit of bickering between the two old ladies as Bernice's shouted, "You're too close to the car on your right! Be careful you don't run over those kids! Don't hit the truck to the left!"

"Shut up, Bernie, before your granddaughter receives an inheritance from a grandmother she's never seen!"

Bernice worried as she changed into her watermelon shorts and a Trek-Fest T-shirt. How would the outfit look soaking wet? Should she wear a shower cap to keep her hair dry? Would the hot springs wrinkle her skin beyond repair? She dug around in a closet for a beach towel as she waited patiently for Grandy to squeeze into a black, one-piece swim suit with an aquamarine skirt. Soon the ladies were waddling towards the mineral hot springs pool. They stopped to pick up information and pool rules. Bernice was quick to blurt out one of many concerns.

"The brochure says, 'If you are over 50 or have high blood pressure, avoid soaking for more than ten minutes at a time.' I don't have a watch on. How will I know when it's been ten minutes?"

"When you start to pass out, I'll pinch you so you can get out."

"What if you start to pass out?"

"Then you pinch me."

"What if we both start to pass out at the same time?"

"For crying out loud, Bernie. Did you think about the option of getting out of the pool at the first sign of feeling a little too warm?" Grandy's was highly irritated by this time.

Both gals suppressed giggles as they observed two elderly gentlemen exit the hot springs.

"Well, it definitely isn't the fountain of youth," Grandy remarked as the wrinkled grandpas walked past them.

Bernice gingerly dipped her toe into the pool, pulled it back out and began whining, "It's too hot."

"It's not too hot, just jump in fast."

Minutes later, Bernice was up to her neck in the soothing swells. She let out a giant sigh, "Oh this is heaven."

"Told ya."

The girls spent the next couple of hours, ten minutes at a time, soaking their troubles away. They went into great details about their childhoods and laughed at their memories of the retirement home. The soothing qualities of the hot springs seemed to magically transform them back to their youth.

Evening offered a sunset of rainbow pinks and purples. Grandy put her head underwater one more time before the ladies exited the pool.

Back inside the motor home, the elderly women took showers and put on clean, cotton nightgowns. Supper consisted of peanut butter and jelly sandwiches, a handful of potato chips, and tall glasses of milk.

That night, Bernice and Grandy slept more soundly than they had in years. The next morning, they were up before the sun, ready for one last dip in the pool.

"Grab the cell phone, Grandy. We gotta call Chet in a few minutes."

Once inside the mineral springs, Old Red dialed Chet's number and then put the phone on loud speaker.

"Good morning, Ladies. And what have we been up to?"

"Well right now we're taking a bath," answered Grandy.

Silence filled the airwaves as Chet had a frightening visual flash through his mind.

"Don't worry, Chet, we're not naked or anything like that. We're at the Hobo Hot Pool in Saratoga, Wyoming. You know, the calming effects of a mineral hot springs."

"Yeah, Chet, it's pretty nice," added Bernice.

"Well, your voices seem more relaxed than usual. Tell us more about the hot springs? How hot is the water?"

"Somewhere between 102 and 128 degrees, depending on where you stand in the pool." Bernice's voice had the presence of importance.

"Sounds awesome! Grandy, you still there?"

"Yeah, I'm still here."

Chet could hear sounds similar to that of someone splashing wildly about in the water.

"Grandy?"

"What, Chet?"

"I have a surprise for you."

The splashing sound stopped and Grandy was breathing heavily into the phone.

"What is it?"

"I have somebody on that line who claims to be a big fan of yours."

"Yeah? Who would that be?"

"I'll let him speak for himself."

"Hi Sweetheart."

"Lester?"

Chapter 31

"Hi, Honey! How's it going? Haven't heard from you in awhile." Lester's voice was a thick syrup of insincere greetings.

"What do you want, you old, womanizing freeloader!"

"Now, Grandy, is that any way to talk to your husband?"

"Ex-husband. We haven't lived together for over 20 years!"

"Technically speaking – "

Chet interrupted the banter before he or his program were kicked off the air. "Say, Grandy and Lester, how about you two continue your little reunion off the air."

"No, thanks." A dial tone filled the airwaves as Grandy abruptly hung up the phone.

The two ladies stared at each other – Grandy with an angry expression and Bernice with the look of confusion. Red began to mumble under her breath about Lester, shovels, and the desert.

"Why do you think Lester wanted to talk to you, Grandy? You two haven't been in touch in years."

"He wants money, and since he apparently found out I have a new motor home, he's looking to claim half of it."

"Can he do that?"

"Don't worry, Bernie, if Lester ever catches up with us, it'll take forensic investigators three years to find a body part big enough to figure out who he is. By then, we'll be too old and famous for anyone to care."

Bernice let loose a horrified gasp, "Don't talk like that, Grandy. If something ever did happen to Lester, you would be the main suspect."

"Yeah, but I wouldn't be the *only* suspect. You think Lester hasn't made a few enemies out of all the bimbos he's jilted?"

"Doesn't matter, Grandy, don't let other people hear you talking like that. What about your sons?"

"What about them?"

"Wouldn't they care if something happened to their father?"

Grandy played with her frizzy hair as she pondered the question. "I can handle the boys. I don't want to talk about this anymore. We need to head into town and do some laundry. I'm running out of bloomers."

* * *

"Bernie, look there's a rodeo this weekend," Grandy read from a colorful poster on the laundromat bulletin board.

"But it says it's in Riverside. We can't go all the way back to Riverside."

"Riverside, Wyoming, silly."

"Oh," Bernice sighed. "How far is that?"

"Let's ask that old fart sitting outside, it'll be faster that looking it up on a map."

The two friends escaped outside from the heat of the laundromat only to be confronted by the high, dry temperature of the Wyoming sun. An unpleasant odor met them as they approached a dark brown, wrinkled man sitting in the shade of a tobacco store front.

Bernice grabbed Grandy's arm and spoke to her in a hushed frantic voice, "I'm not talking to that strange man, he smells."

"Bernie, don't be so paranoid. Excuse me, do you know where Riverside is?"

"Yup."

"Well."

"Well what?"

"Well, where is it?"

"You didn't ask me where it was. You asked me if I knew where it was."

"Well, now I'm asking where it is."

The old man paused to spit on the sidewalk. "That way," he pointed down the street.

"Do you know how far?"

"Yup."

"Let me rephrase that. How far is it?"

"Well, as the crow flies, about ten, fifteen miles."

"Thanks."

"Yup."

A refreshed attitude washed over Grandy as she and Bernice went back inside the laundromat and grabbed baskets of clothes.

"Come on, Bernie, we're goin' to the rodeo."

Chapter 32

Grandy's tough and rough persona would not allow Bernice to see her deep concern about Lester and Avis. With all the technical communication devices available, it was only a matter of time before they would catch up with her. "Maybe," Grandy thought to herself, "they'll get tired of chasing me all over the country. Or better yet, I'll stage it so it looks like me and Bernice were abducted by aliens."

Before detailed plans could be laid out, Grandy's thoughts were quickly diverted to another subject when she heard Bernice loudly placing items on the counter.

"What are you doing, Bernie?"

"Trying to find the new bottle of nail polish I bought yesterday. I'm sure I put it in my basket here in the bathroom."

"Was it the color of pink lemonade?"

"Yeah, did you see it?"

Grandy cringed as she remembered that she had "borrowed" Bernice's nail polish to paint Felix's claws. "Yes, I did see it and I used just a teeny bit of it."

"Where's the rest of it?" Bernice's voice was becoming high pitched and irritated.

"It's sitting next to your side of the bed."

"I swear, Red, you are stacking up a heap of I.O.U.'s you will never be able to repay!"

"Look Bernie, I'm really sorry about your nail polish. But it's no big deal. I'll buy you a new bottle. I'll even buy you two. Quit fussing and let's git going towards that rodeo. Those young buckaroos are calling my name."

"I don't want to go to any dusty, dirty, smelly animal abuse event!"

"Aw, come on Bernie. It'll be fun. Besides, we need to stay incognito for a couple of days. Don't wanna give Lester any clues on where we are. We may have to study the map and come up with a different route to L.A."

"We're going to get lost, I just know it."

"No Bernie, we're not gonna get lost. Now put your seatbelt on and let's go. You ever been to a rodeo?"

"Nope."

"It's a lot more fun than you think, you're gonna love it. We'll have to buy us each a cowboy hat, though."

"Oh, joy." Bernice knew she was in for another weekend filled with oddball characters, wicked tasting food, and the possibility of jail. "How much longer before we get to L.A.?"

"We're not punching a time clock. We'll get to L.A. in due time."

Bernice put on her usual pouty face and kept quiet.

Grandy was thrilled that in less than a half an hour they would be in Riverside, Wyoming. Two miles out of that "wink-and-you'll-miss-it" kinda town, the ladies noticed a small, fawn-colored creature in the ditch. It was limping and cowering as vehicles passed by. Grandy slammed on the brakes, giving Bernice a minor whiplash.

"What are you doing?"

"We gotta help that dog."

"Oh no, Grandy. We're not going to stink up the motor home with dog smell. Besides, you don't even know if he wants help. He could be wild or have rabies or something."

Grandy ignored her friend's ravings and jumped out of the motor home and walked quietly towards the dog.

"Here Doggy. Let me help you. Here Doggy, Doggy." Grandy's hand was extended towards the small canine staring at her with large, frightened eyes. Bernice watched in amusement as the injured animal tried to decide whether or not to trust the old lady with hair the color of fire.

After a few moments, Grandy came back into the motor home, rummaged around for a treat for the dog, and then went back out to continue her pursuit. Figuring he was not in any real danger, the dog finally allowed Grandy to scoop him up in her strong, thin arms and bring him into the motor home.

Bernice's silver, suspicious eyes studied the mangy mutt. "Now what?"

"We find a vet in Riverside and get this poor guy fixed up."

"After he's fixed up, you are going to find a home for him?"

"We'll see."

"Grandy, we're *not* going to keep the dog! I'm not traveling the countryside with a pesky pooch!"

"Hang onto your dentures, let's worry about that later. Now keep a look out for a veterinary hospital. There's got to be one around here someplace."

The ladies cruised through Riverside but only saw a grocery store and a gas station. What they did notice was an abundance of fishing and hunting lodges, cabins, campgrounds and motels. They pulled the motor home into the Lazy Acres Campground and went inside.

"Good afternoon, Ladies. Can I help you?" An elderly gentleman dressed in a blue, long-sleeved cowboy shirt, Wrangler jeans, and a gray Stetson cowboy hat, smiled as he spoke to the motor home mamas.

"We need a vet, now!" Grandy's short demeanor and wild-eyed look startled the campground host.

"Ummm, Doc Anderson, lives just six miles north of town, brown house with an old, John Deere tractor parked in the front yard."

"Thanks." Grandy grabbed Bernice's arm and pulled her towards the camper.

"Ouch! You're hurting my arm!"

"We need to get that dog help and we don't have time for you to be flirting."

"Flirting! What are you talking about? All I did was stand next to you while you asked that man a question."

"I saw the way you two looked at each other."

"Grandy, you've been eating too much SPAM. Your brain has turned into a ground up ham sandwich."

* * *

Doc Anderson was a middle-aged, petite woman who, with great tenderness, wrapped the broken hind leg of the dog and gave strict instructions to Grandy on his care.

"Bring him back in a couple of weeks so I can check on his progress."

"I'm not sure we'll be around here in a couple of weeks. Can't I just take him to another vet?"

"Suppose so. Just make sure you do."

Bernice put her hand over her mouth to hide the smile as she watched the interaction between the saucy veterinarian and Grandy. It was good to see someone who could match her friend's coarseness.

Grandy scowled as she counted out money to pay the bill.

As they headed back towards Riverside, Grandy tried to balance the mutt on her lap as she drove.

"Why don't you put that thing down while you drive, you're going' to have an accident."

"His name is Ditch."

"Ditch? What kind of name is Ditch?"

"That's where we found him, in a ditch."

"That's not a very attractive name."

"So, he's not that pretty. Besides, I like the name."

Chapter 33

The flight of butterflies in Bernice's stomach was something she hadn't felt in a long time. Yet, there it was as Grandy pulled back into Lazy Acres Campground.

"Think you can keep from drooling all over that old man while I check us in?"

"Grandy, I never said a word to that man the first time we were here."

"Well, just keep your panties on, we don't have time for any on-the-road love affairs."

There was no use in arguing, so Bernice pursed her coral-painted lips and marched ahead of her disagreeable friend into the campground office.

"Well, well, look whose back! How's the puppy doing?"

" Ditch will be just fine," said Bernice with gooey sweetness.

"Ditch? Interesting name. Glad to hear he's going to be okay. Can I help you with a camp site?"

"Of course, why else would we be here," Grandy said with a touch of saltiness.

Walt, the campground owner, chuckled and shook his head.

* * *

The next morning, Bernice was able to talk Walt into looking after Ditch so that she and Grandy could take the Woodchopper Stagecoach back into town for the parade and opening ceremonies. While there were no Klingons or Vulcans at this parade, the kinship of like minds was similar. Grandy transformed naturally as her childhood was reminiscent of the Old West. Bernice, again, found herself the outcast. The extent of her frontier days consisted of watching an occasional episode of Rawhide on television.

Passing a booth of Western gear, Grandy insisted they exchange their urban clothes for a more countrified look. Bernice's reluctance was halted by Grandy's reminding her of the matching, pink T-shirts on national television. Bernie in turn, reminded her of the Vulcan ears. The standoff was settled by the purchase of yellow T-shirts with horses running across the front and straw cowboy hats. A pair of pink, pint-sized cowboy boots caught Bernice's eye and she purchased them for little Jackie.

"Buck will appreciate these, since he's from Texas."

The parade was replete with stagecoaches pulled by matching pairs of horses, covered wagon floats with smiling and waving 4-H kids, cowboys and cowgirls demonstrating lariat tricks, and antique cars decorated with a queen or princess of something. The spirit of the crowd was contagious and Bernice was actually looking forward to the other activities.

After the parade, the old biddies wandered over to a wooden stage awash with men in sequined shirts and ladies in matching dresses. The dancer's petticoats keeping time with the square dance calls. It was contagious enough to cause both Grandy and Bernice to clap their hands and move their hips. After an hour though, the long day had caught up with them and it was time to head back towards the camper.

For some unknown reason, the comforting smells of sawdust and high thrills of the rodeo reminded Grandy of her three sons. Avis, Grandy was sure, was beating the bushes trying to find her, Howard was probably sharing a beer with Blackie, and Dakota... how she wished she knew where he was. She missed his easy-going manner punctuated with dry sense of humor. As soon as she and Bernie's visit was over with Joyce and her family, Grandy was determined to do three things; visit crop circles, attend the UFO Crash Retrieval Conference in Las Vegas, and find Dakota.

As the two travelers wandered towards their portable home, Bernice saw a young girl in her teen years, racing her horse around a set of three barrels. It brought back a memory of when Joyce begged for a horse when she was that age. Thankfully, it was the one time Jack did not give in to his daughter. The girl also helped Bernie realize how fast children grow up. So, as much fun as the new grandma was having, she wanted to skip all the sightseeing and get to L.A. When the time was right, she would put her foot down and tell Grandy it was time to get serious about going to California.

* * *

The weekend became a blur of bright colors, greasy food, and more hat tipping "howdy, Ma'am's" than the ladies had ever encountered. Sunday night, they packed away souvenirs as they discussed what they would talk about with Chet Monday the next morning.

* * *

"Hello, Ladies. And how was your weekend?"

"Hi, Chet. We had the best time." Bernice spoke first.

"Tell us about it."

Bernice rambled on and on about the rodeo. Grandy watched in amazement at her usually subdued friend carrying on as though she'd drank too much of her homemade acorn coffee.

"Sounds exciting. How about you, Grandy?"

"Well, I entered the cow chip throwing contest. Could've won first place but I let some little kid win."

"Well, that was really nice of you, Grandy." Chet's voice denoted a bit of skepticism.

"Won a fake bronze cow chip for second place, maybe I'll send it to you."

"Thanks, Grandy, I'll mount it on the wall."

Bernice chuckled as she told America about her travel companion's win in the chaw spitting contest.

"Interesting," was all Chet could think to say so changed the subject, "Where was this rodeo?"

"Somewhere in Wyoming."

"How about the name of the town, Grandy?"

"Can't do that, Chet. Since Lester is looking for me, we're on the lam."

"On the lam? There isn't a crime involved in all this, is there?" Concern crept into Chet's voice.

"Not yet."

"Not yet?"

Bernice jumped in to salvage the conversation. "Chet, I just want to say that if my daughter, Joyce is listening, I'm on my way, Honey! Looking forward to seeing you and Jackie and Buck real soon!"

"Okay, Ladies, that's all the time we have for today. Look forward to talking to you tomorrow."

"Bye, Chet."

"Bye, Bernice. Bye, Grandy." ... "Grandy?"

"She left, Chet, I think she's making an antenna out Q-Tips and aluminum foil."

Chapter 34

"Grandy, why don't you see if you have any messages on your cell phone, I bet you've have lots of them. Lord only knows how many are from Joyce. She probably thinks we hate her or that we died or that – "

"Shut up, Bernie. More likely than not, they're all from Avis. He just wants me committed so he can have all my money." She hastily tossed the phone to her whiny friend and said, "Call Joyce, but don't stay on too long. They might be tracking me through my cell phone."

Bernice shook her head as she dialed her daughter's number.

"Hello."

"Hi, Honey, it's Mom."

"Mom, where are you? I've been worried sick. I called Grandy's cell, but you never answered any of my messages."

Bernice scowled at Grandy. "Well that's because Grandy doesn't check her messages. How's the baby doing?"

"Oh, she's doing great, growing like a weed. She's in size 3 months already and she's only a month old."

"I can't wait to see her."

"Where are you and when are you going to be here?"

"Not sure. We're in Wyoming right now. I just went to my first rodeo."

"Really? You? That's unbelievable."

"I know. I can't believe it myself. It was fun."

"Are you feeling okay?"

"Feeling great. Is everything okay there?"

Grandy looked at her watch and pointed.

Bernice turned her back to Grandy.

"Well, looks like we're moving to Texas."

"Texas? Really? When?"

"We close escrow on the business in about five weeks. We've got a couple of people interested in the condo, so it just depends."

"Well, congratulations. I remember you guys talking about that. Are you okay with it?"

"I can't wait to get out of this town. It's no place to raise a family."

"I agree... Well, Grandy's giving me dirty looks, so I have to get off her phone. I'll call you when we get to California. It shouldn't be too much longer, I hope."

"Okay, Mom. Hope you don't mind the mess. I've already started packing, I'm so anxious to get out of here."

"No problem. Just don't leave before we get there."

"Oh, it's going be a while. And you know, you're still welcome to move in with us. We'll have lots of room in Texas."

"I'll keep that in mind. Say hi to Buck and hug Jackie for me. Oh, I almost forgot. We're on the radio every morning, I guess it would be 7 a.m. your time."

"What?"

"Yeah, we're doing a call-in show with a guy named Chet Baxter."

"Oh, I've heard of him. How'd you get hooked up with that?"

Grandy cleared her voice loudly.

"It's a long story. I'll have to tell you later. Gotta run."

"Okay, I'll listen for you. I love you, Mom."

"I love you, too. We'll see you soon."

"Okay, bye."

"Bye, Hon." Bernice tossed the phone back to Red. "You really should listen to the rest of your messages, Grandy. Your family is probably worried about you."

"Fine, give me the phone, if it'll make you feel any better." There was a long uncomfortable silence while Grandy listened to messages. She twisted her lips and closed her eyes as she bobbed her head back and forth. Her voice was a low hiss as she said, "I told ya so. Avis. Avis. Avis." It pitched several notes higher as she shouted, "Take that you back stabbing son!" and hit the button to delete the messages. She stopped short her tirade. "Uh-oh, there's one on here from the retirement home."

"What do they want?"

"Shhhh, I'm trying to listen."

" Hope it's not about that Nick incident."

"Oh, I forgot all about that."

"Hi Grandy, this is Lillian from *Passage of Time*. Sure miss you guys. Wanted to warn you that Avis has been here looking for you. I think Irene gave him some information. I thought I'd better let you know, she may have told him where you were headed. I'm not sure if they have an address or phone number for Bernice's daughter on file, but just wanted to give you a heads up. I remember what you told me about him. Hope you're doin' okay. Be careful. Bye."

"Oh, swell. Does Irene have Joyce's phone number?"

"I'm not sure. Maybe Jack gave it to her when we first moved in. Why?"

"Well, now Avis probably knows right where we're going. Can you call Joyce back and tell her to play dumb if Avis calls her?"

"I can't ask her to lie."

"She doesn't have to lie, just pretend she has amnesia or something. You wanna go to LA, don't you?"

"Yes, of course I do."

"Then call Joyce while I check the map. We're gonna have to lay low for a couple of days, off the main drag, just in case he's on our trail."

Grandy spread the map out on the kitchen table, while Bernice called and gave Joyce the quick message.

"Let's see," Grandy thought out loud as she studied the map. "If we go down here, that should throw him off for a while. We're gonna have to be really careful when we talk to Chet. We don't wanna give out too much information on our whereabouts. "

"Well, that would be lying, too."

"Bernie, it's not lying. We tell him the truth, but we'll just be a day or two ahead of our stories, that's all."

"It's still lying."

"No its not. You don't understand. Avis is a lawyer. He can convince anybody of anything, and I could lose my freedom. And then where would you be? Texas? You really wanna get stuck down there?"

The new grandma took a moment to process Grandy's words before she said, "Maybe."

Chapter 35

A late June morning sun broke through the motor home windows, its light waking three sleepy travelers. Ditch stretched his small body, his toenails digging into Bernice's back.

"Ouch! Get that mutt off the bed, Grandy! He stinks and his claws are scratching me!"

Old Red turned over, pulled the dog closer to her and responded to the complaints in a dry, lazy voice, "Cool your jets, Bernie, he's just showing a little affection."

"Hummph! He still stinks."

It wasn't until it was time for the daily chat with Chet that the ladies spoke to one another again. Grandy set the cell phone on speaker mode.

"Good morning, Ladies. And how was your weekend?"

"Oh, fine," said the travelers in unison.

"What's the latest?"

"Go ahead, Bernie." Grandy whispered in her ear "Stick to the plan."

"Yeah, um, sure... We're ... still in Wyoming. Yeah, that's right. That's where we are."

Bernice wanted to tell about their adventures at the Fossil Valley RV Park in Colorado, but she was afraid Grandy would leave her out in the wilderness to die.

"And, um, we went to the Wyoming Frontier Prison. Right Grandy?"

"Right."

"And, um. Oh, yes. We went there in the daytime and then they told us to come back at night because it would be more interesting."

"So did you go back at night?" asked Chet.

"We sure did, but I think the daytime would have been just fine."

"Well, I disagree. I think the nighttime tour was the best." Grandy was barely able to complete her sentence as a deep cackle spilled onto her words.

"It's not funny, Grandy!" Bernice said with a tightness in her voice.

"What happened in the prison, Gals?"

"Nothing!"

"Aw, come on, Bernice, tell your listeners about your latest adventure."

"I'll tell ya," Grandy butted in. "First they took us down past all the cells. It was pitch black, cold and damp. Then they told us stories about how many prisoners hung themselves right in their cells. To make the whole thing more interesting, out of no where, this figure of a body flew out right in front of us."

"Well, that doesn't sound so awful. What really happened to upset you so, Bernice?"

Grandy continued her story in a half dramatic tone mixed with shakes of giggles. "Could be it had to do with the trip into the gas chamber. We each took turns getting strapped in. You should've heard Bernie when I shut the door on her. She let out the loudest scream. She sounded like Faye Rey. Ya know, in *King Kong*? I read somewhere Faye Rey got hired just because she was a good screamer."

"Go on."

Chet was trying to stifle a laugh while Bernice narrowed her eyes and pursed her lips at her inconsiderate friend. She thought about interrupting the dialogue with her legitimate explanation, but felt at this moment the whole country was more interested in her misery than her pride.

"Anyway, where was I? Oh yeah, I shut the door on Bernice and then couldn't get it opened – "

"I couldn't see anything. I have never been so scared in my life!"

"Oh, the door wasn't stuck. I just said that to get you riled. The tour guide thought it was hilarious too and went along with it. I think he was sorry he did when Bernie came out swinging. She hit him with her purse so hard it knocked his tooth loose."

"The young whippersnapper deserved it. I should have knocked your teeth out as well, Grandy. That stunt was not funny."

Before the bickering turned into a fist fight, Chet asked Bernice to tell the listening audience more about the history of the prison.

"Let's see." she thumbed through the brochure. "It was in operation from 1901 to 1981. They filmed a movie there called *Prison* in 1987. I bought a book called *Petticoat Prisoners*. It's a collection of stories, first-hand accounts of some of the women prisoners who were there in the earlier years."

"Yeah, she wants to see if any of her relatives are in it," Grandy said snidely.

Because she felt she had more class than her psycho friend, Bernice ignored Grandy's last comment and continued to give a narration of fascinating facts about the prison.

"Thanks for that captivating description of Wyoming Frontier Prison. We do have time for one short phone call. Someone on the line says he's related to you, Grandy."

"Oh no, not Avis," Grandy mumbled under her breath.

"Hey, Sis!"

"Is that you, Dog Face?"

"It's me alright. Hi Miss Bernice."

Bernice's spine felt like a cold, steel rod as she recognized the redneck drawl. "Hi, Dale," she said in a pale voice.

"What's up, Dog?" Grandy's voice exuded excitement, but only because it wasn't Avis, or Lester.

"Well, I heard ya on the radio. Been trying for a week to get through."

"Do you wanna talk to Bernie?"

"You bet. How ya doin', Miss Bernice?"

"Okay."

"Looking forward to getting together sometime."

"Uh-huh," answered Bernice, as she punched Grandy in the arm.

"Oh, Grandy, I wanted to let you know your scooters and bicycles arrived. I did like you said, I put 'em in your secret hiding place."

"Thanks."

"Well, I hate to break up this family reunion, but we're just about outta time. We'll talk to you ladies again tomorrow. Happy trails!"

"Thank you, Chet," Bernice said in her most prim voice.

"Bye Miss Bernice," Dog Face sounded like a jackal waiting to steal a lion's dinner.

Chapter 36

"We're almost to Salt Lake City. We can get back out onto one of the main highways from there." Grandy glanced at her frazzled friend when she didn't respond. "Bernie! You okay? You look like a load of wash someone forgot to wring out."

"I want to see my daughter, and granddaughter. I need a manicure and a haircut. And I've run out of my prescription stool softener." The list of complaints was accented in a drawn-out, high-pitched whine. Bernice wiped the tears away from the corner of her eyes.

Old Red didn't know whether to be angry at her friend or feel sorry for her. "Okay Bernie, which highway do you want to take to California, 80 through Nevada or 15 through Utah? It's your choice."

"Which one will get us to L.A. the fastest?"

"I'm not sure, but you need to decide before we leave Salt Lake."

A sliver of a smile spread across Bernice's face. "Does that mean we won't be stopping anymore till we get to California?"

"No. It just means you get to decide which route we're taking to get there."

"Oh." The grey-eyed grandma seemed to melt into a pool of sorrow.

"Let's look for a Wal-Mart so we can get your prescription filled. Tomorrow there probably won't be anything open."

"Oh, yeah, it's the 4th of July. I almost forgot."

"I never forget the 4th of July." Grandy thrust her chest out and stiffened her back.

Bernice was amazed that her friend was so patriotic. "I used to love to visit my sister, Char on the 4th of July and watch the fireworks from her high-rise apartment in San Francisco. Maybe someday we can visit her. It's been about fifteen years since I've see her."

"How come so long?"

"Oh, she was so much younger than me. Then she got married young and left home, and then right after Jack and I got married. I moved to Minnesota We both had our own separate lives. She has Alzheimer's now and I'm sure she doesn't even know who I am."

"Then why do you want to see her?"

"She's still my sister, Grandy. And I guess I'm looking for some kind of closure. What's your favorite thing about the 4th of July?"

"The fact that the whole country throws a party for my birthday."

"Your birthday is tomorrow? How come I didn't know that?"

"For the same reason I don't know yours. We never asked each other."

"How is it that we're such good friends and didn't ask that question?"

"I don't know, Bernie. Maybe because when we get to our age we don't want to be reminded that we should be fitted for caskets instead of mini skirts." A mile of silence occurred before Grandy said, "There's a Wal-Mart. I'm going next door to the liquor store for a box of wine while you get your prescription. I'll meet you at the Wal-Mart check out counters in half an hour."

"But, Grandy, this is Utah."

"So."

"Well, isn't Utah a dry state?"

"The whole state can't be dry. And certainly this very religious population of people knows that Jesus drank wine. Besides, I just want to enjoy a few sips, not drink the whole thing at one time."

"Remember what happened when we flew to California?"

"That was a different situation than this."

"How so?"

"I had two things I really needed to blank out of my mind at the time."

"What else besides the plane ride?"

"You."

* * *

After Grandy purchased a box of white zinfandel wine and a six-pack of beer, she went into Wal Mart and bought a few more items; a box of Whitman's assorted chocolates, a bag of dog food, a turkey baster, and the latest literary rags next to the checkout line. She also purchased a surprise for Bernice.

As the ladies headed back to their motor home, Grandy asked what all her traveling companion had bought.

"Oh, not much, just my prescription, a box of Depends, film for my camera, and a few other things."

"I suppose you bought me a birthday present."

"That's awfully presumptuous of you, Grandy. What makes you think I would get you a birthday present?"

"Because that's the way you are, Bernie, all soft and prim and proper."

"As opposed to being, what? Like you?"

"What's wrong with me?"

"Mainly, that you have the demeanor of a mosquito looking for blood."

"You still didn't answer my question. Did you get me a birthday present?"

"Grandy. First of all, you never *asked* me if I bought you a present and secondly, even if I did, it's not your birthday until tomorrow."

"Fine."

"Fine."

The girls soon pulled into a KOA campground. Suppertime was fast approaching so they decided to wait until morning before venturing out into the city. After hooking up the motor home, they gorged themselves on a meal consisting of spaghetti, garlic bread, and salad. Grandy started on her second glass of wine.

"I thought that wine was for tomorrow night, to celebrate your birthday."

"There's enough for tomorrow. Besides, I still have the beer. Why don't you have another glass?"

"No, thanks. One of us needs a clear head."

"Hmmmph, bet I can't tell the difference in you whether you've had six glasses of wine or none."

Chapter 37

Bernice thought for sure her friend would sleep in because of her late night companionship with the wine, so she was quite surprised to be greeted by singing as she walked past the bathroom door. The song was almost unrecognizable because of Grandy's deep, harsh voice that turned song notes into a collage of mismatched sounds. "Grandy, are you okay?" Bernice rapped softly on the door.

"Of course, I'm okay, why wouldn't I be?"

"No reason." The fairly new grandmother made her way to the kitchen and started making coffee. As she waited for the morning eye-opener to finish brewing, she spotted Grandy's box of chocolates. Resentful because she only got one piece the night before, Bernice quickly stuffed both cheeks with the irresistible decadence. It was difficult to chew two pieces at the same time and soon chocolate drool was oozing out of Bernice's mouth. She thought the singing had stopped, so she tried as quickly as she could to chew and swallow the chocolates before her friend came out. At the same time, she replaced the two empty candy wrappers with pieces of chocolate-covered prunes. The surprise gift Grandy had bought for Bernice.

"What's this?" Bernice had said last night as Grandy handed her a package.

"They're chocolate-covered prunes. They'll work better than them stool softeners."

"But I'd rather try one of your Whitman's. They make the best chocolate-covered cherries."

"I'll give you one cherry, if you try the prunes first. I went to all that trouble of getting them for you."

A fussiness arose inside of Bernice as she also remembered how Grandy had thrown a fit when she wanted to give Ditch a piece of chocolate. "Chocolate is deadly to dogs. Don't ever give him chocolate!" she had warned.

* * *

It was another ten minutes before Grandy exited the bathroom. Her hair was once again another shade of red, and much to the shock of Bernice, Ditch was now the same color.

"What did you do to him?"

"I had a little cream rinse left over. Looks good, doesn't it?"

"No. It looks stupid. Are you trying to make him look like you?"

"You sayin' I look stupid?"

"No, but I'm saying he does."

"Well I think he looks great. Come here, Ditch. Bernie's not being very nice." She coddled the pooch as he licked her face. "I think you are just a cutesy wootsey, widdle puppy dog."

"That's disgusting."

"You're just jealous."

"Yeah, whatever. Happy birthday, by the way. This is for you." Bernice pulled a small, plastic bag and a card from her bathrobe pocket and handed them to Grandy.

"Thanks." The card was whipped out from its envelope and read quickly. "Blah, blah, blah. Mushy, but cute." Contents from the plastic bag were dumped onto the table. Grandy frowned as she held up a coffee mug that read, *"If you don't believe in extra terrestrials, you haven't met my ex-husband."*

"That's almost an insult Bernie, using ex-husband and extra terrestrial in the same sentence. If Lester had been an alien, we'd still be together. Instead, I was married to solid mass of deformed chemicals and cells."

"That explains everything Grandy," Bernice said matter-of-factly, "Do you think any of your boys will call and wish you a happy birthday?"

"I doubt it. Avis will probably have my granddaughter call. Howard might, depending on how much celebrating he did himself. And Dakota ... I wish he'd call, but I suspect he's in a cave or on an ice glacier or something like that. I worry about that boy. I'll check my messages later... Do you want to eat something before we head downtown?"

"I'd better not. Wine and prunes haven't exactly felt like a down pillow to my stomach."

"Well then, Bernie, paint your face and put your dancing shoes on, we're going to town to celebrate my birthday!"

133

Chapter 38

As the ladies and waited by the bus stop, Grandy commented, "It's times like these I wish we had those scooters. We just might have to figure out a way to get a hold of them. Wonder if Dog Face would haul them out to California for us?"

Bernice's stomach did a quick somersault at the mention of Dog Face's name. She quickly changed the subject, "What did you put in your purse? It looks heavy."

"Beer."

"Beer? Couldn't you just buy some in town?"

"No. It's a holiday. The liquor stores are closed."

"How you going to keep it cold?"

"If I drink it right away, I won't have to worry about that, now will I?"

Bernice sighed, adjusted her large, round sunglasses, and smoothed the wrinkles on her red, striped shorts. Gratefulness washed over her as she saw the bus approach their stop.

An abundance of colorful tourists left only two seats available on the bus for Grandy and Bernice – but not next to each other. Bernice sat next to a 9-year-old boy, sticky from a melting, orange Popsicle. She tried not to touch the kid with any part of her body or belongings. Unfortunately, her spreading derriere and thighs soon came in contact with the boy's gummy leg. She winced as she felt cold, gooey Popsicle juice on her skin.

Farther back in the bus, Grandy encouraged Ditch to growl at the elderly man to whom she was torpedoing evil glances. The man had propositioned her to become one of his many wives. He tried to assure her that she would love the rustic beauty of the sprawling compound and his close-knit family. If he hadn't had one of his children sitting on his lap, Grandy would have sideswiped him with her beer-laden purse.

Within a few short minutes, the bus stopped at a large park decorated with red, white, and blue banners, balloons, and food booths. Somewhere in the distance, a band played patriotic tunes. Throngs of spectators created a human casserole of activity. Bernie and Grandy (with Ditch cradled in her arms) searched for a picnic table in the shade, one they hoped they wouldn't have to clean or share. Grandy handed Bernice a can of beer.

"No, thanks. I'm going to clean myself off with a moist towelette. Are you sure it's okay to drink in a public park? Maybe we should get some food first. I smell a barbecue close by."

"Well I'm gonna start celebrating. Birthdays only come once a year."

While Old Red sipped on her beers, Bernice wandered over to a food booth which offered curly fries and pork chops on a stick. She purchased enough vittles to feed a family of four, returned to the picnic table in time to see Grandy smashing her third beer can against her forehead and tossing it into the nearby trash receptacle.

"Boy, I sure was thirsty," Grandy said with much of gaiety in her voice.

A young police officer, his face flushed from the summer sun, approached the table. "Good afternoon, Ladies."

"Nice party," Grandy replied.

"You realize alcoholic beverages are not allowed in public places."

"No, I didn't realize it. Can you make an exception? It's my birthday today and we're just doing a little celebrating," Grandy's speech wavered and her demeanor naturally combative.

"I'm going to have to ask you to dispose of the beer."

Grandy chugged down the beer she had just opened and handed the officer the can. "There, you happy now?"

"Ma'am, I'm sorry, but I'm going to have to take you in."

"What for?"

"Being drunk in public is against the law."

"Well you told me to get rid of it. By the way, what's your name? And I want your badge number."

The officer was losing his patience, while Bernice perspired profusely, more from nerves than the 100+ degree heat.

"Well, now you're under arrest for having alcohol in a public place, and for being drunk in public. You're both going to have to come with me."

"I wasn't drinking," Bernice whined.

"I'm in no mood to argue. Let's go. And you should know better than to have a pooch out here in this heat without any water. That's animal endangerment. And what did you do to his fur?"

"He came that way. We rescued him off the road."

"I saw you giving him beer."

"Just a sip."

"Well, he'll be held up at the pound until you are released."

"What about all this food I just bought? And the fireworks? We came to see the fireworks." Bernice began to cry.

"You can take your food with you. Let's go. You both need to dry out."

"But..."

"But nothing. Get in the car and let's go."

The ladies argued all the way to the police station. After being booked, printed and photographed, the two sat in a cell and bantered back and forth until Grandy fell asleep. Bernice asked for a drink of water several times and tried to sweet talk the officer.

"I swear to you, I haven't had one itsy bitsy sip of alcohol. My crazy ET-loving companion is the one with a drinking problem."

"Yes, Ma'am, whatever you say."

135

Later that evening, Chief of Police Ben Williams made his daily supervisory appearance at the jail. "What do we have?"

"A couple of old women drinking in the park."

"How long they been in here?"

"Oh, about six hours."

Chief Williams studied the paperwork on the women. "You know, these ladies' names sound familiar."

"What? You know them?"

After a long pause, the Chief replied, "Now I remember! They're the two old ladies traveling around the country in a motor home. They're on Chet Baxter's show every morning. You got to let them out, immediately. You want it all over national radio how we lock up poor, old, defenseless women?"

"But they, or at least one of them was drunk in public."

"I don't care. Let them out."

"What about their dog?"

"Where's their dog?"

"At the pound."

"Well, get them their dog and let them be on their way. Give them your most sincere apology. Try to be extra nice. We don't want the mayor to hear about this on the radio."

"Sure thing, Boss."

Bernice overheard the conversation between the officers. "Grandy, wake up, we're getting out."

"What?"

"Yeah, they think we're famous. You know, we're on the radio and all."

The officer who had arrested them gave the ladies and a ride to their motor home, offering regrets for the "little misunderstanding."

"Little misunderstanding my butt," Grandy mumbled as the police car exited the driveway. "I don't much like this town. Let's leave tonight."

"Fine with me, if you're up to it."

"I slept all afternoon. Fix me a SPAM sandwich, Bernie and throw on an extra slice of cheese."

Bernice was irritated that her traveling companion had landed them in such an embarrassing and uncomfortable situation. Then to be ordered to cook and serve her was almost more that she could tolerate. The grey-haired grandma tried to think of a way to sabotage the sandwich. After a few minutes, she grinned to herself as she melted butter in a pan to fry the SPAM then added a couple of finely chopped prunes to the mixture. She handed Grandy the sandwich and tried to act like her normal self.

"What'd you do to this sandwich? Tastes like last week's hot dish," Grandy's face was scrunched up as she took a second bite.

"Just the usual Grandy. Maybe the beer you drank gives it that aftertaste."

"You better hope so Bernie. If I find out you've tried to make my meal healthy by adding some of your vitamins, I'll – "

"Look Grandy! Bernice pointed out the windows and the ladies fell into silence as the first darkness of night entered and fireworks filled up the sky.

Chapter 39

Bernice awoke to a grayness outside. She wasn't sure if it was overcast or early dawn. She glanced at the clock that read 5:33 a.m. The motor home was slowing down and pulling off to the side of the road.

"What are you doing?"

It's time for your first driving lesson. Besides, I'm tired and it's your turn at the wheel."

Panic began to strangle Bernice as she saw the determination in her friend's face. "Not without a license I'm not."

"You old fool! The roads don't get any straighter than this, and there's no traffic."

"What if a cop sees me? I could go to jail again!"

"Just put your sunglasses on, smile, and wave to him. Unless you're speeding or driving on the side of the road, he won't have a reason to pull you over."

"I don't know, Grandy, I'm – "

"Come on, it'll be okay. Just a couple of miles. You gotta get used to it in case of an emergency."

"Emergency. What do you mean?"

"In case sometime I can't drive."

Bernice weighed her options should something happen to Grandy out in the middle of no where and reluctantly crawled into the driver's seat. She surveyed the dashboard and thought it probably resembled that of a space shuttle.

"There's too many buttons. This is confusing."

"Stop your whining and do as I tell you."

"What's this?"

"Don't touch that one. Or that one, either."

The scared senior fumbled with the seat belt and gripped the steering wheel with such force her knuckles immediately turned the color of bread dough. She continued to study every knob and gadget. "What's cruise control? Is that like auto pilot?"

"Sort of. Don't worry about that. Just put your right foot on the brake and pull this handle until it's on the 'D.' That's 'Drive.' You do know which is the brake, don't you?"

"Yeah, I know. I wasn't born yesterday."

"Now take your foot off the brake and put it on the gas pedal, lightly and you need to look out your side mirrors."

"I'm really nervous, Grandy. Are you sure I should be doing this?"

"Oh, Bernice, this thing practically drives itself. Now go!"

The reluctant and uninsured driver lurched forward as she tried to maneuver their small home. After a few jerky starts and stops, she began cruising at about 15 miles an hour in the left-hand lane of the long, straight Utah road.

"At this rate, we might get to L.A. in about six years. Do you think you could go a little faster? We don't want to get a ticket for going too slow."

Just as the silver-haired grandma was about to accelerate, an eighteen wheeler loaded with hogs seemed to come out of nowhere and pulled alongside the motor home. The scruffy driver waved to Grandy and motioned for her to roll down her window. Grandy complied and began shouting answers to the man's questions. Bernice, meanwhile, was beginning to feel faint from fear and the strong pig smells. Her knuckles whitened even more since she could not hear what was being said above the wind. After a few moments, Grandy rolled up the window, attempted to fix her red, knotted hair, and waved to the truck driver. He in turn, smiled, waved back and sped past the ladies.

"What did he want?" Bernice's voice was taunt and tiny.

"He asked if everything was okay since we were going so slow and driving in the left hand lane."

"What'd you tell him?"

"The truth. That you had never driven before."

"Why did you have to tell him that?"

"What was I supposed to tell him? That you were driving slow because you were waiting for him to catch up with you?"

Bernice unfastened her seat belt and crawled out of her seat, with the motor home still in drive.

"What are you doing, trying to get us killed?" Grandy grabbed the steering wheel and gave her roommate a deadly look.

"I'm not driving anymore. I don't know what I'm doing and I don't need people making fun of me."

"Okay, fine. Hurry up and get out of my way before we end up wrapped around a telephone pole."

"I thought you said it drove itself?"

* * *

With no city lights on the horizon, Grandy was concerned about the fuel gauge. For the second time that morning she pulled off to the side of the road.

"Now what's wrong? Are we lost?"

"No, we're not lost. I just wanna know how far to a gas station. I forgot to get gas in Salt Lake because I was so mad, and I don't want to run out."

"Nice goin', Grandy."

"So, divorce me. Take Ditch outside while I study the map."

"Can I just hold him outside the window until he pees?"

Another angry look was forwarded to Bernice before Grandy began studying the map. The dog was taken outside and left to do "his thing" while his caretaker grumbled beneath her breath and watched for whatever in the early stages of the day. Once back inside the motor home, Bernice began a barrage of questions.

"So how far to the gas station?"

"Too far. I don't know if we're gonna make it."

"So what are we supposed to do?"

"We'll see how far we get, and then we'll figure it out."

"We're gonna die out here. You should've asked that truck driver if we could borrow some of his gas."

"First of all, semis use diesel not gas, secondly, we use gas not diesel, and thirdly, how would you have gotten the fuel into our tank?"

The unhappy passenger ignored the comments and question and strained her eyeballs out the windshield, hoping a gas station would appear like an unexpected oasis in the desert.

"Look, the Nevada state line. I bet there's a gas station close by."

Bernice was afraid to relax too soon, but a thought overtook her apprehension. She remarked with regret, "Hey, we forgot to pick up a Utah bumper sticker."

"We'll get one next time we pass through."

Chapter 40

"Hi, Sugar, how was your day?" Buck kissed Joyce on the forehead. She responded by placing their new baby in his arms.

"And how's my little cowgirl?" The tiny bundle of pink looked at her daddy with large, blue eyes. He, in turn, smiled and kissed her on the forehead, too.

"I'm worried about Mom."

"Why, what happened?"

"I got a phone call from Grandy's son, Avis."

Buck moved his gaze from his daughter to his wife. "What'd he say?"

"He told me some things about Grandy, and, well, I don't know. Maybe it isn't the best idea for Mom to be hanging around her."

"What'd he say about her?"

"He said she's crazy as a loon and belongs in an institution."

"I don't know, Honey. She seemed different, but I think she really cares about your mother. When I was alone with Grandy at the hospital, she told me her son was after her money. What'd you tell him?"

"I really didn't know what to tell him. I remembered Mom's last phone call and how she told me to 'play dumb' if he called."

"Did you tell him they were on their way here?"

"I didn't have to, he kept telling me to be sure and call him when they arrived."

Buck sighed, "Well, I'm sure it wasn't hard to figure out your mom would want to come out here and visit her new granddaughter."

"What are we going to do, Buck? I don't want to ruin things for Grandy, but I also don't want Mom dragged into a dangerous situation."

Daddy placed Jackie in the bassinet and sat next to Joyce with his arm around her shoulder. "I think you need to not worry so much, I'm sure they'll be here soon and we can get this whole mess straightened out."

"I wish that weird, old, redhead would answer her cell phone."

"How about calling the radio show?"

"I didn't even think of that. Do you think I could get through?"

"I don't know why not. Surely, Chet would patch through Bernice's daughter."

"I don't want Mom to think there's something wrong with the baby. She might have another stroke."

"Well then, just tell them you want to talk to your mother."

"Okay. I'll give the show a call tomorrow." Exasperation was clearly evident in Joyce's voice.

"It'll be fine, Joyce. I think Grandy is a much better person than you give her credit for."

"You're probably right." Joyce gave Buck a smile and kissed his cheek. "Dinner's ready. You hungry?"

"Always, Darlin'."

Chapter 41

Ditch's brown, button eyes watched for falling breakfast crumbs. His owner and her friend were hastily eating scrambled eggs and toast before their daily phone call to Chet. Grandy set her plate on the floor for the nearly healed dog, then began slurping down a glass of tomato juice.

"Don't let that mutt eat off our plates! That's disgusting! That's –"

"Zip it, Bernie. He has fewer germs than you or I."

"I doubt that. He licks his butt."

"Never mind the dog. I'm dialing Chet's number right now. And remember, don't mention our jail term in Salt Lake City."

Bernice gave her unpleasant traveling companion the first of many angry looks of the day. "You think I'm stupid? I know better than to mention that."

"I don't think you're stupid. Sometimes you just forget."

Grandy had Chet on the phone line before Bernice had a chance for another retort.

"Good morning, Travelers!"

"Good morning, Chet."

"Sounds like you're in perfect unison today."

"Not hardly," Grandy said in her standard, dry voice.

"Chet, we saw the most awesome fireworks while in Salt Lake City, and have you ever had a pork chop on a stick? It practically melts in your mouth." Bernice moved the conversation forward in a hurried tone.

"And, it was Grandy's birthday, too."

"You were born on the 4th of July, Grandy?"

"Sure was, in the backseat of my daddy's 1934 Hudson. Was conceived there, too. Weighed 9 lbs. 3 oz., 'bout ripped my mother in half, so she said. Don't really remember."

"Well, happy birthday, Grandy. Bet you had quite a celebration between the 4th of July and your birthday."

"You can say that again."

Bernice interjected, "It was hotter than blue blazes."

"Yeah, and did you know that in Utah you're not allowed to drink alcoholic beverages in the park?"

"No, I didn't know that, Grandy. I'll try to remember. So how did you stay cool?" Chet cringed as he realized too late his last question could produce some very inappropriate responses from Grandy. He desperately hoped he would not hear the words "naked or fire hydrant."

"We turned the AC on in the motor home and left town."

"What else can you tell us about the holiday and birthday celebrations?"

"Not much to tell, Chet, enjoyed good food, meeting new people, toured the city, you know, the usual." Bernice tried to sound nonchalant.

"Any chance you ladies can tell us where you are?"

"You know, we don't wanna get too specific. Gotta save that element of surprise," said Grandy.

"Well you just stay in your air-conditioned coach and enjoy the scenery while we take a few phone calls. Bessie from Oklahoma, you're on the line with the happy travelers. What's your question?"

"Hi, this is Bessie from Oklahoma. And I'm 78 years old."

"Yes, Bessie, what's your question?"

"Well, um, I'm a little nervous. I've never been on the radio before."

"Hey, Bessie, how you doing?" a polite Bernice said.

"Oh Grandy, I loved to travel before I had my stroke and sure wish I could do what y'all are doing. Me and my friends, we live down here in a retirement home, and you are our hero!"

Bernice frowned at the omission of her presence by the old broad and her friends. She tried to summon a remark that would remind *all* radio listeners that she was just as much a part of this adventure as Grandy was.

"Bessie, this is Bernice. If you put your mind and heart to it, you could do the same thing we're doing."

"Thanks for your advice, Bernice, but what we're really wondering is if we could get a few autographed pictures of you two." Then, sounding very computer savvy, the old woman added, "And could we get the picture on a CD? We want to start a web page for our fan club. And we want to have matching T-shirts made up with your pictures on them."

Bernice and Grandy were both speechless.

"We can arrange that, if it's okay with the ladies."

"Sure," Bernice said with great enthusiasm.

"I don't –"

"It'll be fun, Grandy. Of course, we'll do it!"

"We can post the picture on our web page and if you'll talk to the call screener, you can give her your address where to send the pictures."

"Thanks, Chet."

"No problem, Bessie. Okay, we've got Joyce from California on the line."

Bernice's heart skipped a beat.

"Hi, Mom."

"Joyce, are you okay? How's the baby? I'm so excited. I can't wait to see you."

"Calm down, Mom. How are you, is the question?"

"I'm just great, now that I've heard your voice. I can hardly wait to see you and the baby, and Buck, of course. Is everything alright?"

144

"Everything's fine, here, Mom. I was just worried about you. Could you please call me after the show so we can talk in private?"

"Of course, Honey. Chet, this is my daughter. She lives in Los Angeles and she just blessed me with my first granddaughter and we're going to see her, finally."

Grandy grabbed Bernice by both shoulders, looked her in the eye and shook her violently. "What are you doing?"

"Stop it, Grandy. What are you doing?"

"What's going on?" asked Chet.

"Oh, nothing. I think we better get going, Chet," answered Grandy.

"Yeah, we're about out of time. Nice to meet you Joyce. We'll talk to our travelers tomorrow. Happy trails, Ladies."

"Bye, Chet," Bernice replied.

* * *

"What was that for? You almost shook my eyeballs out of my head."

"Nice goin', Bernice. You just told the whole world where we're going."

"So."

"Does the name Avis ring a bell? How about Lester?"

"Oh, I forgot. I'm sorry. But I was so excited. I can't wait to get to L.A."

"Well if you can't wait, maybe I should just put you on a plane and you can go right now."

"Really, you'd do that for me?"

"Sure. As long as you buy your own plane ticket. "

Bernice thought for a moment, and decided it would be selfish of her to leave Grandy out in the Nevada desert alone. She would never be able to forgive herself if something happened to her. "I'm sorry, Grandy. I'd rather go with you, really I would. You know, I'm just excited."

"Yeah, well, now I'm sure Avis and Lester are going to be hot on our heels. We'll probably have to abandon the motor home and get disguises. You'll have to learn to walk without a cane and I'll – "

"For crying out loud, Grandy, you're getting a little out of control. I'm sure we'll be fine. Why don't you let me use the cell phone and call Joyce. We'll figure out a way to avoid your son and ex."

"You'd better. But before you call Joyce, I want to check my messages, just in case somebody called to wish me a happy birthday."

Chapter 42

"Well?"

"Well what, Bernie?"

"Any messages?"

"There's one from Lillian. Aw. She remembered my birthday. Gonna have to give her a call one of these days and find out the gossip at the home... And Augusta, of course, reading the script her dad wrote." Grandy listened intently to the next message. Her facial expressions covered a wide array of emotions, from joy to total shock.

"What is it?" asked Bernice.

"It's Dakota."

"What's wrong?"

"Nothing's wrong. He loves and misses me and it seems as though I have a grandson."

"Wow! That's a shocker."

"What do you mean? My son has always loved me."

"I don't mean that part. I mean about the grandson. Congratulations, Grandy. You should call and talk to him. Find out more about your grandson. Do you know where Dakota is?"

"No. But we'll meet up soon. We can't stand going too long without seeing each other."

"How will we catch up with him?"

"He'll call me when the time is right."

"What's Dakota's wife like? You've never mentioned her."

"Didn't know he had one."

"Aren't you a little hurt he didn't tell you?"

"I suppose a little. But if she's good to my son then that's what matters the most."

Grandy turned away from her friend and slipped into silence. She began vigorously scrubbing the already clean counters of the motor home. Bernice was at a loss of what to say to the woman who seemed to treat the good and bad things in life in the same manner. She then picked up a brush and started humming softly as she groomed the red-tinted mutt.

"What are you doing?"

"Brushing."

"No, not that. That strange noise you're making."

Bernice gave Grandy the "squinted eyes and tight lipped" look, then said in a terse voice. "Think I could use the phone to call Joyce?" Old Red tossed her the phone and said, "Make it quick."

Joyce picked up on the first ring. "Mom. Is that you? Finally."

"Yeah, Honey, it's me. Sorry, Grandy was checking her messages. I'm so glad you called the show today. It was good to hear your voice. How's my Jackie?"

"She's great. But I'm worried about you, Mom. Are you okay? Where are you?"

"We're in Winnemucca, Nevada. We should be there real soon."

Grandy slapped her travel companion's arm.

"Ow!"

"Mom, what's wrong?"

"Don't tell her where we are!"

"It's okay, Honey, I just bumped my arm."

"Ask her if she's had any calls from my darling son," Grandy interrupted.

"Joyce, Honey, have you gotten any calls from any of Grandy's relatives?"

"As a matter of fact, that's why I'm worried. Avis called."

"What did he say?"

"He asked when you'd be here."

"What did you say?"

"Nothing. I played dumb, like you said."

"Don't worry, it'll all work out. Everything will be just fine."

Grandy started yelling from the background, "Tell Joyce I'm not crazy! Tell her my son just wants my money! Tell her – "

"She knows, Grandy. Now be quiet, I'm trying to talk to my daughter."

"I'm worried about you, Mom. I want you to come live with us, now."

"Oh, Joyce, I can't do that. Grandy needs me. And right now she's a little emotional."

"I am NOT!"

"Mom, what is going on?"

"Nothing. Tell me about Jackie. How big is she now? Is she smiling yet?"

Grandy decided it was time for fresh air and coffee. She picked up and left the motor home, shutting the door loudly behind her.

"What was that?"

"Grandy just went outside. We can talk in peace now."

"Is she treating you okay? I want the truth."

"Oh, don't worry. She's just a little outspoken, that's all. Why, she even offered to send me to L.A. on a plane."

"Great! So when do I pick you up?"

"Oh, no, Dear. I told her I'd rather stay with her. We're really having a good time. We've seen a lot of interesting things. We'll be there before you know it, I promise."

"Are you sure she's not making you say those things?"

"Grandy's a little eccentric, but she really is harmless."

"Well, okay. But I'm still worried."

147

"Don't be. I'll be just fine. Give Jackie a kiss for me."

"Okay. But you be careful."

"I will. Bye now."

"Bye."

* * *

Bernice went outside to check on Grandy who was no where to be seen. "She just needs a little time alone to think things through," Bernie thought to herself as she went back inside to wait. "This is a good time to paint my toenails."

Chapter 43

After Ditch finished his business, Grandy scooped him up and began walking towards Griddle Café, about a half a mile from the motor home. As she meandered along the side road, she began filling her over-sized handbag with tarnished highway treasures. "A paperback book, only missing the back page," the old redhead commented to herself. "Hmm, this ink pen just needs a new refill and looky here, a brand new jar of mustard, wonder if it's expired?" She decided to leave the pink panties and half can of deodorant behind.

The restaurant cooled Grandy's over-heated body, and strong breakfast aromas caused both Grandy and her four-footed friend to lift their noses. They found a booth and nestled in for a large, leisurely, morning meal.

"What can I get ya, Honey?" A waitress longer in years than Grandy, also displaying a head of artificial red hair, instantly appeared next to the booth.

"I'll have biscuits and gravy, hash browns, a side of bacon, and a cup of your strongest coffee."

As the waitress wrote down the order, she noticed Ditch on Grandy's lap. She nodded towards him and said, "You know, pets aren't allowed in here, but because you and your little pal are intimately acquainted with my shade of Miss Clairol, I'll let it slide. And if anyone says anything, just tell them he's your hearing helper dog, okay?"

"Okay."

* * *

Her plate empty, Grandy prepared to pay her bill, when an hurly-burly group entered the restaurant. She stared at a dozen women, clad in purple dresses and red hats of different shapes and sizes. Their shrill cackling made Grandy roll her eyes and shake her head. Unfortunately, one of the Red Hat Society members had a long conversation with Jack Daniels in the early a.m. and did not find Grandy's expression funny.

"What seems to be your problem, *Red*?" The hefty woman said in a snobbish voice as she sized up Grandy. "And what did you do to that dog of yours?"

Grandy ignored the large lady's second comment but responded to her first. "You're my problem. Can you please move your giant, grape-colored behind, I need to get by."

"Careful or I'll -."

"You'll what? Kill me with your looks or your breath. Both are in need of a full aisle of beauty supplies."

The woman was about to retort back but the group she was with ushered her to the back of the restaurant.

* * *

The late morning sun felt glorious on Grandy's face, so she decided to take her time getting back to the motor home. She talked to in a soft, crusty voice as she strolled by tourist shops and city businesses. An infant's pajama set caught her eye in one of the stores. It was black with neon green planets on it and it advertised as a glow-in-the-dark product. Grandy thought she might buy it for her new grandson but had no idea when she would see him. Her visits with Dakota were always few and far between, so she had little hope for frequent reunions with her son. "Maybe when me and Bernie are done roaming the countryside and Dakota gets done doing whatever it is he does, we can spend more time together," Grandy muttered to no one in particular. Gazing at the sleeping outfit one more time, the saddened grandmother decided it was too cute to pass up, so she went inside the store and purchased it for Ditch.

Passing a beauty shop, Grandy suddenly remembered her friend back at the motor home. "I should probably make a hair appointment for Bernie. She might be a bit mad at me for leaving her behind." Once inside, Grandy surveyed the décor of the shop and the beauticians standing at the two stations. There was not any particular theme, just a different primary color on each wall and the floor a mixture of black and white tiles. Indistinguishable music irritated Grandy's ears as she approached the beauticians. They were identical twins except for one having blue hair with yellow streaks and the other yellow hair with blue streaks. One was rolling a perm for a dark-haired, elderly woman.

One of the hairdressers smacked her gum as she smiled at Grandy and said, "Whatcha need, Hon?"

"I don't need nothin'. It's my friend, she needs an appointment. You got anything open this afternoon?"

"I could squeeze her in about 2:30 with Tina. Will that work? What's she need done?"

"Just put her down for the works. Her name is Bernice."

"Phone number?"

"651-555-6872. My name's Grandy and we're just passing through."

"Okay, then. We'll see Bernice at 2:30."

"Thanks."

After Grandy left the beauty shop, the sisters looked at each other and simultaneously realized that a celebrity had just left their salon.

"It's them! They're the ones on the radio! Let's call the girls."

* * *

Grandy returned to the motor home to find Bernice scrubbing the toilet. She donned a pair of bright yellow, rubber gloves and was holding a toilet brush in one hand and a spray bottle of cleanser in the other.

"What are you doing, Old Woman? The toilet's not that dirty."

"Where have you been? I've been worried."

"Yeah, you really look worried. I got you an appointment."

"This is what I do when I'm worried. Helps me not think about how worried I am." Bernice paused. "An appointment for what?"

"You've been complaining about needing your hair fixed, so I set it up."

Bernice peered at her traveling companion over her spectacles. Her look was one of skepticism. "Oh, yeah? Is this a regular hair salon or some fruit stand along the side of the road?"

"This place is as normal as any place you or I would go to."

"You and I don't go to the same place for our hair. I patronize certified, high-class salons, and you go to the places of beauty school dropouts."

"Never mind then!" Grandy was miffed at Bernice's attitude, so she stomped to the front of the motor home, sat down in the driver's seat, and started up the vehicle.

Panic attacked Bernice and she shouted at her friend, "What are you doing?"

"We're leaving. You don't appreciate my kind gesture so to heck with you."

"No! No! I do appreciate it. I'm sorry Grandy. Don't go! Please." The silver-haired grandma was nervous, scared, and hyperventilating.

Grandy turned off the engine and sat quietly.

"What time did you say my appointment was?" Bernice humbly asked, then continued to ramble on. "You can't take seriously everything I say, Grandy. Why I'm sure these cleanser fumes are affecting my mind."

"You don't need cleaning fumes to muddle your mind," Grandy grumbled softly.

"What?"

"2:30."

"2:30. That's perfect. Are you getting your hair done, too?"

"Why? Do I need it?" Grandy's voice was tight.

"No, no, of course not, I was just wondering." Bernice silently prayed for forgiveness for her small, white lie.

"Depends on how your hair turns out. I'll decide after I see how you look."

Chapter 44

A strong grumbling tumbled from Grandy's mouth as she tried to find a place to park near the beauty shop. It seemed like the quiet street earlier that morning had erupted into a parking lot for a major sporting event. Frustrated she could not find a space, Grandy doubled parked the motor home.

"What if those cars need to get out?" Bernice remarked.

"Too bad, they'll have to wait."

Before exiting the coach, the ladies glanced in their respective visor mirrors to pull and pick at their hair. Bernice applied another layer of red lipstick and Grandy struggled to pull up her knee-high nylons.

Entering the salon, the grandmas were bombarded with bright colored balloons, streamers and a loud, out-of-tune rendition of *For She's a Jolly Good Fellow*. Grandy and Bernice gave each other a puzzled look.

"What goin' on?" Grandy asked with suspicion.

"We're part of your fan club," said a chorus of young and old women.

"Fan club?" Bernice clapped her hands, her gray eyes sparkling with appreciation.

The beautician with blue hair and yellow streaks approached her and said, "Hi, Bernice, I'm Tina. I'll be doing your hair today, free of charge."

"Free? I have money, I can pay."

"I know, but it's a gift from your Winnemucca Fan Club." Tina turned to Grandy. "You can have a free hairstyle too. My sister, Toni, rearranged her schedule for you."

Grandy gave a weak thank you to the hair stylists and surrounding crowd.

A white-haired woman wearing a royal blue T-shirt with the words "Go Grandmas!" written in white shoe polish stepped forward. "Could we please get your autographs? You are such an inspiration to all of us. We love you!"

"Yeses and amens" came from all directions of the room. "Can we get a few pictures, too?"

Grandy pulled Bernice aside and whispered in her ear. "How much do you think they'll give us for photographs?"

"We can't do that. They're paying for our hairdos."

"So. How about autographs?"

"No, is that all you think about is money?"

"No, but – "

"But nothing. You be nice to these people, enjoy your hairstyle, shut up and smile." Bernice's voice was low but harsh.

Grandy was taken aback by her companion's display of brashness. She complied with her friend's wishes by straightening her shoulders, finding a broad grin, and walking over to the group of ladies. They all took turns standing between Grandy and Bernice for photos.

The last woman in line was a familiar, old broad in a red hat and purple dress. She was clearly uncomfortable and when she spoke, her voice was subdued.

"Sorry I insulted your dog, I didn't realize who you were!"

"It's okay," Grandy said with softened sarcasm. "Your hat was probably too tight."

After the crowd left, the celebrities sat down to have their hair transformed by the beautician twins. It always felt like heaven for Bernice to have her hair done, so she closed her eyes and let Tina's long fingers do their magic. When the experience was over, she put her glasses back on and looked at herself in the large mirror.

"Well, what do you think? Do you like it?" The young hair dresser was eager for her customer's approval.

Frankenstein's Bride was the first thought to cross Bernice's mind. Gray highlights of various shades crowned her head. Tina's attempt to update the old ladies' hairstyle had produced the look of a muted skunk with too many different colored stripes.

"It's just fine." Bernice tried not to sound too feeble or disappointed. She glanced over at Grandy and was selfishly pleased to see a similar disaster on her head.

"I love it!" screeched Grandy. She played with the strands of hair that ranged in color from a deep burgundy to an almost light pink.

The hair designers smiled at each other as they removed the black capes from the famous duo.

Chapter 45

Bernice tried on a purple, felt cowboy hat with a multicolored scarf around the crown. She pulled it forward on her head then pushed it backwards. Her mouth formed an S-shape as she concentrated on herself.

"That hat looks stupid, Bernie, wear your straw one," Grandy remarked.

"Nothing can look more stupid than my hair. Maybe the colors of the hat will detract from the disaster on my head."

"You know, I can fix your hair if you want. I was thinking about doing something with Ditch's, since we don't match anymore."

"Aw, leave the poor mutt alone. He's been through enough. And I'd rather wear this hat and wait for my hair to grow out than to let you mess with it."

"Fine. But the cowboy hat still looks stupid." Grandy turned away from her fashion-challenged friend and began checking the price tags of Montana silver belt buckles.

"Can you believe the price of these pieces of tin? Let's go Bernie, we need to call Chet."

The two traveling tourists left the Western apparel store and stood outside their motor home as they placed a call to Chet.

"Good morning, Ladies."

"Good morning, Chet. You sound different, like there's an echo or something," Bernice said.

"That's because I'm not in the studio. I'm out on location. Actually, I'm in Reno."

"Reno? We're on our way to Reno."

"You are? How wonderful!"

"Ow!"

"Bernie!"

The sound of scuffling and low voices could be heard before Grandy took over the conversation.

"We're not going to Reno, Chet. Bernie got her towns mixed up. We're headed in a different direction."

"I see." There was a slight pause before Chet continued. "It's a shame you won't be able to join me in Reno. I'm here for the Rock, Paper Scissors Tournament."

"There's actually a tournament for that?" a baffled Grandy replied.

"Yes there is. You oughta see these people. They come from all over the country to compete. This is really big time stuff."

"Sounds dumb."

"Well, if you change your mind, we're at the Hilton. I can get you two in for free."

"Can't show up, Chet, we have people looking for us."

"I understand. By the way, what have you two been up to?"

Bernice wrestled the phone away from Grandy and began speaking in a hurried tone, "We visited a place called Imlay."

"Tell us more."

It was a railroad town from the mid-1860s. Now part of it looks like a tornado hit. It has dirt streets and roof shingles in disarray." She continued, "Then outside of town this Indian guy named Rolling Mountain Thunder built these monuments out of concrete and turned the place into a sort of spiritual community for the Indians. Lots of other people have come in and added their contributions to the shrine. All kinds of sculptures. There's one made from a pile of bones and skulls. That was kind of creepy."

"Do they give tours?"

"You do your own tour. And Rolling Thunder's kids still live there. The whole thing was interesting, but a little strange."

"Thanks Bernice, for sharing that fascinating information about Imlay. Let's take a couple of calls before our time is up. Gladys from Ukiah, California. You're on the air."

"Ladies, you really oughta go to Reno if you're close. Take in a show, do a little gambling. And they even give you free drinks while you gamble. Me and my friends take a bus up there twice a year. It's a hoot."

"Thank you, Bernice. Tom from Reno is on the air."

"I wasn't gonna go the tournament, but if you two are going, I'll be there. I'm rich, good looking and very a-vai-la-ble."

"And humble, too. Next caller?"

"Hi Ladies, this is Velma from Virginia. You've got quite a following in this part of the country. Will you be visiting us anytime soon?"

"Well, if we do, we can't tell you when."

"Grandy, why don't you just let that ex-husband of yours follow you to Virginia. I'm sure my brothers could 'talk' him into leaving you alone."

"Leave your phone number with Chet and I'll give you a call sometime."

"You bet I will! You gals have a great one!"

"That's about all we have time for, Ladies. Look forward to talking to you tomorrow. Hope you change your mind about Reno."

"Thanks, Chet. But Grandy is giving me a dirty look so I doubt we will. Have fun and we'll catch up with you tomorrow."

"Bye."

"Bye."

"What do you think, Grandy? Just a quick stop to say hi to Chet?" Bernice attempted to flash a wide-eyed sorrowful look at her friend.

Old Red responded by shaking her head no but muttered an "Okay."

"Yeah! Maybe we can see a show."

"Don't get too excited. If I suspect we're being followed, you'll have to call Chet and have him stand on a street corner so you can wave to him as we drive by."

Chapter 46

Avis' voice was firm and serious as he spoke to the private investigator, "Stanley, I know my mother *will* go to Reno. You need to be there as soon as possible. She shouldn't be hard to find with that red hair of hers."

"You don't think she changed the color of her hair, do you?"

"Not a chance. Her hair color is her biggest pride. Besides, you'd better have a way to find my mother other than her hair color."

"I do. I was able to find their motor home permit number, perhaps the local police will help track it down."

"I don't care how you find her, just find her."

* * *

Grandy pulled the motor home into the RV Park behind the Hilton Hotel. She hollered to Bernice who was in the bathroom primping, "Grab those rolled nickels I have stashed in the Tupperware container of brown sugar. I wanna go try my hand at the slots."

"Just a minute! I'm trying to do something with this hair."

"There's nothing wrong with your hair, just find me them nickels."

"Grandy, you can never win on those rigged machines. Let's just see a show." Bernice tried pulling her hair in a tight bun which only made the outlandish highlights stand out more. She then rummaged through a drawer of Grandy's stuff until she found a baseball cap. It was a Hawaiian print with the words "I got leid on Waikiki Beach." Her face soured as she tried to decide which looked worse, the baseball cap or her hair.

"What kind of show were you thinking about?"

"Is this the only baseball cap you have? I can't wear this in public."

"What kind of show, Bernie?"

"Oh, you know, Wayne Newton or Glen Campbell or the Beach Boys."

Grandy stared at her friend while loading up her large handbag with rolls of coins, a bag of marshmallows and Ditch. "That hat doesn't match your outfit, maybe you should change."

Bernice was getting pretty good at giving her traveling companion the evil eye so it was with little effort she gifted her one. She also said with authority, "You cannot bring that dog into the casino. It's against the rules. Besides, he'll be more comfortable in the motor home than suffocating in your purse."

"Fine." Grandy took Ditch out of her bag and placed him on the bed. "Let's go. I hear them cherries calling my name."

The ladies entered one of the many casinos outlined in bright, multi-colored lights. Smoke, crowds, and loud voices mixed with the sound of winning bells assaulted their senses. Grandy's elbow punched an elderly lady who had bumped

157

into her in her rush to take over a particular slot machine. "Dumb Broad," she muttered.

Bernice scanned the room for her favorite activity. "I see it!"

"See what, Bernie?"

"Bingo. I'm going to play bingo."

"Fine. These rolls of nickels are getting heavy. I'm going to deposit them in the winning slot machines. Find me in a couple of hours and we'll go eat at the two-for-one steak buffet."

"Okay." Bernice almost skipped away with giddiness, her hand in her purse wrapped around her bingo stamper. She entered the bingo parlor with enormous anticipation. What she saw caused her heart to leave the building – hoards of people feverishly playing a dozen or more computerized cards at a time. It looked like a finger feeding frenzy. The dejected woman turned around and slowly began to make her way through the casino to look for her traveling partner. When she found Grandy, she stood next to her, her wrinkled face stretched out in a long, sad expression.

"What's the matter with you? I thought you were playing bingo."

"They play like a dozen cards at a time and it's all computerized. That doesn't look like fun. Can we get tickets to a show or something?"

"You'll have to wait a minute. This Star Wars machine is giving me the galaxy."

"When are we going to eat?"

"In a while, Bernie. Play a slot machine or roulette or something."

"I don't have any nickels."

"Put in a dollar bill."

"A whole dollar!"

"Go buy us some show tickets then. Here's money for mine." Grandy handed Bernice a five dollar bill.

"There's no show you can get into for five dollars."

A vexed Grandy handed her annoying friend a twenty then turned her attention back to the slot machine. A short time later, a cheered up Bernice returned with tickets in her hand.

"I got tickets to a 'Broadway' cocktail show. We get three cocktails each. It starts in a couple of hours. Can we go get that steak dinner first?"

Grandy perked up when Bernice mentioned cocktails.

"Cocktails? You did good, you old coot. And since you don't hardly drink, that means I get yours, too."

"Not all of them, I get at least one."

"Fine."

"Let's go eat, Grandy. I'm getting bored."

Grandy knew she wasn't going to enjoy the slot machines with her whiny friend hanging over her shoulders, so she cashed in her winnings.

* * *

After dinner, the two women found a small gift shop to buy souvenir T-shirts, large, fuzzy dice and a Reno bumper sticker. Grandy contemplated sending Leisure Suit Larry a postcard with beautiful, scantily clothed showgirls on it. She thought it would be funny if she wrote "Wish you were here - NOT!" But the old dame decided Larry was not worth the 35 cents for the card or the postage to send it.

Finally, the ladies made their way to the theater and stood in line. They looked at each other in bewilderment, wondering why so many of the future audience members seemed to be drunken men in business suits. After being seated, Bernice ordered a white wine cooler and Grandy ordered a shot of whiskey.

"Better drink up. They're pretty weak and yours will be even more watered down if you let the ice melt."

"I don't care. I want mine to last through the whole show," Bernice answered.

The lights dimmed and the music began to play.

"Isn't this exciting?" Bernice exclaimed.

"Yeah, sure." Grandy was more interested in finding a server so she could order her second drink. She waved her scrawny arm and yelled, "Hey, You!" to a young woman carrying a tray full of glasses.

"Sssh, the show's about to start," Bernice hissed.

Grandy ignored her friend and glanced towards the stage.

"Bernie," Grandy said in a low voice, "what kind of show did you get tickets for?"

"Broadway." Bernice was now paying close attention to the activity happening in front of them. "Oh my gosh!" she gasped. A cabaret of bare, tasseled breasts bounced across the stage. Long legs accented bare bottoms and large, white smiles, topped with towering neon colored feather headdresses.

"This isn't Broadway, it's Burlesque."

"Let's get outta here," Bernice turned her head and tried not to look as the dancers came closer to the edge of the stage.

"Didn't you see what kinda show it was before you bought the tickets?" Grandy was clearly aggravated once again with her naive friend.

"Sorry. It said it was a show with bright costumes, singing, and dancing."

"It is, Bernie, except they forgot the costumes."

As the gals made their way to the casino doors, a tall, black man of medium build left the winning slot machine he was playing and began to follow them.

Chapter 47

"Get up, Bernie."

"What?" Bernice moaned as she pried her eyes open. "It's too early."

"No more wine for you at night. Now get up. I wanna go catch the all-you-can-eat breakfast."

Bernice slowly peeled herself out of bed and hobbled into the bathroom.

"Did you see that black man as we were leaving the casino?" Grandy hollered to Bernice from the doorway.

Bernie flushed the toilet. "No wonder you had me walking so fast. Why didn't you tell me last night?"

"Because I knew you'd get all paranoid and keep me up all night worrying about it."

"How do you know he was following us?"

"Because my intuition is always right."

"What'd he look like?" Bernice peered out the bathroom window.

"Fortyish, tall, Black and bald."

"Which way did he go?"

"I don't know. I knew we shouldn't have come here. There's lots of reasons why they call this place 'Sin City.'"

"Yeah, I think we found that out last night. And hey, not a word to Chet about that 'Broadway' show."

"Yeah, whatever. Just get yer face on so we can go eat."

The ladies looked in every direction as they exited the motor home and walked briskly toward the restaurant inside the hotel. After feasting on a smorgasbord of pancakes, bacon and omelets, they discussed their next move.

"Are we going to the tournament?" Bernice whispered.

"Why are you whispering?"

"That guy might be listening."

"Don't worry. I can handle him. Just hang onto your purse. We can pop in to the tournament, but I really wanna get on the road."

* * *

The ladies entered the large hall where men and women of all ages, shapes and sizes were playing "Rock, Paper, Scissors."

"I'm not sure I remember how to play that game," Bernice remarked.

"Here, let me show you." Grandy made a fist. "This is a rock." She held her hand out flat, "this is paper." She then extended her forefinger and middle finger and noted "This is scissors."

"I know all that, I just can't remember how you win."

160

"Well, paper covers the rock, scissors cut the paper, and the rock smashes the scissors. Got it?"

"I think so." Bernice watched as the contestants performed the gestures. "How do they think so fast?"

"Oh, you get the hang of it after a while. My brother and I used to play all the time, especially since we spent so much time in the car."

"Hey, there's Chet." Bernice pointed to the radio booth.

"I almost didn't recognize you." Chet searched for the right compliment. "You've been to the beauty shop, haven't you?"

"Yeah, remember, we told you we got free hairdos? Are we on the air?" asked Grandy.

"You sure are."

"Well, then, howdy to Tina and Toni and the gang in Winnemucca," Grandy hollered into the microphone.

"Are you two enjoying Reno?" asked Chet.

"Oh yes, it's been wonderful. The food has been great and we went to a show last night."

"Really? My wife is traveling with me and I was hoping to take her to a show. What show did you see?"

"She'd love this one." Grandy chuckled.

"I don't think so." Bernice clenched her teeth.

"I can't remember what it's called but it's at that casino across the street."

"So who's winning the tournament?" Bernice changed the subject.

"A little early to tell, but it's been interesting. You two mind sticking around for a few minutes to talk to the crowd? Word has it you've got quite a following right here in Reno. Lots of people have been asking about you two, if you were going to show up."

"Sure," answered Bernice.

"Make it quick, gotta get on the road."

A group of ladies approached the booth. "They're here! They're here!" A larger crowd congregated, firing questions at the two grandmas.

"So what was Bob Barker like?" asked one white-haired woman.

"Dreamy," answered Bernice.

"Oh, he wasn't that hot. He was nice enough. Gave us a ride in his limo," Grandy stated nonchalantly.

"You got to ride in Bob Barker's limo?"

The multitude of fans grew larger and louder with each minute. Grandy noticed out of the corner of her eye a tall, dark figure. She tried not to stare, and as soon as she was sure who it was, she addressed the crowd.

"Look, look! Over there! It's Michael Jordan!"

The crowd reacted on cue, and as they converged upon the man, with a voice of urgency Grandy whispered to Chet, "Gotta go" and quickly scurried down the hall and out the back door to the RV parking area.

"Hey, I wanted to see Michael Jordan."

"It wasn't Michael Jordan, Bernie. It was that guy. Now let's get outta here."

Chapter 48

"I wanted Michael Jordan's autograph, too."

"Bernice, for the tenth time, that was not Michael Jordan."

"Then why'd you say it was? And what about all those other people? They thought he was," Bernice lamented.

"Because they wanted it to be Michael Jordan. People believe what they wanna believe. Now let's get outta here. I didn't think you even knew who Michael Jordan was."

"I know who Michael Jordan is. I've heard his music."

"Oh, really?"

* * *

Comforting, cool air marinated the ladies as they entered their motor home. They had left the vehicle running, but Grandy had insisted it was the only way Ditch would not become a baked casualty.

"Aaaaah, this feels better than skinny dipping in the town fountain." The dippy redhead pulled her shirt up and stood in the pathway of a stream of cold air. Bernice refrained from comment and pushed Grandy out of her way as she headed for the bedroom.

"Hey! You – "

"I'm going to lie down for a bit, I feel a headache coming on." Bernice shuffled a few more steps before her shrill voice caused Grandy to look her direction. "What on earth?"

Standing on the bed and staring at the two old ladies was Ditch. In his mouth was an object that resembled an overgrown, grey mustache.

"What is that in his mouth?" Bernice wrinkled her nose as she squinted her eyes and leaned over for a better look.

"Oh, no!" Grandy moaned. "It's Felix. Ditch ate Felix." She began wagging her finger at the bewildered pooch, "Bad Dog, Bad Dog! Oh, Bernie, why do you think he did that?"

Bernice pretended to sympathize with her distraught friend. "Well, maybe he was upset because you left him alone." She smiled inside at the thought of the ugly, beady-eyed, stuffed ferret no longer staring at her as she tried to sleep at night. She quickly tracked down a garbage bag, handed it to Grandy, and said in a forced sincere voice, "That's too bad, Grandy, let's give Felix a proper burial, and then we can be on our way."

"Bury him where? We're in an asphalt parking lot. I'm not dumping him in a garbage can. We'll find just the right place as we travel. Put that garbage bag away, I'll find something else more respectable to lay him to rest in."

Bernice reluctantly complied with Grandy's wishes. She stood by silently as her nutty roommate placed Felix's remains in a worn Tupperware bowl with a cracked seal. Several layers of masking tape were wrapped around the bowl to ensure the contents would not be attainable by other creatures. Grandy then placed the unit on the floor next to her as she started up the motor home. Since there was nothing else for Bernice to do, she pulled back the bedspread and laid down for a nap. It wasn't long before the sounds of the engine and a barely audible song on the radio put her to sleep.

* * *

Sometime later, Bernice awoke to silence. Grandy and Ditch were no where in sight, so she decided to look outside for them. She frantically looked for the pair of shoes she had been wearing but couldn't find them, so settled on her pink bedroom slippers. Cautiously, she opened the motor home door and peeked outside. Thirty yards away, Grandy was standing in front of a tree full of shoes. Bernice walked over and stood next to her. They stared at the unusual landmark for several, long moments before Bernice spoke.

"What's the purpose of throwing shoes up in a tree? Especially ones that are almost brand new."

"It's a form of communication with our alien friends. I just don't know how to interpret the message. But I threw your shoes up there so you and I would be represented."

"You did what? How come you threw mine up there? Why didn't you throw your own?" An uncomfortable tightness formed in Bernice's stomach as she spotted her recently washed pair of white Nikes.

"Mainly because Ditch didn't pee in mine. And besides, maybe the aliens will make contact faster if they see footwear from non-believers showing support." Grandy laughed and elbowed Bernice. "Support, get it, support, like – "

"I get it, Grandy," Bernice's voice was stiff and barely above a whisper, "you owe me a new pair of shoes."

"Fine. I'll buy you a new pair of tenny runners. How about a pair like mine?" Grandy stuck her foot up in the air and flashed her red, white and blue high-tops. "They'll go nicely with your pink, watermelon shorts."

"I don't want any cheap imitations. I want a pair just like those," Bernice whined as she pointed up in the tree.

"Which ones? There's about a hundred pair."

"Like the perfectly good pair that your mangy dog ruined."

"Well, maybe if you were a little nicer to him. I'm gonna get a shovel from the motor home so we can bury Felix."

"You go ahead. I'm gonna fix something to eat. I need to take a pill."

"A chill pill, I hope."

"What did you say."

"Nothing."

Chapter 49

Back inside the motor home, Bernice fixed herself a sandwich, while she watched her loony companion bury tufts of fur. She couldn't hear what Grandy was saying, but knew it was quite the sermon based on her exaggerated arm gestures. Sermon. Bernice got to thinking about how little she had been to church over the last few months. Perhaps she could use this Felix incident to convince Grandy to stop by a church this weekend for a service.

After about five minutes, Grandy entered the motor home, a look of determined peace on her face. "Felix said he'd let me know when our space buddies arrive."

"Happy to hear that, Grandy. How about if we stop by a real church this weekend. I miss the reverence of the hymns and hearing God's Word."

"Okay."

"Okay?" Bernice was taken aback at the ease of respect her friend displayed for her request. She quietly buckled up as Grandy started the Fleetwood and headed down the highway.

An hour passed before Bernice spoke, "So where are we, anyway?"

"Somewhere near Fallon, Nevada. I think we're gonna stay here the night and then go back down and hit I-80 west."

"Will that take us to Los Angeles?"

"Well, it probably won't, but I bet we can find a road that will."

"How long do you think before we get to L.A.?"

"Don't start that again. You sound like a little kid. *Are we there yet? Are we there yet?*"

"What do you expect? Seems like we've been on the road forever. My granddaughter will be graduating from high school before I get to see her." Bernice was pouty and hoped the church service would help free her from negative thoughts.

Grandy was hoping the same thing, that church would give Bernice a new attitude and perhaps get her to enjoy this cross-country adventure. She also planned to pray for just enough misfortune on Lester, Avis, and whoever else to keep them from their pursuit of her and Bernie. And last, but certainly not least, she figured a shot of that communion wine would give her a little added Holy Ghost intervention.

* * *

Sunday morning greeted the ladies with an overcast sky and strong wind. They ate a breakfast consisting of a mixture of scrambled eggs, SPAM, and cheese. Toast, coffee, and orange juice evened out the meal. Even Bernice didn't complain because she knew in the near future she would be sitting in the spiritual comfort of a church pew. As soon as she had consumed her food, Bernice hurried to the bedroom to change into appropriate church attire. She put on a black, pleated, polyester skirt, white blouse, a necklace and matching black, plastic earrings and pumps. Her pinstriped hair was pulled tight to her scalp in a bun and adorned with a large, black, silk bow. When she exited the bedroom, Grandy stared at her.

"Why you dressed so fancy?"

"For church, of course. What were you planning on wearing? A green spacesuit and your red Converse shoes?"

"No. But I'm sure as heck not dressing up like that. A pair of slacks and top will work just fine."

"You wear whatever you want, Grandy. This is a treat for me to get all dolled up, plus it shows respect to our Lord."

"I sure don't remember the Bible talking about Jesus wearing a suit and tie to the temple. He wore a toga."

"It wasn't a toga," Bernice sighed. "Never mind, Grandy. Let's just find a church."

* * *

A few miles out of Fallon, Nevada, Grandy spotted a small, white church on a hill. About two dozen cars sat in the parking lot, mostly older models awash in dust. Grandy pulled into the lot, nearly side-swiping an elderly lady exiting her car.

"Careful Grandy, or you're going to be asking forgiveness for more than just your wardrobe." Bernice snickered.

The redhead punched her friend in the arm as she slammed on the brakes.

Bernice continued to rub her arm as they entered the church. A middle-aged man was playing a guitar in the front of the sanctuary as the congregation sang along. Most of the small crowd had their arms in the air and their eyes closed as they swayed to the rhythm of the music. Except for one elderly couple in the front pew and a Native American with feathers in his braids, the congregation was dressed in jeans and T-shirts.

Bernice felt very out of place and looked around for a hymn book. All she found was a crudely typed pamphlet with unfamiliar songs. She tried to sing along but wasn't sure which song they were singing.

Suddenly, Grandy's gravelly voice rose to a pitch Bernice had never heard before. She watched in a combination of shock and terror as the redhead waved her arms and shouted, "Hallelujah!"

The song ended and a young man approached the pulpit. His attire was the middle ground between Bernice and the others. He was small in stature with skin that looked like it had never been in the sun, and black hair. In an unexpected, baritone voice, he welcomed members and visitors to the service. Announcements and prayers were taken care of. Just as the pastor was about to read from the Holy Scriptures, the Native American stood up.

166

"I have an important message I must share."

A streak of nervousness appeared on the pastor's face. "May I ask what type of message?"

"Listen and you will understand." And with no opportunity for further discussion, the Native American raised his hands, closed his eyes, and began chanting. Worshipers watched and waited in silence as the monotone voice would occasionally crescendo. Bernice glanced over at Grandy, then elbowed her when she heard her softly chanting along.

"Knock it off, Grandy, you're being disrespectful," Bernice's voice was a whispered hiss.

Grandy ignored her traveling companion, raised her voice an octave, and went and sat cross-legged in the church aisle.

Chapter 50

Staying for the rest of the service was more than Bernice could handle. A hammering pain the size of Grandy's wild imagination was in full residence in her head. It was out of character for Bernie to interrupt or be rude, but today she was making an exception. She ignored inquisitive stares and slid her blooming bottom to the end of the pew.

"I'm going to go lie down for a while," she muttered to her friend who was still enraptured with the holy chantings of a displaced Native American.

Grandy shot off a rather disingenuous "Jesus loves you," and the peace sign as Bernice exited her seat.

* * *

Back at the motor home, Bernice was finally able to fall asleep, once she convinced Ditch that she was not going to share her pillow with him. She wasn't sure how long she had been sleeping when the slamming of the coach door woke her. Her dream of buying little Jackie a cute, pink and white lace dress and taking her to Sunday school was evaporating as quickly as her belief that she would ever see her new granddaughter before she was 12.

"Going to church was the best idea you've had this whole trip." Grandy's exuberance filled the motor home like a poisonous gas.

"You call that a church? That was more like a circus." Her voice was thick from drowsiness and sarcasm.

"Call it what you want, but I am enlightened." Grandy began singing a mixture of hymns and Native American chants.

"Knock it off, Grandy. I want to go to California and see my family."

"After we go to the flea market I just heard about. It's right down the road and it's supposed to be huge."

"We don't need any more junk."

"I owe you a pair of tennis shoes, remember?"

"Second hand?"

"Yours were second hand."

"Not when I bought them."

"Well, they were when I threw them up the tree. Come on. It'll be fun."

Her body and mind too tired to argue, Bernice ran a comb through her bed-head hair and announced, "I need to eat something."

"We'll find a hotdog stand or something."

"Hotdogs are nasty."

"Fine. We'll find you a hamburger then."

* * *

At the flea market, the ladies found a concession stand offering hotdogs, hamburgers, chips, lemonade, and candy bars. Bernice tried to daintily eat a greasy hamburger while Grandy stuffed a hotdog suffocated with ketchup, onions, and relish into her mouth. A glass of watered-down lemonade followed a pill down Bernice's throat. A melting Milky Way candy bar left chocolate traces on Grandy's thin lips and fingertips.

Moments later, the old women were staring at rows upon rows of tables constructed of cheap plywood. Most of them were piled with chipped, ceramic knickknacks, old rusty tools, used plastic toys, and dozens of T-shirts emblazoned with designs ranging from the cute and cuddly to the borderline obscene. In stark contrast were the vibrant colors of imported clothing, vases, and vegetables.

Bernice could taste the heat and feel the dust. She saw nothing of interest and wished Grandy felt the same way. She was about to complain to her traveling buddy that it was time to leave when she noticed her friend's distraction. Grandy was admiring an old, dilapidated wheelchair with an American flag embossed on the seat back.

"No Grandy! We don't have the room for it."

"Yes, we do. There's plenty of room if I throw out all your bottles of nail polish. Besides, I gotta have it."

"Why?"

"I miss my old one."

"You miss your wheelchair?"

"Yeah, it was a part of me for a long time."

"You just miss the sympathy you get while riding around in it."

"So."

"So! That's deception Grandy. That's not moral or ethical or something like that. You were just in church, remember?"

Grandy ignored the comments and handed the booth owner five one-dollar bills. She promptly sat down in the wheelchair and started down the crowded walkway. Those that dared to stare were greeted with sorrowful eyes or a smile conducive to a lottery winner. Now that she had a more expedient way to get around and an easier way to carry items, Grandy bought several odds and ends that she didn't need but thought she couldn't live without. Bernice remained quite a distance behind her, grumbling and shuffling. Completely ignoring anything around her, she concentrated on a speech to put Grandy in her place.

"I found some shoes for you, Bernice!" A scratchy voice hollered from the next aisle over. Grandy was holding up and swinging a pair of olive green boat shoes with a small, red apple print. When Bernice was able to see them close up, she just shook her head and walked away.

"What's wrong with these? They'll go good with your watermelon shorts."

"I'm leaving. I just wanna go to L.A. and see my granddaughter."

"What about the shoes?"

169

"Buy them for yourself, Grandy. Maybe you can find some water tower to hang them from." Bernice instantly regretted the comment. It would probably give her psycho roommate the idea to paint their names on one.

* * *

Monday morning Bernice awoke to a repetitive squeak coming from the motor home living room. Her groggy eyes pried themselves open and she got up to investigate the source of the noise. It was Grandy, rolling her wheelchair back and forth, humming and stroking Ditch who sat on her lap. The poor dog, once again, was subject to his owner's appetite for the most unusual fashion trends. Today, he wore a collar created from Bernice's empty pill bottles. They had been strung on a piece orange yarn and Grandy had put a small dog treat in each pill bottle. Bernice couldn't tell whether the dog tolerated the collar because it had treats in it or if he actually liked wearing it around his neck. She did decide though, that once they were at Joyce's house, she would take Ditch to a park or something and let him go free. Grandy would be plenty mad at her, but at least the poor mutt could live a life free from nail polish and aluminum foil. Bernice decided to groom herself for the day and then prepare for her meeting with Jackie.

"What are you doin', Bernie?"

"Getting ready to meet my granddaughter. We should be there today, right?"

"No."

"What do you mean 'no?' Can't we drive through California in one day?"

"Probably. But I don't want to."

"I do."

"I don't wanna drive that fast. It's hard to read the billboard signs."

"Who cares about the signs. I NEED to see my family!" Bernice's voice was wrought with anguish and frustration.

"Put a lid on it. Go get whatever you were getting ready, ready."

The depleted grandma turned around as if every cell of life was taken out of her body. She slowly began to pack the presents she had bought for her granddaughter.

"Don't forget those stuffed Klingons in the closet I bought for Jackie!"

Bernice took another look at the Klingons and wondered if they might give the child nightmares. Considering the source, she was slightly grateful for the gesture and placed the stuffed toys in the bag with the other gifts.

"Hey, it's time to call Chet." Grandy hollered at Bernice while dialing the number.

* * *

"Hey, Ladies. Nice to hear from you. Where'd you disappear to on Saturday? A lot of your fans were disappointed they didn't get to meet you."

"Yeah, well, we left Ditch in the motor home. Didn't want him to get overheated." Grandy replied as she winked at Bernice.

"I understand. You should have brought him in for us to meet."

"Next time."

"You there, Bernice?"

"I'm here." Bernie's voice was cheery but low.

"What do you have to share with America today?"

"We saw a tree that was full of shoes."

"Really. Where was that?"

"In Fallon, Nevada. Yeah, and Grandy threw my brand new tennis shoes up in the tree."

"Really?" The pitch in Chet's voice didn't rise too much as he was becoming quite accustomed to the redhead's strange behavior. "What is the purpose of throwing the shoes in the tree?"

"I don't know and I don't care. All I know is that I lost a good pair of shoes."

Grandy butted in, "I tried to buy her a new pair but she wouldn't take them."

"Well, Ladies. Do you have any other places of interest to talk about?" It was important to keep the conversation on neutral territory as it otherwise frequently turned into a verbal bloodbath between the two seniors.

"We went to church yesterday."

"And how was that, Grandy?"

"Very enlightening."

"How so?"

"I felt like God and the whole world were talking to me at the same time."

"And what were they all saying to you?" Chet fought desperately to maintain a sincere tone of voice. His stomach, meanwhile, was in agony as it roared in silent laughter.

"Peace."

"Peace?"

"Yeah, peace. Like you know, anti-war, love thy neighbor kind of peace."

"How about you Bernice? Did you have the same experience?"

"Can't say that I did. It wasn't my kind of church."

"I'll say. Can you believe it Chet, Bernie got up right in the middle of the service and left?"

Bernice punched Grandy's arm.

"Ow."

"We have time for maybe one call this morning, Ladies."

"Sounds good, but before I forget, we have to curtail the calls for a couple of days."

"Everything okay?"

"Oh yes. We'll just be in an area where cell phone reception isn't very good."

"Well, you be sure and take notes. We'll want a full report when you get back in range. Now here's the caller waiting to talk to you. Roscoe, you're on the line."

"Is that you, Grandy?"

"Roscoe, from Iowa?"

"It sure is! So are you almost to Area 51?"

"You betcha." Grandy dominated the call while Bernice seethed in anger at her holier-than-thou friend's previous comments about church.

"I'm already here. Maybe we can hook up."

"Yeah... uh... sure. Can we continue this conversation off the air Roscoe? Still on the lam, ya know."

"Gotcha Grandy. I know what you mean. Never know when our buddies are listening in."

Chet interrupted the dialogue before it turned into some government conspiracy soap opera. "Good luck, Grandy and Bernice. You ladies have a safe trip, and be sure and call us as soon as you can. We'll be here waiting."

"Sure thing."

"Bye, Chet."

"Bye Bernice. Bye Grandy."

Once they were off the air, Grandy filled Roscoe in on why they had to be secretive about their whereabouts. He was disappointed there would be no rendezvous with his new friend at Area 51, but understood the situation and promised not to tell a soul of their travel plans.

"One more thing, Grandy."

"What?"

"If you wear undergarments with the wires from old CB radios attached to them, our you-know-who friends can't read our minds. Those old wires somehow scramble their communication systems."

"Why do they have to be sewn to underwear?"

"It's more comfortable than taping it to the skin."

"Gotcha. I'll get right on that, Roscoe. Thanks."

"You're welcome, Grandy."

Chapter 51

Avis wanted to jump through the phone and strangle his overpaid private eye. "How could you lose them?"

"I got a little side tracked, giving out autographs." The smile in Stanley's voice added to Avis' frustration.

"Autograph? Who in the world wanted your autograph?"

"A lot of people. I bear a strong resemblance to Michael Jordan."

"I don't care who you look like, I'm not paying you to give out autographs. You're supposed to be incognito. Remember? Pri-vate investigator? I suppose my mother figured out who you were?"

"Well...."

"She did, didn't she?"

There was a silence at the other end of the line as Stanley tried to figure out how to answer that question. Before he could speak, Avis snapped out, "You're fired. I'll take care of this situation myself." Avis hung up the phone and hollered to his secretary.

"Yes, Mr. Wayland?"

"I need a flight to Los Angeles as soon as possible. And book me a room at the Sheraton."

"How many nights do you need the room for?"

"Book it for five nights."

"Yes, Sir."

* * *

Preoccupied with watching *Wheel of Fortune* on the small TV, Bernice did not hear Grandy slide up next to her.

"Bernice."

The grandma nearly spilled the cup of tea resting on her lap. "Lord Almighty, Grandy! Don't sneak up on me like that. You about gave me a heart attack." She reached over and turned up the TV volume.

"You need to call Joyce and tell her we're not gonna make it to her place."

"What?" Bernice stood up too fast, the tea cup slipped from her hand, and the brown liquid saturated her dandelion yellow blouse and shorts. She shut off the TV and turned to face Grandy.

"What are you talking about? We've come all this way and now we're not going to Joyce's? I knew it. I knew you were just leading me on. Take me to an airport. I've had enough of your stupid games." With a dampened dishrag she tried to remove the stain with the same fury as her words.

"There you go, getting your knickers all twisted up again. I didn't say we couldn't visit Joyce. I said we aren't going to her condo. I've been thinking that it wouldn't take much for Avis to find out where Joyce lives and show up there to

173

wait for us. He'll probably hire a couple of thugs to kidnap me and take me to some desolate nursing home in Mexico."

Bernice pondered her friend's theory and decided part of it could be true, but that the other part was an idea over-cooked in her miswired brain. "So what are we going to do? How am I going to see Joyce and Jackie?"

"Call Joyce and ask if we can meet somewhere safe. Try to use a code just in case somebody has her phone tapped."

"You really think that's possible? I thought that only happened in the movies." Bernice's voice was full of skepticism.

"Get real Bernie. It happens all the time."

The bewildered roommate wondered how Grandy would know this, but decided not to pursue the subject. Grandy tossed the cell phone to Bernice.

"Call Joyce."

* * *

"Hello."

"Joyce, its Mom."

"Mom? Where are you?"

"We're at a campground near Sacramento."

"So you'll be here in a few hours, then."

"Well, I'm not sure. Could be tomorrow. Say, Honey, we need to meet somewhere besides your condo. There's a good chance Grandy's son might show up at your place and that would create a pretty uncomfortable situation."

"We can do that. Besides, we sold the condo and the place is full of boxes." Joyce paused before continuing in a softer voice, "Are you okay, Mom?"

"Yeah, I'm just tired and I miss you and I want to see my new granddaughter so bad I can hardly stand it." There was a suspension in conversation before Bernice asked, "When are you moving?"

"I miss you too, Mom. We're moving in a couple of days. It was a cash deal, so there's a real short escrow. When I see you I'll give all the new address info."

"Sounds good. Now, back to meeting somewhere else."

"Let's meet at the mall. It's just two exits past the one to my place."

"Sounds just fine, Honey." Bernice turned to Grandy and repeated the suggested location. Old Red grumbled an okay as she melted butter in a skillet to fry her sliced SPAM.

"Grandy said that should work. So we should see you probably tomorrow."

"Sounds great, Mom. Call me tomorrow and let me know where you are."

"Okay, bye."

"Bye."

A euphoric aura radiated from Bernice after she hung up the phone. Even the sight of her friend's SPAM and cabbage sandwich could not puncture a hole in her buoyant thoughts. "This time tomorrow I should be holding and hugging my Jackie!"

174

"Depends."

"Depends on what, Grandy?" Bernice's voice was on its way to panic.

"I wanna go to the Winchester Mystery House tomorrow."

"Why?"

"Because its supposed to be a neat old house with lots of stairs, doors, and stuff going nowhere. I think ghosts might be involved too."

"Oh great. You abandoning UFO's for ghosts?"

"No, just adding an interest."

"Well, I don't want to see that old house. I don't care about your interests, Joyce is leaving in a couple of days, and I JUST WANT TO SEE MY FAMILY!" A bowl of peanuts and raisins scattered across the motor home floor as Bernice tried to pound the table and instead hit the bowl by mistake. One of the raisins landed on Grandy's lunch. She ignored the outburst and continued eating the sandwich, raisin included. Knowing she would never be taken seriously by her traveling companion, Bernice grabbed her bright, red sweater and left the trailer.

An hour passed before Grandy decided she'd better find Bernice. If anything ever happened to her, Grandy didn't want to have to explain to Joyce that her mother met with some unfortunate demise.

Old Red slapped an army camouflage hat on her hair, tucked Ditch under her arm, and headed out to find her frustrated friend. As she kicked rocks along the gravel driveway, she noticed RV's and campers quickly filling up the campground. A group of black leather clad men with motorcycles were pitching tents in a small meadow not far from the Fleetwood.

"Nice bikes," Grandy announced in a loud voice.

"Thanks." The chorus of voices was a river of grateful sincerity.

Grandy wandered closer to their camp. "You seen my friend? She's got frizzy, grey hair and is dressed like a banana."

Brief interaction among the bikers revealed no information about Bernice, but they invited Grandy to come back and visit after she had found her. Losing interest in finding her friend and not wanting to miss out on stories of the open road, Grandy abandoned her quest for Bernice and planted her bottom on a nearby lawn chair. For the next couple of hours she drank, sang, and even pranced around the campfire.

* * *

On the other side of the campground a tired and saddened Bernice strolled purposefully towards the motor home. Day after tomorrow, another 48 hours and Bernice would find another way to L.A. if she wasn't holding little Jackie in her arms by then. Traveling across the country did not afford as much pleasure as she had hoped. Yes, there had been small dots of fun and it was better than the retirement home. Yet, she wished they would just get to L.A. Upon arriving at the Fleetwood, Bernice went inside and packed a small suitcase. When she was

175

finished, she tucked it in back of her miniature closet on her side of the bed. She then curled up and read an outdated *People*.

* * *

On the way back to the motor home, Grandy took a detour hoping to discover something of interest or value. Seated on a picnic table beneath a Pine tree, a young girl toyed with the black straps of her red backpack. Her dyed green hair shifted in the sultry breeze. Melting mascara slid down her cheeks like a runaway inkwell.

Ditch barked at the unusual sight and Grandy gently tapped his paw to quiet him. She walked up to the girl and said, "What's wrong?"

The teenager stared at the unmanaged red hair of the senior citizen and replied in an indignant tone, "Nothing."

"Something's wrong, you're crying like the Mississippi River."

"Why do you care?"

"Didn't say I cared, just wondered what was wrong."

"Ran into a little bad luck is all, nothing I can't handle."

An uncomfortable silence passed before Grandy spoke, "My name's Grandy. What's yours?"

"April June."

"That's a different name."

"So is Grandy."

A few more moments of silence passed between the two females as they assessed each other's attire. April June wore a tight, black tank top with sequenced letters spelling out the words, "Kiss My Grits," black, knee-high boots and black, leather shorts. Old Red's outfit was in stark contrast, a cheery blue, seersucker short outfit accented with the words "Vacation Naked" in white letters.

"Where ya from, April?"

"Oregon. My boyfriend and I were on our way to L.A. Then he dumped me for some tramp in San Francisco, so I hitched a ride and ended up here. I decided to go to L.A. without him. Stole his iPod, though." A fraction of a smile escaped from the emotionally twisted girl.

"Good for you. Say, me and my friend, we're on our way to L.A. How about you ride with us?"

"Are you sure it wouldn't be no trouble?"

"Naw. It'll be nice to have somebody to talk to who doesn't complain all the time."

"What's your dog's name?"

"Oh, this is Ditch. Nice to meet you." Grandy motioned a salute with Ditch's front paw. Come on April, we need to get to the camper before my roomy has a fit."

The two walked slowly, sharing life stories and misfortunes with men. Grandy didn't think much of April's eyebrow and lip piercing but was enthralled with the entire solar system tattoo stretched across her back.

"Well, here we are. Home Sweet Home."

"You sure your friend won't mind me being here?"

"Oh, she'll act like she minds. Don't take it personal. She's just moody. I'm taking her to L.A. to see her new granddaughter, and that's all she talks about, when she's not whining about something else."

Bernice was snoring loudly when Grandy returned with her new friend.

Chapter 52

Once inside the motor home, Grandy folded down the dinette set to make a bed for April June, tossed her a pillow and blanket and said, "See ya in the morning." The new roomy dropped her backpack in the middle of the floor and strategically placed her slab of florescent orange gum on top of the counter. Before crawling into bed, she found a banana to eat and took a long drink from the carton of milk in the refrigerator.

* * *

Howard became annoyed as the phone interrupted his Wednesday night poker party.

"Blackie! Answer the phone!"

"I can't! I'm busy making your damn Cheez Whiz snacks!"

"Sorry, Guys. I'll be right back." Howard grabbed the receiver and barked, "Yeah."

"Howie. It's Dakota."

"Don't call me Howie, Brother, I'll have to punch you in the face again. Haven't heard from you in months. What's going on?"

"Thought you might want to know you're an uncle."

"I know I'm an uncle."

"I mean you're an uncle again. I have a son."

"Really? That's cool, I guess. You get married. too?"

"Yeah, did that first."

"How come you never told me?"

"Been kind of busy and all. It was a short private ceremony."

"Does Ma know?"

"She does now. That's kinda why I called. You know what Dad and Avis are trying to do to her?"

"I know they're trying to find her. She's off on some half-crazed trip in a camper she won on T.V."

"Ma does have some different ideas, Howard, but she doesn't deserve to have her family chasing after her, trying to take what little she has."

"Don't lecture me, D. I'm right in the middle of a poker game."

Serious yelling resonated in the background, "Come on, Howard! Tell 'em you'll call 'em back!"

"Be there in a minute! Drink another beer! I'm talking to my brother!"

"Look, Little Brother, I think we should help Ma out. Let's go to L.A. and tell Avis and Dad to lay off. Nothing good could come of them trying to commit her or take what belongs to her. Besides, I want to introduce you to my son Rain."

"Rain? What the hell kind of name is Rain?"

"It's what was happening when his mother and I were in the middle of –"

"I get the picture. I can't believe you'd name your kid that, though."

"How about it? Will you go to L.A. with me?"

Howard thought for a moment before responding. "Let me see if I can get time off work. Call me back in a couple of days."

* * *

Saluting the next morning with a half-cup of optimism, Bernice shuffled towards the coffee maker, still dressed in her pink, floral nightgown. She wasn't aware of the backpack blocking her path because she was rubbing her eyes. When her bare feet tripped over the object, her hands reached out to grab onto the counter to keep from falling. One hand landed They landed on the counter, one hand directly on April's wad of gum.

"Aaaaah!" Bernice's outcry set in motion an early morning chaos. As she tried to figure out what she fell over and what was sticking to her hand, April June peeked out from under the covers, her green hair spread out like fresh grass clippings. Just as the frightened grandma opened her mouth to scream again, Grandy came out of the bedroom.

"What's wrong with you, Bernie?"

"Who is that?" Bernice was possessed with a fear that radiated from her voice.

"That's April June. We're giving her a ride to L.A."

"We're what?"

"You heard me. Quit staring and make some coffee. I'll fry up some eggs and SPAM."

"First I have to get whatever this orange stuff is off my hand."

"It's my gum," April said in a quiet but firm voice. She sat up, yawned, and vigorously rubbed her face with her hands.

"Why didn't you put it in the garbage?" The disgusted senior citizen picked at the sticky mess.

"Because I was planning on chewing it again today, it's the last piece I have."

Bernice wasn't sure how to respond, so she muttered a small "sorry," and handed what was left of the wad back to the strange-looking girl.

* * *

After breakfast, Grandy told April to wash up the dishes while she and her roomy prepared the Fleetwood for departure from the campground. During the act of making the bed, Bernice whispered to Grandy, "What do you know about that girl? How do you know she's trustworthy?"

"She's just as trustworthy as I am."

That statement gave absolutely no comfort to Bernice, so she began checking her drawers for jewelry she may have forgotten to pack earlier.

"What are you doing, Bernie?"

"Nothing."

"You are too!" Unexpectedly, Old Red launched into a lecture on Christian love. "That poor girl in there, her boyfriend dumped her, left her with no money and you're worried about your stupid bobbles. You're the one who's always preaching about being a good Christian. How could I just leave her out there in the dark? You need to start practicing what you preach, Bernie."

"I'm done with the dishes. I'm going outside for a smoke." April yelled from the kitchenette. Bernice quickly shut her drawers and gave Grandy a look of disgust.

After the door slammed shut Bernice asked, "Did you know she smoked?"

"No. Does it matter?"

"Of course it matters! I'm not going to allow that nasty smell in our motor home."

"She went outside, didn't she? What makes you think she would smoke in here?"

"I don't know. Anybody that would dye their hair green –"

"Chill, Bernie. Let's get going. I really want to see the Winchester Mystery House."

Chapter 53

"Can I sit up front?" April June asked Grandy, "I get car sick real easy."

"I don't care, but you'll have to talk Bernie into it."

"Well Bernie, is it okay?"

The wide-bottomed grandma tried a sincere smile as she replied, "Why don't you sit at the dinette table, you could look out the window and that should help with your car sickness."

"Oh." April said in a deflated tone then instinctively started rapping her hair around her finger.

"Let her sit up front, Bernie. Your butt fits just fine on the dinette seat."

"Thanks, Grandy." April plopped herself into the front passenger chair and reached for the radio buttons.

Red slapped the teenager's hand and snapped, "Keep your grubby hands off things."

"Fine." April scowled then began snapping her gum.

"Can you read a map?"

"Yeah, but why don't you use your navigation system?"

"It doesn't work."

"How come? I thought this was a brand new unit?"

"It is, but maps are easier."

April stared at the wild-haired old lady. "You sure are grouchy sometimes."

"And you're rude. Show some respect or I'll drop you off at the next campground."

* * *

Meanwhile, Bernice was as irritated as a bumble bee trapped in occupied underwear. It was bad enough Grandy operated on a level different from most people, but now this teenager from outer space had landed her ship in their parking space.

Nobody said a word when they pulled into the parking lot at the famous Winchester Mystery House near San Jose, California. Towering before them was a stunning, adult gingerbread-looking house surrounded by gorgeous gardens.

"Wow!" April was the first of the three to start a chorus of utterances of disbelief.

Three pairs of eyes stared at the sprawling structure of turrets, fountains, and balconies. The immaculate exterior of the place reminded the ladies of an adult's playhouse.

As Bernice applied another layer of Sunset Red lipstick and teased at her streaky hair, Grandy grabbed her shotgun out of the corner.

"Look at this, April." She pointed to the inscription on the firearm.

"What's it say?"

"Winchester."

"Well, there ya are. Winchester, as in Winchester Mystery House."

"How do you know it's the same Winchester?"

"Because I know these things."

"Cool."

"Quit messing around, Grandy. Let's get this tour over so we can get to L.A." Bernice's voice had a firm tone to it as she exited the motor home. April followed behind. Old Red was a couple of minutes later because she had to open the motor home windows for Ditch. She also tossed a string of battery-operated, miniature lights and a red onion in her large handbag.

* * *

"One senior," Bernice grumbled as she pulled the entrance fee from her purse. "Sure is a lot of money to look at a pretty house."

"I swear you invented negativity, Bernie. This will probably be the greatest landmark we've seen our entire trip and you're already pissing and moaning about it." Grandy paid for her and April's fees, then turned to her new friend and began to read aloud from the brochure. "See, I was right. Sarah Winchester, Winchester Rifle heiress. It took 38 years for her to build this thing."

"How come it took so long?"

"Had to do with her husband and baby dying, ghosts, and other stuff."

"What kind of stuff?"

"You'll hear all about it on the tour."

April shrugged her shoulders and followed along. Inside the front door, most tour members were in awe of the gold and silver chandeliers and Tiffany art glass windows. The creativity even impressed Bernice. "Look at the detail" she said with growing interest.

Their tour guide was a short, round, spike blonde-haired young man who managed to squeeze off a wink to April before launching into his oration.

"Ewe."

"What's wrong, April?"

"That tour guide winked at me."

"So."

"So! Grandy, he's not my type. I'm not ready for another relationship."

"That sounds like something Bernice would say. He only winked at you."

"Yeah, but – "

"Hush. I want to listen to him."

"Welcome to Winchester Mystery House. My name is Zeke and I'll be your tour guide today. Please feel free to ask questions at any time during the tour. Construction of the Winchester House began in 1884 and took 38 years. There are 160 rooms. It was unlike most homes of its era, not just because of its size, but because of its modern heating and sewer systems. It has 47 fireplaces and 52 skylights."

As the sightseers wandered through the house, April kept her distance from Zeke while marveling at the home's oddities.

"This is cool." April said softly to herself as she noticed the stairs that went no where and the window built into the floor.

The tour guide continued. "The reason behind the continuous building is believed that Sarah Winchester was convinced by a medium that the non-stop construction would appease the evil spirits that were killed by her father-in-law's invention of the Winchester rifle. It was also supposed to give her eternal life. In 1906, Sarah was trapped in a bedroom by the big earthquake. It took her servants over an hour to find her because they didn't know where to look since she slept in a different bedroom every night. Sarah decided the earthquake was a message from the spirits that they did not like the way the house construction was going, so she had the front 30 rooms boarded up, never to be used again. And from then on, she slept in the same bedroom every night, where she died in 1922."

Grandy's delicate, blue eyes slyly glanced at her best friend. She was pleased to see Bernie absorbed in the tour guide's words and her hands gently caressing some of the more ornate architecture.

"Now we come to the Séance Room, a secret room where Sarah would go every night at midnight and consult the spirits about her building plans. They would direct her in what to build next. There are three exits to this room, but only one entrance. One door opens into thin air where there is a 10-foot drop to the kitchen. Did you see the stairs that go nowhere?"

"Yes," everyone in the group answered in unison.

"It is believed that was to confuse the spirits. And the 47 fireplaces, it is believed, were to give the spirits a place to escape. The bell tower rang every night to summon the spirits, and again to tell the spirits to leave."

"Has anyone held a séance in here lately?" asked Grandy.

"Not lately, that I know of," answered Zeke. He ushered the tour group out of the room but made sure his arm lightly brushed against April's. In response, the green haired beauty popped her gum. Meanwhile, Grandy whispered in Bernice's ear, "Maybe we can get a hold of Jack."

"I don't think so. Let's get outta here. It gives me the creeps."

When they reached the next point of interest, Bernice and April realized the red-haired grandma was no longer with them.

"Where's Grandy?" asked April.

"She was right here – I bet that old woman is somewhere she shouldn't be, like the Séance Room," answered Bernice.

The two allowed the tour group to wander ahead before they slipped back towards the Séance Room. There inside sat Grandy, cross-legged in the middle of the floor with her hands clasped together.

Bernice recognized the chant and began laughing out loud – not only for the sound coming out of her roommate's mouth, but also for the priceless look of shock on April's face.

"What's she doing?"

"I'm trying to reach Mrs. Winchester. Why don't you join me April?"

"Grandy, I don't think she was an Indian," said Bernice.

"So. This is not for the unbeliever. Go outside and wait for me."

Clearly outnumbered and at a loss of what to do, Bernice slipped out of the room, closed the door, and silently prayed no one would come and arrest them.

After a moment's hesitation April sat down next to Grandy and began chanting too.

A few minutes later, April leaned into her crazy friend and whispered, "What are we saying?"

"Sssssh! You'll upset the spirits."

Still in a hushed voice April continued her questions, "How can I upset them if I don't know what I'm saying?"

Grandy flashed an irritated look to the confused young girl. She then took the onion out of her purse and took a large bite out of it. Handing it to April, Grandy waited for her to also take a bite. After a slight pause, April gave it back.

"No thanks, Grandy, onions give me hives."

* * *

After what seemed like an eternity to Bernice, Grandy and April came out of the room.

"Well?"

"Well what?"

"Did you talk to her?" Bernice said in mock concern.

"We're not telling, because you wouldn't believe us if we told you."

"Fine. Let's catch up with the group before we get arrested or something."

"We won't get in trouble."

"How do you know?"

"'Cause Sarah told me so."

Bernice closed her eyes and shook her head, "Whatever you say, Grandy."

* * *

As the July sun was reaching its hottest peak of the day, Joyce had just laid Jackie down for a nap when the doorbell rang.

"Who's there?" she asked through the closed door, while staring through the peep hole at a middle-aged man dressed in a grey suit and blue necktie. His eyes darted around him as if he was looking for something or someone.

"My name is Avis Wayland, Grandy's son."

"Just a minute." She unlatched the door.

184

"May I come in?"

"Let's talk on the porch, I don't want to wake up the baby."

"I understand."

Avis tried to peer inside before Joyce could shut the door behind her. She offered him a seat on the porch swing. "How can I help you, Mr. Wayland?"

"Please, call me Avis. I know my mother may have told you some things about me that don't project me in the best light. I can assure you she has a tendency to exaggerate and that I am only looking out for her best interest."

"I understand Avis, but how does that concern me?"

"I know she is on her way here and I was wondering if you had heard from her?"

"No, I've only spoken to my mother."

"Do you know when they are supposed to arrive?"

"No, can't say that I do."

"Well, here's my card. That's my cell phone number. I'm staying at the Sheraton and I'd appreciate it very much if you would call me as soon as you hear anything. My only real interest is the safety of my mother, and yours of course."

"Thank you for the sentiment, Avis. I'll let you know if I hear from them again."

"Thank you. Joyce. Good day."

"Good day."

Joyce watched Avis get into a rented Mercedes and drive away. Even if her mother had not said a word, Joyce felt Avis' false demeanor and how it reeked of ulterior motives concerning his mother. She went back inside and locked the door.

185

Chapter 54

April sat in the passenger seat of the motor home, singing along to a rap song on the radio. Grandy's recently dyed hair looked like runaway burgundy cotton candy as she bobbed her head to the beat. Hoping to befriend the other senior, Ditch attempted to lay his head on Bernice's lap. She paid little attention to his move as she watched the desolate countryside rotate past her. The few scattered farms and orchards lacing the landscape had her worried, as she was sure Grandy had changed her mind and was heading for Area 51. When her eyes caught a road sign that read "Los Angeles - 130 miles," she breathed a sigh of relief.

"It's getting late. I think we'll stop here for the night," Grandy yawned, as she pulled into McDonald's in Buttonwillow.

"But it's only two hours to L.A.," Bernice protested.

"Relax, Old Woman, we'll be there tomorrow."

"Can I call Joyce and tell her?"

"Yeah sure, but don't give her a time. You never know what we'll find along the way."

"Maybe some crop circles, huh Grandy?"

"Nah, the best ones are across the pond."

"Across the pond?" April asked the question but both she and Bernice gave the "arched eyebrow" look to the redhead.

"Yeah, you know, over in England and places like that. Now, let's go get a hamburger."

There was no answer when Bernice dialed Joyce's number, so she left her a rambling message about their current location and plans for the next day. She then contemplated whether to join April and Grandy in the restaurant or scrounge up something to eat in the nearly barren motor home cupboards. Their young, green-haired passenger had turned into a human tapeworm, eating their healthy supply of food almost to extinction. Bernice didn't think she could digest one more fast food item, but since all that was left in the refrigerator was four sips of skim milk and half a can of dog food, her stomach decided it could deal with a visit from a few chicken nuggets.

"Wait for me!" Bernice used her cane furiously to try to catch up with her roomies.

"Hurry up you Old Woman, I'm hungry."

Bernice scowled at Grandy and opened her mouth to spit back a response.

"Dinner's on me." April blurted out and held up a handful of coupons. Her action stopped the preface to an argument.

"Where'd you get those?"

"Oh, I've been saving them. Every time my boyfriend and I, or my EX-boyfriend I should say, stopped to eat, we went to McDonald's. We were hooked on their Monopoly game, but all we ever won was an order of fries here, a Big Mac there. I think I have enough here for all of us to eat for free."

"Maybe you should save them for yourself, you might need them later."

"I have lots of them. Besides, I hope I can get a job in L.A. walking dogs for rich people. Then I'll be able to afford to eat at higher class restaurants."

"Honey, I have more money than you and I can't afford to eat at higher class places." Bernice's voice was filled with regret. The taste for processed chicken quickly soured her appetite, so she opted for a salad and diet Coke instead.

"What are you having, Grandy?" April inquired.

"Big Mac and orange juice."

It was no surprise to the elderly women when April inhaled two Quarter Pounders with cheese, fries, a chocolate shake, and apple pie.

"Where do you put all that food? You're no bigger than Ditch's tail," Grandy said with slight amazement.

"High metabolism. Runs in the family."

"Speaking of family, Ditch is probably waiting for his fish sandwich."

* * *

Once they were back inside the trailer, April unwrapped the fish sandwich and held it out for .

"Take it out of the bun and scrape off the tarter sauce," Grandy scolded, "otherwise he'll get the runs."

"Sorry."

The search for a nearby RV park yielded only an undersized site next to the highway that was in need of rescue. Hook-ups were disabled, so Grandy sternly lectured her companions on the conservation of water and toilet use. Ditch was forced to forego his nightly teeth cleaning ritual, while his owner wet a wash cloth to scrub her armpits and face.

An overwhelming anticipation of the next day's meeting with her family caused Bernice to completely ignore any pre-bedtime routine. She lay down early in the evening trying to relax, hoping she would get a great night's sleep.

April changed into an oversized T-shirt that read "The voices in my head tell me what to do," lay down on the pulled out sofa, and fell asleep with her stolen iPod headset still playing on her head.

* * *

Intense, eye piercing sun rays woke all three ladies on a Friday morning. Obviously, Bernice was the first one to get dressed, mask her face with make-up, and begin tidying up the motor home. "I cannot believe I finally get to hold Jackie today. I was beginning to think it would never happen."

Barely audible mumblings greeted her comment and when Grandy and April joined Bernice in the minuscule kitchen, both were replicas of characters out of a "Living Dead" movie.

"Hurry up, Gals! Let's get going, I'll make breakfast while we're driving towards L.A."

"We don't have anything to make breakfast with, Bernie. We haven't been food shopping for days." Grandy's voice was a low crackle.

"I'll find something, now go get dressed so we can – "

Strange music interrupted Bernice's comment. The three females gave each other a puzzled look.

"April, is that your cell phone?" Grandy asked.

"No. I don't have one. I just borrowed yours, didn't think you'd mind."

"That's not my cell phone, that's Chet's phone."

"Who's Chet?"

"Tell you later, April. Answer the phone Grandy," said Bernice.

Grandy pushed the talk button and put the phone to her ear. "What?"

"Is that you, Grandy? This is Chet."

"Yeah. What do ya want?"

"I'm worried about the two of you. I've received several phone calls from your son, husband and numerous fans. They're worried about you, too."

"Lester and Avis ain't worried about me. They're worried about my money. Next time either of those two call, tell them to kiss off."

"Okay Grandy," Chet replied with a smile. "Can we put you on the air now? We have a lot of fans that have been missing you."

There was a hesitation while Grandy tried to decide if it was safe to do so.

"What do you say, Grandy. America is waiting."

Against her better judgment, Grandy agreed. While she put the phone on speaker mode, she turned to Bernice and said, "Put your lipstick on, we're goin' on the air, watch what you say."

"Good morning Bernice and Grandy! It's great to hear from you again! My listening audience and I have missed our daily chats. What have you been up to?" Chet's demeanor over the phone displayed a mountain of sincerity.

"We picked up April at one of the campgrounds." Grandy's voice had tints of pride and a mother's protectiveness.

"Picked up April? What's an April?"

"Not what. Who. April is a poor teenage girl dumped by her yellow-bellied, forked-tongue boyfriend. He should be staked next to a watering hole where crocodiles live."

"Hi Chet!" A faint, high-pitched voice could be heard in the background.

"Hi April. How are you?"

"Fine."

"Where are you from?"

"I was born in Nebraska but my last home was in Oregon."

"What's it like traveling with Grandy and Bernice?"

"Grandy gets kinda crabby sometimes, Bernice is a little too uptight but Ditch is pretty cool."

Chet tried to drive the conversation to a more positive location, "Have you seen any interesting sites?"

"Yeah, but I'm not supposed talk about it because Grandy's looney relatives are after us."

"I see. Well, it's been nice talking to you. Is Bernice there?"

"Yeah."

Silence permeated the airwaves before Chet said, "Can I talk to her?"

"Oh sure."

"Hey Bernice, how's it going?"

"Just fine, Chet."

"Have you seen your new granddaughter yet?"

"Not yet."

"Well, I have a fan waiting to talk to you and Grandy. Go ahead, caller."

"Hello Grandy and Bernice, my name is Sassy Saucer. I'm secretary-treasurer of the local chapter of ISAET, 'I Saw an Extraterrestrial.' I was wondering if you could stop by our monthly meeting tonight about 7 pm. We meet at the Moose Lodge in the town of Dark, only about 17 miles west of L.A."

"Thank you for the invite, Sassy but I'm afraid we won't be any where near LA. Perhaps another time."

The ladies said their goodbyes to Chet and promised to call again soon.

Only a few moments after they hung up the phone, Grandy's cell phone rang. Caller ID showed a Montana number.

"What."

"Hey, Ma."

"Dakota! About time you called me. Where are you? How's the new one?"

"He's awesome, Ma. How are you? Everything okay?"

"You know me, Son, I can handle what comes my way."

"Well, I'd like to meet up with you so you can see your new grandson."

"We're nowheres near Montana. Actually we're almost in L.A."

"That's great. So are we. I can call you when we get there."

"Fine. Then I can tell you where to meet us."

"Are Dad and Avis still harassing you?"

"Yeah. I think your brother hired a private investigator to follow us, but we gave him the slip. I know they've figured out where we're going. We're just planning to meet somewhere other than where they think we'll be."

The conversation continued for another several minutes. There was an inquiry about the baby's mother, but Dakota just said he would tell his mother all about it later.

As soon as Grandy was finished talking to Dakota, she announced, "I'm hungry. Let's go back to McDonald's and get some breakfast."

"McDonald's again?" Bernice complained.

"I've got coupons for Egg McMuffins?" April said with a smile.

Chapter 55

A sheet of 4'x5' weathered plywood with the words "FREE" painted in fluorescent pink letters caused Grandy to slam on the brakes. Had it not been for seatbelts and a table to hang onto there would have been serious injuries to the occupants of the motor home.

"What is wrong with you, Grandy? You nearly killed us all!" A spaghetti thin voice several octaves higher than normal escaped from Bernice.

"Free stuff, Bernie, I think I saw Augusta's next birthday present."

"No more junk, Grandy. We don't have room in here for plastic plants or chipped knickknacks."

The blue-eyed grandma gave her friend "the look," grabbed her monstrous handbag, put Ditch in it, and exited the coach. Not sure what to do, April shrugged her shoulders at the other elderly woman and left the vehicle. Bernice decided that maybe her presence would put pressure on Grandy to hurry up and/or limit the amount of useless items she picked up, so the extremely agitated old lady also headed towards the pile of garage sale rejects.

The house behind the ditch of unwanted items was characteristic of generations of a family not familiar with pride in appearance or appreciation of possessions. Minute patches of paint somewhere in the color of an icky blue shade clung with desperation to the pitted boards of the house and a shed collapsed on one corner. The front yard was a cemetery of faded, plastic toys, rusted out vehicles, and other unidentifiable objects.

"Perhaps," Bernice thought to herself, "this is why Grandy wanted to stop here. Someone or something most people can't relate to lives here."

"What do you think, April?" In her hand Grandy held a pogo stick in an almost fairly decent condition.

"What is it?"

"It's a pogo stick. I might give it to my granddaughter, Augusta, for her next birthday."

"What does it do?"

"I'll show you."

"NO Grandy. Don't get on that thing, you'll hurt yourself." Bernice was working her cane hard to get to her friend before she did serious damage to herself.

"I'll be fine. I used to play on one of these things all the time when I was growing up."

"That was over 50 years ago, and you don't know for sure if that pogo stick even works, it looks bent."

"It's okay, just one or two jumps."

"Grandy – "

"Hush, Old Lady, I'm trying to concentrate."

Grandy gripped the handles of the head busting toy, put one foot on a peg, then tried quickly to put the other foot on the other peg. It looked like she might have known what she was doing if the one peg hadn't fallen off and Grandy's right ankle twisted as it landed on the ground.

"Ow! Son-of-a-!" Old Red threw down the pogo stick and grabbed her ankle.

"Grandy, you alright?" April rushed to her side and tried to look at her injury.

"Of course I'm not alright, you young whippersnapper. I hurt my ankle."

"I told you not to get on that thing," Bernice tried to sound concerned but a streak of I-told-you-so seeped through.

"Just hand me those crutches next to that lawnmower."

Bernice dutifully gave her crazy friend the wooden crutches held together by duct tape. She and April then helped Grandy to the motor home.

"April, bring that pogo stick along. Maybe Dogface can glue the peg back on. And don't forget my purse with Ditch in it."

Inside the camper, Grandy sat down and elevated her leg. The hurt ankle was swelling up like a white water balloon. Bernice made up an ice pack to put on it and April handed her friend a can of Mountain Dew. Grandy took a sip and began to cough.

"What is this?"

"It's Mountain Dew, you know, soda pop." April's voice hinted of anger and hurt.

"It tastes like cow pee."

"How would you know what cow pee tastes like? You ever drink it?"

"Of course not you young fool. But I've smelled it and this smells like cow pee."

"It does not. Just drink it."

"Here, you drink it. This stuff will chew holes in my stomach lining."

April shared a look with Bernice that said "I'm beginning to see what you mean."

"Grandy, how bad is your ankle? Are you going to be able to drive?" Panic was becoming an eruption in Bernice's voice.

"I can drive," April announced.

The senior girls looked over at the young gal snapping her gum and twirling her green hair. Doubt was the only emotion displayed on their faces.

"Do you have a driver's license?"

"Of course I have a driver's license." April pulled it out and tossed it to Bernice since she was the one who had asked. The old woman lifted up her glasses and squinted at the photo then glanced up at April.

"Your hair is purple in the photo."

"So, that has nothing to do with driving a car."

"But this is a big motor home, April, maybe – "

192

"Do you wanna drive, Bernie?"

"Oh, no."

"Then let April drive. I'm sure she can do it better than you. Besides, I'm getting tired of driving. I need to sit back, relax, and watch the scenery."

"But we're almost to L.A.. Will she be able to get around on those freeways? How about all that traffic? And what about driving this large rig?"

"Calm down, Bernie, she'll be fine. Here, have some Mountain Dew."

Chapter 56

A nightmare woke Avis at 4 a.m. In the dream he was riding in a motor home with a woman, who had a wild look in her eyes and her hair was fanned out like a red broomstick. She was driving on only two wheels while she rambled on about being late to a meeting with the mother ship.

There was no going back to sleep, so Avis took a shower, dressed, then sat down to answer e-mails on his laptop. Halfway through the third reply, he stopped and ran his hands through his quickly thinning hair. He then rubbed his tired, green eyes till he saw spots.

"Oh Ma, how come you insist on creating all this chaos?" he mumbled to himself.

At 7 a.m. Avis turned the hotel radio knob until he found The Chet Baxter Show. If luck was on his side today, he would hear his mother call in. If he was really lucky, she or her friend would drop a hint on where they were headed next. Although he knew for sure they were going to L.A., he would prefer to catch up with the ladies before they reached the home of Bernice's daughter.

Energy found its way into Avis as he heard his mother's voice. Turning up the volume, he listened intently to a caller extending an invitation to his mother and roommate to attend some kind of meeting in a town named Dark.

"Dark. Where the hell is Dark?" Avis went to mapquest.com on his laptop to find directions. Grandy had said they probably wouldn't be going there, but somehow Avis believed she would not be able to resist meeting up with others who shared her bizarre interests. It would be worth the trip to Dark to see if she showed up.

Just as Grandy's eldest son was leaving his hotel room to get some breakfast, his cell phone rang.

"Avis Wayland."

"Avis, where are you?"

"Dad?"

"Have you heard anything from your mother?"

"No, but I'm going to check out a place tonight where she might show up."

"Really? Where?"

"What's it to you?"

"I'm her husband and I'm going with you."

"Quit saying you're her husband. You know darn well you haven't lived as husband and wife for years. Just because she won a few prizes on a game show doesn't make you a couple."

"Quit lecturing me, Son. I'm in west L.A. at the Happy Campground. So I might as well be your backup."

"I don't think – "

194

"No more arguing Avis. Just pick me up when you're done farting around with whatever you're doing."

A loud sigh escaped from Avis as he realized leaving his father out of his plans would only backfire on him later on down the road. Reluctantly he asked, "What camp site number are you in?"

"Can't remember the number, just look for my '68 pickup."

"Okay Dad, I'll see you later this afternoon."

Avis had no sooner hung up the phone, when it rang again.

"Avis Wayland."

"Avis, it's me, Howard. What's up with Mom?"

"I think I've found her. Dad and I will be picking her up tonight."

"So you and Dad got it handled? That's good. I was calling to let you know I'm not going to make it back there to help, Blackie got a new piercing the other day and it's become infected. I should stick around and make sure she'll be okay."

"Thanks for sharing that, Howard," Avis said dryly, "You always were just like a blister, showing up after the work's all done."

"You're all heart, Brother."

"Say, I have another call coming in. It's an important one. I'll call you when I get back to the Cities."

"Yeah, whatever. I'll talk to you later."

Avis cut over to his other call. It wasn't as important as he let Howard believe, he just didn't want to spend any more time on the phone with relatives. He was especially not looking forward to having a possible meeting between his mother and father.

* * *

A highway patrolman behind the Fleetwood followed closely with his lights flashing.

"What does he want?" April's voice was shaky with fear.

"Pull over and you'll find out." Grandy, sitting in the passenger seat, looked over at April suspiciously. "You don't have any warrants out against you, do you?"

"NO! And I'm not speeding either." It was April's turn to throw an unpleasant look towards Old Red.

"Well, pull over then."

April turned the coach sharply to the right, knocking her passengers back and forth violently.

"What are you doin?" Grandy bellowed, as horns honked and tires squealed behind them.

"You told me to pull over."

Once the motor home was safely stopped the highway patrolman eased in behind them.

"Oh my gosh!" Bernice began to hyperventilate. "Now we're in trouble!"

"Hush up Bernie, you'll draw unnecessary attention to us."

Grandy turned around and noticed Bernice was clenching the small kitchen table with her left hand and crossing herself with her right hand.

"You're not Catholic, Bernie."

"It can't hurt."

The officer walked up to the driver's side window and spoke to April, "Good morning, is everything okay?"

"Yeah sure," April flashed him an angelic smile.

"You were driving rather erratic the last four miles."

"Sorry, I'm not used to driving this big a vehicle." April pointed to Grandy as she continued, "This is Grandy's motor home but she can't drive right now because she hurt her ankle while jumping on a pogo stick."

The handsome young officer peered over at the old woman with hair the color of sun-starved oranges. "Can I see your license, insurance, and registration please?"

"Sure."

As Grandy scrambled for the proof of insurance and registration, April hollered to Bernice to bring her backpack up to the front. Once the patrolman had the documents, he went back to his car to check for verification.

"Isn't he hot, Grandy?" April said with way too much enthusiasm.

"Not really. I thought you were done with guys for awhile?"

"I can handle a date or two with him."

"You shouldn't flirt like that, it'll probably get us all in trouble."

"Relax Grandy. I haven't been in trouble with the law since last summer."

* * *

Fortunately for the unstable three travelers, the kind officer let them off with a warning to drive more safely.

"That was close," said Bernice with an exaggerated sigh of relief.

"Here." Grandy tossed her cell phone to her nervous friend. Call Joyce and get some directions to the mall. We're almost there."

It was all Bernice could do to dial her daughter's number. Excitement boiled in her like a pot of Midwestern potatoes.

"Hello."

"Hey, Hon, it's Mom. We're finally here in L.A.! We need directions to the mall. What exit do we take? And how far is it from where we are? What's the name of the mall?"

"Where are you?"

"Coming down some really steep highway that twists and turns."

"Are you on the Grapevine?"

Bernice glanced up at Grandy and gave her a look of "help me please."

"Hang on a minute, Joyce."

Grandy held out her hand and took the phone from her nervous friend. As Joyce and Grandy talked about directions, the new grandma sat back down. Ditch laid his head on Bernice's lap, hoping just once her hand would scratch his head. It did not, so he jumped down, went to the bedroom, and curled up on Bernice's pillow. When the best route to the mall had been figured out, Grandy hung up the phone.

"Why did you hang up? I wanted to talk to her some more."

"You're gonna see her in a few minutes. You'll survive until then."

"There's Magic Mountain. You want me to stop?" April sounded like a small child begging for a treat.

"Let's just concentrate on where we're going. My ankle is in pain, and I really want to get to the mall so Bernice will quit her whining."

"I don't whine, Grandy, I merely express my desire to see my family. Unlike you, who have relatives trying who hunt you down like some animal."

"That's only because they're jealous of me."

"I doubt that. It's because they think you're looney as a cartoon."

"Hmmph! I wouldn't talk if I were you, Bernie. Traveling with you has been like living in somebody else's dirty underwear drawer."

"Why, I'll have you know – "

The badgering would have continued between the old ladies had April not interrupted and demanded they both help watch for road signs to where they were going. "I swear, you two sound more like sisters every day. Be grateful you have each other."

Chapter 57

"Who is this?" Grandy's voice sounded more brusque than usual on the cell phone.

There was a petite pause followed by a short chuckle, "Hi, Mom. It's Dakota."

"Hi Son. What's so funny?"

"Nothing, you just sound like you're ready to hurt somebody."

"Maybe I am."

"Anybody I know?" You could hear the middle son smile as he spoke.

"Its better you don't know."

"Where are you now, Mom?"

"L.A. We're getting ready to meet up with Bernice's family. How's my grandson?"

"He's great. I can hardly wait for you to see him."

"Me too. Where are you?"

"I'm almost to L.A. Where are you meeting Bernie's family?"

"The parking lot of The Grove at the Farmer's Market. It's a swanky mall next to an outdoor market. Look for the clock tower. We'll be in the back parking lot."

"How do I get there?"

Grandy did her best to give Dakota directions to the Farmer's Market and they hung up, both in great anticipation of seeing each other.

"This must be where all the rich people shop. Look at the fancy cars," April exclaimed. She was rubber necking as she drove through the Farmer's Market parking lot.

"Pay attention to what you're doing," Grandy snapped, "I don't want you smashing my motor home."

"Don't' worry. I got us through the L.A. traffic, didn't I?"

"You still need to watch what you're doing."

"Maybe we'll see some movie stars."

"April, Dear, movie stars and rich people are no better than anybody else," Bernie chimed in.

"Yeah, you shoulda seen Bernie when she saw Bob Barker."

"Who's Bob Barker?"

"You've never heard of Bob Barker?" Bernice's voice was incredulous. "How about *the Price is Right* show?"

April thought a moment, "I think I might have seen it once. Is Bob Barker part of the show?"

"Of course he's part of the show, he *is* the show. Oh April, you need to watch more T.V."

"No she doesn't, Bernie, there's more to life than game shows hosts."

"Well, he's just the most handsome, dreamiest game show host who ever lived, that's all."

"Did you meet him in person, Bernice?"

"Did I meet him?" Her voice rose an octave or two as the grandma in her watermelon shorts remembered fondly her rendezvous with Bob. "Why Honey, I got to ride in his limousine and give him a kiss on the cheek."

"Did you meet him too, Grandy?"

"Yes."

"Was he as dreamy as Bernice said?"

"No."

"You didn't like him?"

"Didn't say that, just said he wasn't dreamy."

Bernice couldn't stand the way the conversation was going so she butted in, "Didn't Grandy tell you how she got this motor home?"

"No."

"My stars, April, we'll have to tell you – "

The ringing of Grandy's cell phone ended the rambling dialogue.

"Who is this?"

"Hello, Grandy. It's Joyce."

"Hey Joyce. Suppose you want to talk to your mother?"

"Yes I would, thank you, Grandy."

Bernice had a greedy, hungry look in her eyes as she held out her hand for the phone. Her voice was close to the hyperventilation stage as she said, "Joyce? Where are you? We're here in the Farmer's Market parking lot."

"Mom, we're just entering the parking lot. I see a white motor home with blue trim. Is that yours?"

"Yes, yes it is!"

"We'll be there in ten seconds."

"Okay!" Bernice hung up the phone, grabbed her cane, and opened the trailer door. The recently coiffed, grey-haired grandma scanned the parking lot for a vehicle approaching her direction. When she saw a maroon minivan pulling up beside the motor home, Bernice almost fell trying to get to it. After a long hug and a few tears, Joyce unbuckled the little bundle from her car seat and gently placed it in her mother's arms.

"Oh Joyce, she is so beautiful." Bernice touched Jackie's silken cheek and kissed her on the forehead. "She has the most unbelievable, blue eyes. She looks a lot like you did when you were a baby." In a somewhat clumsy manner, the overcome-with-emotion grandma hugged Joyce and the baby at the same time. "What does Buck think of her?"

"When he's around he hardly puts her down. When it's time for a feeding, it's practically a three-person sport."

They both laughed then Bernice said, "You look great, Honey, it's so good to see you again."

"It's wonderful to see you again too, Mom. Your hair looks nice."

"Thanks. Say, let's go inside the motor home to visit, it'll be a bit more private than the shopping mall."

"What about Grandy? Is that alright with her?"

Bernice continued to stare at her granddaughter and softly said, "If I say it's alright, then it's alright. Don't worry about Grandy."

The family of three entered the Fleetwood and after Bernice shooed Ditch off the pint size couch, they sat down. Grandy and April were still sitting in the driver and passenger seats.

"Hi Grandy."

"Hey Joyce." Grandy glanced up from cleaning her fingernails with a pocketknife and produced a half smile for the visitors. "Good to see ya, how's the little one?"

"She's awesome, Grandy. Want to come join us so you can see her?"

"In a minute. April here needs to get my crutches."

"Hi." April gave the newcomers a slight wave.

"Hi. Crutches? What happened, Grandy?"

"Just a little accident, twisted my ankle a bit. Nothing to fuss over." Grandy tried to sound as nonchalant as possible. She glared at Bernice though as she heard her giggling.

"She tried to ride a broken pogo stick she found along the side of the road."

"Well, that's too bad. I hope you get better soon." Joyce put as much sincerity as possible into the sentiment.

"Yah, yah. Where's Buck? You leave him, too?"

"Heavens no, Grandy, he's in Texas getting our new house ready. He'll be back later tonight, just in time for the movers tomorrow." Joyce looked over at April. "Have you been traveling long with my mother and Grandy?"

"Not really. Grandy found me at a campground and insisted I come along. I'll probably stay in L.A. if I can find a job."

"I didn't insist you come along. I invited you." Grandy stood up and chose to hop on one foot towards the couch instead of using the crutches.

"And the cute little dog, where did you find him?"

Bernice's eyes never moved away from Jackie's face as she said, "Alongside the highway, just like the pogo stick."

"He's cute. What's his name?"

"Ditch."

"Ditch. That's an interesting name. Joyce moved closer to her mother as she noticed Grandy was getting ready to sit down on the couch.

"Look Grandy. Isn't she just adorable?" Bernice could not keep the wonderment out of her voice.

"She looks like a baby." The usually grouchy roommate reached across Joyce and gingerly stroked Jackie's tiny fist.

Bernice barely glanced at her friend but said to Joyce, "Did I tell you Grandy's got a new grandson?"

"No, you didn't. Congratulations, Grandy."

"Thanks."

"Have you seen him, yet?"

"No. Should see him sometime today, though. I just talked to his father. They're here in L.A., but I'm not sure where."

"L.A.'s a big city. Could take a while, depending on where he was when he called. Do you know?" asked Joyce.

"No, I just figured I'd wait here. Really nowhere to go right now." Grandy placed her swollen foot up on a chair, hoping for some sympathy.

The chit chat was becoming boring for April so she grabbed her backpack and said, "I think I'll go check out the mall, maybe I can even find a job there."

"April, take my wheelchair outside. I think I'll see what kind of high buck stores are here. Bernice, I'm leaving Ditch with you."

"Fine. What about Dakota?"

"He'll call me when he gets here and then we'll meet in the mall. Nice seeing you Joyce, and your kid, too. She's not bad looking."

"Thanks, Grandy."

"When you see Buck, tell him I said hi."

"I will. Nice meeting you, April."

"You too, Joyce."

As Bernice and Joyce watched April push Grandy towards the mall entrance, they looked at each other and began laughing hysterically. It was worth the price of an admission to watch them go across the parking lot – April's green hair, Grandy's red hair, and a dilapidated wheelchair with a bumper sticker on the back that read, "I like Mr. Spock's tips."

Chapter 58

Joyce's smile fluctuated between genuine and artificial as she pulled the baby gifts for Jackie out of a shopping bag. It was obvious which ones Bernice had purchased and which ones Grandy bought.

"This is interesting. What is it?" The new mother held up a small purple object, triangular in shape with flashing orange and yellow dots.

"I'm not sure. I told Grandy it was too sharp for babies, but she said it contained some kind of protective powers against a planet somewhere in the Milky Way. Sorry, Honey, it's easier to give it to you and let you get rid of it than argue with her." There was a deep sigh before Bernice continued, "How I wish I had been there when my grandbaby was born." She looked lovingly at the photos of Jackie first two months of life.

"Don't worry about Grandy's gifts, I'll keep them in a safe place." Joyce chuckled as she placed all the presents back into the bag. "And thanks Mom, for everything. I love the sun dress with watermelons on it."

Mother and daughter grinned at each other before starting a new subject of conversation.

"What do you know about this April, Mom?" A dash of concern now lay in Joyce's voice.

"Not a whole lot. Just that her boyfriend dumped her on the highway and Grandy felt sorry for her. She's not too bad, just a little weird."

"You two better be more careful. You just never know about people."

"Well, if somebody wants to mess with Grandy, good luck to them."

"Even so, knowing Grandy, she'll pick up somebody else."

"I know her judgment seems a little crooked, but her heart is in the right place. I just wish her mouth reflected it more. She can be curt – and rude – and annoying."

"Have you thought anymore about moving in with us?"

"Lots of times. But despite the differences between me and Grandy, it's kind of fun seeing the more unusual sites of this country."

"Well, don't forget, the offer always stands."

"I won't." Bernice watched Jackie's tiny mouth yawn and the baby's mother wonder at her God-given miracle. "You know Joyce, I think I will come and stay with you, Jackie, and Buck for a little bit. I can help you settle into your new home in Texas."

"That would be awesome Mom! When do you think you'd come?"

"Let me talk to Grandy and I'll give you an exact date. If it works for her, probably in the next few of weeks."

Joyce stood up and gave her mom a tender hug. "I can hardly wait!"

"Me neither. Say, I'm getting kind of hungry. Let's walk over to the mall and I'll buy you lunch."

"Let me buy you lunch."

"No, I insist, I'm buying."

"Okay, but I'm buying you a new pair of shorts."

"What's the matter with my shorts?"

* * *

After lunch, the three generations wandered through the mall. Bernice pushed the stroller past a musical fountain of dancing waters and they stopped to marvel at its unique display.

"Do you need to sit and rest for awhile, Mom?"

"No, I'm fine, Honey." Fifteen minutes later Bernice noticed the pink neon sign of a hair salon.

"I wonder if they do manicures."

"Go for it, Mom."

"I'll treat you to one."

"Thanks anyway, I think the fumes are a little strong for Jackie. I'll just sit out here."

"Are you sure? I don't have to."

"You go ahead. I need to call Buck anyway."

Bernice felt like a queen as the manicurist held her hand.

"This feels so good! It's been forever since I've had a professional manicure. By the way, my name is Bernice."

"I'm Rosa, happy to meet you. It does look like you're overdue."

"I've been traveling the last couple of months. And my friend doesn't like taking a lot of time for beauty treatments."

"That's too bad. Where have you traveled to?"

"A Rock, Scissors, and Paper contest in Reno, a hot springs in Wyoming, and a Star Trek Convention in Iowa – "

"Star Trek Convention? Are you a Trekkie?" The thinly plucked, black eyebrows of the manicurist arched in a manner that projected skepticism.

"Heavens no! Grandy is."

"Grandy?"

"Yeah, that's my friend."

"Wait a minute. Are you Bernice of 'Grandy and Bernice,' the ladies on the Chet Baxter Show?"

"Yes I am." Bernice smiled liked she owned the airwaves.

"Hey, Marta," Rosa yelled over to a middle-aged stylist with an extreme case of frosted hair. "You're never gonna guess who this is?"

"Who?"

"It's Bernice, you know, from Bernice and Grandy on the Chet Baxter Show."

"No way!" The two middle-aged, Hispanic manicurists scurried for paper and pen for an autograph.

"We've had a few famous people in here, but you're the best! We just love listening to your tales. Tell us about some of the places you've not mentioned on the radio."

"Yeah, and are you still being chased by Grandy's son and ex-husband?"

The flurry of questions had Bernice stammering for answers currently just out of reach in her mind. Before she could reply, another inquiry was thrown at her.

"Where's Grandy?"

"Oh, she's somewhere in the mall."

"Can you call her? We'd like to give her a manicure or haircut, whatever she wants, it's on us. We'll do her for free just like yours will be."

"You don't really have to do that."

"We want to. This is the highlight of our day."

"Well, instead of calling her, when I see her later I'll let her know about your offer."

"Sounds good. Now let's finish what I started with you," Rosa said with a soft smugness as she gingerly filed away on Bernice's nails.

Rosa reluctantly accepted Bernice's tip. As she exited the parlor, she admired her bright red nails sculpted with white roses.

"Wow, Mom. Pretty fancy."

"Got it done for free."

"How'd you swing that?"

"I'm a celebrity." Bernice described how the same thing happened in Winnemucca with their hair.

"Sounds like you have quite a following."

"I had no idea." Bernice's modesty was mixed with a hint of pride.

"Buck says hi."

"Oh, how's he doing?"

"He's just great. I can hardly wait to get out of this town. He says our new place is beautiful."

"I'm looking forward to seeing it."

"I'm looking forward to living there."

"Now, let's go find some shorts for you – preferably without any fruit on them."

Bernice picked out a pair of shorts, but then gasped when she looked at the price tag. "I think I'll go to Wal-Mart."

"Don't worry about the price tag, Mom, I told you this was my treat."

"Yeah, but you could pay for a whole year of college tuition for the price of these."

"Don't be silly. Go try them on."

The navy blue shorts with red piping on the pockets were a perfect fit and, although they were not what Joyce would have picked out, she could tell her mother liked them. Bernice changed her clothes and before she could say anything, Joyce grabbed the shorts and took them to the cash register.

"You were always too extravagant with me growing up. For once I'd like to indulge you."

"We did have some fun shopping trips, didn't we?"

"Yeah, when I wasn't being a punk."

"You weren't a punk."

"Yes I was and I'm sorry."

"No more talk of that. The past is the past. Let's head over to the Farmer's Market."

"Sounds good to me."

Jackie's approval in the plans was confirmed by delicate coos and sighs.

Chapter 59

"What else do you wanna look at, Grandy?" April was tired of pushing the wheelchair around the mall and her words squeezed out like slow fart bubbles.

"Let's go over there." Grandy's crooked finger pointed at Izzy's Tattoo Parlor.

"The tattoo parlor? Why do you want to go there?"

"Because I'm hungry for a meatball sandwich. Why do you think I want to go there?"

"Grandy, tattoos hurt. Why would you want to get one this late in life?"

Old Red turned in her wheelchair and squinted at the lost-in-life teenager. "What do you mean late in life? Are you insinuating I'm old?"

A loud gum pop from April preceded her response. "I don't know what insinuating means but look at you. You're not exactly strutting around like a spring chicken."

Indignation filled the four corners of Grandy's body and she jumped up out of the wheelchair, turned to face April then almost fell when her twisted ankle gave way. "Dang it!" she cursed as she had to sit down again. "Listen, I squirted out three babies through a hole the size of a grape, I think I can handle a little tattoo."

"Okay, but don't say I didn't warn ya." April's voice was an extension of nonchalant advice. She wheeled her friend into the red and black, Oriental-themed business. Before the opportunity to absorb their surroundings could occur, a young, Mohawk-haired man covered in tattoos came out from a back room. His brown and gold flecked eyes lit up when he noticed April's solar system stretched across her back.

"Awesome. Who did your artwork?"

"A gal in Oregon."

"You here for another one?"

"No, actually my friend here wants one."

If the tattoo artist was surprised to see an old, fuzzy red-haired cripple looking through sample books for ideas, he didn't show it.

"Tell him what you want, Grandy."

"I was thinking about 'Area 51' right here," she pointed to the center of her chest.

April and the tattoo artist looked at each other with skepticism.

"Are you sure?"

"Of course I'm sure, April, I've been thinking about this for a long time, now let's get started."

"Okay Grandy, we have some paperwork to fill out first." The business owner handed her a clipboard of papers and a pen.

"I'm getting a tattoo, not applying for a loan. How come there's so many forms?" Irritation was clearly at the surface of Grandy's voice.

"I want to make sure you don't have a medical condition or use medications that would interfere with the dye used for tattoos."

"By the way, what's your name?"

"Snake."

"Snake. What kind of name is Snake? Bet you get lots of girlfriends with the name Snake." Grandy's sarcasm was evident.

The young man could not believe this woman sitting in front of him. First, she wants a tattoo where he doesn't want to touch her; secondly, she gives him a bad time about the required paperwork, and thirdly, she insults his name. If it wasn't for the cute chick standing next to the old battleaxe, he would have asked her to leave.

With exasperation in his voice he responded, "I like the name Snake. My birth name is Arnold and I find that a bigger turnoff than my nickname. And just so you know, if you don't fill out those forms, I can't give you a tattoo."

After ten minutes of grumbling, Grandy handed him the forms then asked, "How much is this tattoo going to cost me?"

"My special for the day, fifty bucks."

"Fifty bucks! Are you crazy? For fifty dollars I should be able to get a tattoo the size of Bernie's butt."

April helped the confused Snake. "Bernie's her friend, she has a rather wide bottom."

"Oh." A minuscule pause by Snake then he offered, "Since this is your first tattoo Grandy, how about forty-five dollars?"

"Forty dollars."

"Thirty-five."

"Forty and no lower."

"Fine. Hurry up and get started, I have to meet my son and grandson soon."

"Poor unlucky relatives," thought Snake.

The expectation was that Old Red would complain, criticize, and tell Snake how to do his job. To the amazement of both April and the tattoo artist, the old lady remained quiet and still. The only time she spoke was when she asked Snake about the *Help Wanted* sign in his window.

"I need a receptionist. It gets busy around here and I can't answer the phone or deal with the customers if I'm working on someone."

"Hire April. She should be able to answer a phone."

For a brief second, Snake glanced over at April and smiled. "How about it April, you interested?"

"Pay attention to what you're doing. Arnold. You mess up my tattoo and you'll be feeding hogs somewhere in Central America."

207

The wayward teenager looked around the shop and stared back at Snake. He was kinda cute. Knowing she couldn't travel with Grandy and Bernice forever, April decided this was as good a place as any to put down some roots.

"Okay Snake, I'll take the job."

"Cool. How soon can you start?"

"She can start today. Now, no more talking until you're finished."

When Snake completed the tattoo, Grandy stood in front of the mirror, holding her blouse apart just enough to see her tattoo. "Area 51" appeared etched in block lettering in various shades of emerald green, gold, and the tiniest of silver flakes.

"Won't Bernie be envious of this?" Her voice sounded like soft gravel.

"About that job. What does it pay?" April inquired.

"Oh, I could start you just above minimum wage and if it works out, if things stay as busy as they have been, I could give you a raise in a couple of months."

"Sounds good. Anywhere really, really cheap rooms to rent anywhere? Grandy and her friend are leaving L.A. soon and I won't have a place to stay."

"You're kidding?"

"No."

"My sister's roommate is planning to move out at the end of the month. I bet she wouldn't mind if you slept on her couch till she's gone."

"Really? That would be great. I'll go pick up my things back at the motor home and bring them here. That's okay isn't it?"

"Cool with me."

As Grandy paid for her tattoo, her cell phone rang.

"Who is this?"

"It's me, Dakota, where are you?"

"In the mall." "Where are you?"

"I'm in the parking lot of the mall."

"I'll be there in about ten minutes. Go sit in the motor home."

"Which one is yours?"

"The white one with the blue trim. Knock first, Bernice might have a heart attack if you just walk in."

"Okay Ma, see ya soon."

Tears cascaded down April's eyes as she wheeled Grandy out of the mall and towards the coach.

"Thanks, Grandy, for everything. I really do appreciate it. And I'm going to miss you and Bernice very much."

A long silence was Grandy's volley before she finally answered in a voice also crammed with emotion, "Me too."

Chapter 60

A knock on the door startled Joyce and Bernice.

"I bet that's Grandy's son... Come on in, Dakota."

The handsome, thirty-four-year-old entered, baby carrier in hand.

"You must be Bernice."

"Hi Dakota, we've been expecting you. This is my daughter Joyce and my granddaughter Jackie."

"Nice to meet you."

"Nice to meet you, too."

Dakota tilted the carrier slightly so his son's face could be seen. "And this little guy is my son, Rain."

"Oh look, isn't he cute! Looks to be about the same age as Jackie," Bernice commented.

"He was born June 1st."

"Jackie was born May 31st."

"I know there's not a lot of room, but sit down and relax, Dakota. Your mother should be here soon."

"I just talked to her. She said she's on her way." Dakota smiled at the ladies then said, "That's an interesting toy."

"Yes, it's from your mother," Joyce said as politely as possible. "She gave me a whole set of Klingons. Would you like one for Rain? Jackie doesn't need that many."

Dakota thought for a moment before responding, "How do I know that my mother didn't buy a set for Rain?"

"I don't think she did. We didn't even know you had a baby when she bought them. We were in Iowa."

"Let's wait. Wouldn't want to upset her applecart this early in our visit."

The three adults began laughing, then stopped abruptly when they heard noises outside. Grandy opened the door and hopped up into the camper.

"Ma!" Dakota gave Grandy a huge, warm hug.

"Not so hard, Son, you'll pop my eyeballs out." Grandy tried to counter her comment with a loving hug to her middle born.

"So great to see you, Ma!"

"Good to see you, too. Now where's my grandson?"

The new father carefully lifted Rain out of his carrier and placed him in Grandy's arms.

"He's not bad lookin' Dakota, but kinda small, isn't he?"

"He gets his good looks from me, Ma, and his size from his mother."

"So where is she What kind of mother would go off and leaver her newborn?"

209

"She didn't run off and leave us, Ma. There's a cause she was committed to attend to in Canada. We'll meet up with her later."

"Hmmph!"

"By the way, what happened to your foot?"

"Just a little sprain."

"How'd you do it?"

Bernice interrupted. "She tried to jump on an old pogo stick she found in a pile of free stuff."

"Yeah, see. It's over there. You think you can fix it?"

"I don't know, but I bet Uncle Dog Face could. Wow, I bet this is worth some cash. Were you going to sell it?"

"Well I was going to send it to Augusta for her birthday."

"Oh, Ma. If it doesn't plug in, she wouldn't know what to do with it."

"That's true. So you think I can get a lot for it?"

"Sure. They don't make 'em like this anymore." Dakota admired the design of the pogo stick.

"They sure don't, otherwise she might not have sprained her ankle," Bernice interrupted.

Dakota hadn't noticed the green-haired teenager standing behind his mother. April poked Grandy for an introduction.

"What? Oh, this is April. She was just leaving."

"Not right this second," April scooted closer to the good looking man. She extended her hand and batted her eyes at Dakota, "Hi, I'm April."

Dakota shook her hand, "Hi, I'm Dakota. Nice to meet you."

"You too." The infatuated teenager hung onto his hand a bit longer than necessary.

"Girl, he's old enough to be your father *and* he's married."

April ignored the crabby senior citizen and continued to talk to Dakota. "Your baby is sure cute."

"Thanks, I think so too."

"April," Grandy snapped, "Let go of his hand."

The embarrassed teenager's face turned red as she said, "I need to get my stuff together and get back to the tattoo parlor."

"Tattoo parlor?" Bernice gave Grandy an inquisitive look.

"April found a job at the tattoo parlor where I got my new piece of artwork." Old Red pulled her shirt apart just enough for everyone else to see her "Area 51" tattoo.

Nobody knew quite what to say.

"Well? What do you think? Pretty nifty, huh?"

Bernice and Joyce looked at each other while Dakota responded, "I like it Ma. Glad you didn't go for the ET finger."

Grandy smiled broadly and stared at the other two adults, "Well, what do *you* think?"

"It's unique. Like you, Grandy." Bernice didn't know what else to say without it being a lie or starting an argument.

"Yeah, unique," Joyce agreed.

Grandy's exposed tattoo was making the group uncomfortable so Dakota started a new conversation. "So Ma, where are you headed after this?"

"Got invited to a meeting tonight in a town called Dark, not too far from here I don't think. I got a map off the Internet."

"What kind of meeting?"

"The ISAET. You wanna come?"

"I'd love to, Ma, but ..." Dakota pointed to the baby.

"Bernie will watch him. I doubt she's gonna wanna go inside to the meeting, right, Bernie?"

"Sure." The answer came out in a slow unsure manner. "Don't forget though, that me, Joyce, and Jackie are going over the mall first."

"Fine. Go do what you need to do. Just don't be late getting back here."

As Bernice and Joyce gathered Jackie and various other items, April came walking out of the bathroom. "I'm all set." Her voice was an unsteady mixture of bravado and misery. "Thanks again for everything Grandy. Come visit me sometime, okay?" The green-haired teenager with brown roots hugged her friend tightly.

"Enough with the bear hugs." Grandy struggled out of April's hold. She then held the girl at arm's length before giving her a grandmotherly hug of her own. "Stay away from boys. Start raising Chia pets or something. And here." She reached into her pocket and placed a wad of bills into April's hand.

"I can't – "

"You will if I tell you. Now go. Before you start crying and get mascara all over your face."

April reached down and gave Ditch a scratch behind the ears. "See you later, little guy."

"Is that your dog, Joyce?" asked Dakota.

"No, it's your mother's."

"Really. Where'd you get him, Ma?"

"Found him half-dead on the highway."

"That's just like you." Dakota reached over and pet Ditch. "You're one lucky mutt."

"We're just heading over to the mall ourselves, April, we'll walk with you," Bernice said in a soft, sad voice.

The foursome left the motor home leaving Dakota and Grandy to catch up on the past few months.

"How you really doin', Ma?"

"I'm just peachy-keen. Except for worrying about your brother after me, I've been having a blast traveling around."

"Have you heard from Avis or Dad?"

"I think Joyce said something about Avis calling her. I'm sure he knows we're in L.A. Knowing Avis, it won't be long before he's hot on our trail. But let's talk about you. Where have you been and what have you been doing? How come I don't hear from you more?"

"I'm sorry about that, Ma. Sometimes I end up in places where phone service isn't available. As for my adventures, I'm keeping a journal so that someday I can publish a book."

"Hmmm," Grandy's muted, blue eyes looked at her son with pride. "Good for you, but I still want you to tell me more about where you've been and about Rain and his mother."

The next seventy-five minutes flashed past them as they shared stories of their recent escapades, family memories, and similar interests.

Chapter 61

Inside the mall, April parted ways with Bernice, Joyce, and Jackie, but not before she released enough tears to fill a teacup. It wasn't so much that she would miss Bernice as it was the finality of leaving behind an adventure that was just getting good. She turned her head one last time to watch as the mother, grandmother, and baby entered a children's clothing store.

* * *

A few more purchases included two shirts for Joyce, nail polish and a skirt for Bernice, and a book for Grandy entitled, "How to Identify Your Alien Relatives." Bernice snickered as she put the book in her shopping bag.

"Won't Grandy be insulted by that?" Joyce asked.

"Na, she'll probably tell me she's read it already. I just wanted to get her something and she's so hard to buy for." Bernice thought for a moment before continuing, "I wonder if I should get something for Ditch?"

"I don't think Grandy expects you to buy her dog a gift."

"I know she doesn't expect it, I just didn't want him to feel left out."

Joyce gave her mom a bewildered look but didn't say anything. On their way out of the mall, they passes a PetCo store where Bernice purchased a small pouch of doggie treats for Ditch. The threesome then headed to Joyce's car where the grandmother reluctantly handed Jackie over to her mother after a dozen kisses and hugs.

"Do you have to go right now?" Bernice's voice was tiny and sad.

"'Fraid so, Mom. I have some last minute packing to do. Besides, It'll be easier to feed Jackie her dinner at home. Did I tell you she's eating cereal?"

"Wow! That's great. Bet that's why she's sleeping through the night."

"That's for sure. She doesn't eat much, but it sticks to her ribs."

"She is a beautiful baby, Joyce. I'm so proud of you." Bernice gave her daughter a loving hug.

"We've got plenty of room in the car. Are you sure you don't want to ride with us to Texas and stay a while?"

A light bulb in Bernice's brain came on and she thought for a moment. "Can you wait just a second, I want to ask Grandy something?"

"Grandy!" she hollered outside the camper door, "Can I talk to you for a second?"

"What now?" The door flew open narrowly missing the grey-haired grandma's face.

"Joyce asked me to ride to Texas with her and the baby. I thought I could go down and help her unpack."

Grandy stared at her friend as if she were a stranger, "Go ahead. But I'm headin' up towards San Francisco, thought we could swing by and see your sister."

Confusion suddenly possessed the once determined lady and she went and sat back in her daughter's car. She looked at Joyce with braided emotions. "Grandy says we're going to San Francisco and we could stop by and see Aunt Char, but I also want to go with you and Jackie to Texas."

"Mom," Joyce spoke in a soft motherly tone. "Go see Aunt Char, then you can come and spend as much time as you want with us."

"But – "

"Go. Don't miss this opportunity, I understand. We'll be waiting for you whenever you can come."

"You sure? Because I don't have to."

"I'm sure. Have a great time."

"Thanks, Honey, and don't worry, I'll be fine. I'm so excited! I can't wait to see you in your new home in Texas. And it will be good to see Char."

"Okay, then you keep me posted on where you are this time."

"I will."

"Tell Grandy thanks again for the ... gifts."

"Oh, I will. And say hi to Buck." The teary-eyed grandma opened the back door, leaned over and kissed Jackie one last time. "Bye-bye, my beautiful granddaughter."

* * *

"If all you're gonna do is cry, you should've gone with her."

"I'm just so happy. Isn't Jackie just the most beautiful baby you've ever seen?"

"No. She's not bad but she's not better looking than Rain."

Bernice turned the shade of a Santa suit and stumbled over her words, "I meant isn't she the most beautiful *girl* baby you've ever seen?"

Grandy shook her head and changed the subject. "Dakota's gonna follow us over to the meeting."

"Meeting?"

"Yeah, you said you'd babysit."

"I did?"

"Ma, she doesn't have to babysit. I'll just take him along. He likes riding in his carrier."

The baby fragrance of Jackie was still fresh in Bernice's nose as she looked at Rain, betting he smelled much the same way. "I'd be happy to care for Rain, Dakota."

"You don't have to Bernice. I promise I won't let Ma hurt you if you don't."

A slap from Grandy found its way to her son's upper arm.

"Ow!"

Bernice couldn't help but laugh. "Dakota, I really want to babysit Rain. It definitely will be more fun than that meeting. Now, if you'll excuse me, I'm kinda tired. I think I'll go lie down."

Bernice went into the bedroom and pushed Ditch off the bed with her cane.

"Is she okay?"

"Oh, she's just being Bernie. Finish your SPAM Delight. We have to leave in about a half hour."

Chapter 62

In the parking lot of the Happy Campground, Avis parked his black Mercedes Benz rental car next to his father's old, rusty green pickup. Lester was slouched down in his truck, half of a cigarette hanging out the left side of his bottom lip. "Achy Breaky Heart" was a scallop of a song as it tried to push its way through the last remains of a speaker. Avis slammed his car door in announcement of his presence. Sputtering swear words spit out of Lester's mouth as the sound caused him to jolt out of a nap and drop his cigarette in his lap. He looked over at the source of his upheaval.

"Damn it, Boy! You tryin' to send me to an early grave?"

"Hey Dad. How you doing?" The attorney's voice projected his usual, organized self.

Lester crawled out of his pickup, scratching his private parts. "Can't complain. Wanna beer?"

"No thank you, Dad. I think we should get going. We don't want to miss Ma."

"Don't ya want to give your old man a hug? Haven't see ya in quite some time." The semi-toothless gold digger opened his arms in anticipation of some affection.

The eldest son approached his father with an obvious reluctant demeanor. He could smell an odor similar to that of rotting fish emulating from his relative and held his breath as he stepped in for a quick hug.

"Ahh, that's my son." Lester said as he patted his boy's back. "Get in the pickup Avis. It'll be like old times driving out to see your Ma."

"We can't take that thing."

"Why not?"

"Ma knows your old truck."

"Oh, yeah, right. Guess we'll have to take your wheels. Damn fancy, Boy. What'd this set you back?"

"It's a rental, Dad. Try not to make a mess."

"Hang on a minute." Lester unzipped his pants and relieved himself on the tire of his pickup. Grinning, he turned his head and announced, "Just marking my territory so no one steals this baby."

Embarrassment and panic took over the attorney's face and he tried to block his father's action with his own body. "Dad, you can't do that!"

"Why not? I do it all the time."

"You could get arrested for indecent exposure along with a host of other charges."

"Ahhh, don't worry, Son. You're a lawyer, remember? Let's go, I'm anxious to see your mother."

Avis sighed deeply as he got into the car. He tried to think of the best way to approach talking to his dad and handling the situation with his mom. It was beginning to take hold in his brain that he should have never agreed to meet with his dad.

"Do you know where you're going?"

"I've got the directions. By the way Dad, there seems to be a rather strong smell coming from your clothes. Did you spill something on them?"

"No, I was goin' to ask you if you spilled a bottle of aftershave on yourself."

"No, I didn't."

The two looked at each other, expressions of mild disgust glued to their faces. Lester entertained himself with the large array of dashboard buttons while Avis silently berated himself, "I knew I should've got the extra insurance. They'll probably dock me for the smell."

"Hey, you got any beer?"

"No, it's illegal to have open containers in a vehicle, Dad. You should know that."

"Why are you worried? Do you keep forgettin' you're a lawyer?"

"No, that's the reason I keep reminding you about the laws, because I am a lawyer."

"Hmmph." Staring out the window, Lester tried to think of ways to out-reason his son.

"Dad."

"What."

"Please put your seatbelt on. It's the – "

"I know I know, it's the law." Sarcasm drooled from the old man's mouth.

After an undetermined amount of silence between father and son, Avis dared to speak. "Now, when we see Ma, let me do the talking. In fact, maybe you shouldn't let her see your face immediately."

"Don't be lecturing me, Son. I can handle your mother."

"Yeah, I've seen how you handle my mother."

"Easy, Son. Don't be back-talking your elders. I still could whip your hide."

Avis sized up the body making that statement and decided that, although he would not lose a physical fight with his dad, he sure as shooting would walk away with a few reminders of it. Lester's appearance might bring to mind images of a vulture with missing feathers and one leg, but his son knew the toughness went through the bone.

"You haven't asked about your granddaughter yet."

"Oh yeah, how is little Georgia?"

"Augusta."

"I got the state right. How's the little darlin'?"

"She's just fine, Dad. You know, you could visit her once in a while."

"Maybe I'll come visit ya after I buy myself a new pickup."

"Sure Dad." Avis wished now he hadn't invited his father to his home. The fish smell would throw Liza into a fit and Avis would be forced to burn the house down or, at the very least, move into a new one.

"How's that sexy wife of yours, what's her name, Linda, Lucy..."

"Liza, Dad."

"I knew it started with an L. Just like mine." Lester started to light up a cigarette.

"Please don't smoke in the car."

"Where else am I supposed to smoke? You know in California you can't even smoke in the bars?"

"That's good. Second-hand smoke kills."

"That's hogwash. If that was true, all three of you boys'd be dead."

It was best to change the subject so Avis said, "You know, Dad, we need to have a plan."

"Yeah, when we get there I'm taking the motor home."

"Calm down. I'm serious."

"So am I."

"Just try and think about Ma for one minute and let me finish. When we see the motor home, I'll knock on the door. You stay here in the car."

"And when you get her outside, I'll go in and find the key and drive the motor home."

"That's enough talk about the motor home, Dad. It's not yours. We're here to help Ma. If I can get her to come with me, then you can drive the motor home back to L.A. and park it somewhere until I can get a hold of the pink slip, and then we'll sell it."

"Now you're talkin'. It's probably worth thirty-thousand dollars. Let's see, half of thirty-thousand dollars is..."

"Fifteen."

"What?"

"Half of thirty is fifteen."

"Yeah, I knew that."

"But it's not yours. I will have to use that money to pay her rent when I get her back into the home."

"I must say, Son, it's hard to believe your mother is fragile enough to be in a home for old folks. She always struck me as the type that would outlive you and me both."

"She's not fragile or sick, Dad. She just has become obsessed with some strange ideas and I'm afraid her judgment might end up hurting her."

"She always did have one egg out of the nest."

"Maybe so, but you didn't make things easy for her, either. Your cheating probably helped push her over the edge."

"Careful now, Boy, your mother's lack of libido is what finally turned me away. A man has needs, you know. Your mother was not as hot in bed as I – "

"Enough, Dad! I don't want to hear about you and my mother's sex life."

There was a pause before Avis tried another avenue of conversation. "You haven't asked about Dakota and Howard."

"How are they?"

"Howard's doing fine. He wanted to join us but Blackie got an infection from her last piercing and he needed to stay with her."

"That's nice."

It was obvious Lester wasn't really all that interested in what Avis was saying but the eldest son continued on as if he was.

"Haven't heard from Dakota in a really long time. Has he contacted you in the last few years?"

"I need a beer, Avis."

"You don't need a beer right now, Dad. We'll be to Dark soon. Maybe afterwards we can think about stopping for a quick one."

"Hell no, Son. If we stop, it'll be for a tall one, not a quick one."

Chapter 63

"Hey, Old Woman, get up!" Grandy yelled at her sleeping friend, her gravelly voice at a pitch that sounded like a blender full of cement chips. "We're going to the meetin' and you need to babysit."

Thick dreams of undistinguishable shapes still possessed Bernice's head as she tried to reconnect with the present. Without thought, she fluffed her bed-head hair with one hand as she shuffled out of the bedroom.

"Give me five minutes. I need to freshen up."

"Like a two-month old baby is gonna care if you have your lipstick on," Grandy mumbled.

"A proper woman, which you are not, always tries to look her best." Bernice turned her back on Grandy and went into the bathroom.

"What do you mean by *proper*?" Grandy shouted, "I'll ..." The red-haired grandma was interrupted by a soft knock on the door.

"Who is it?" Grandy snapped.

Dakota entered the motor home, baby carrier and large diaper bag in hand. "Hey, Ma."

"Son, we're only gonna be gone a couple of hours. You have enough stuff to change and diaper Bernice," Grandy snickered at her own joke.

"I know it looks like a lot of stuff, but one thing I've learned about Rain, he sure can go through a lot of clothes in a very short amount of time."

"I'm ready." Bernice hobbled over to the sofa. "Hi Dakota."

"Hi Bernice. Thanks for watching my boy. I appreciate it."

"My pleasure." Bernice reached into the baby carrier and picked up Rain. She held him close to her chest. "You two run along. We'll be fine."

Grandy pulled on Dakota's arm, "Come on, Son, we need to go."

A faded, red-haired Ditch sat on the floor, looking up at Grandy and Dakota as they started to leave. He whimpered softly as Grandy's hand touched the door knob.

" You stay. Don't make the baby or the dog cry, Bernice. We'll be back soon."

* * *

The meeting room was overstuffed with members of ISAET. Dakota's eyes widened as he absorbed the collection of paranormal addicts. His mother seemed to blend in with the group way too easily, but he wasn't concerned. She may have displayed some odd behavior through the years, but she never did anything to harm anyone.

"Grandy!" A voice called from across the room.

A bile of panic rose in Grandy's throat as the voice sounded like Lester. When she saw it was her old friend walking towards her, she let out a sigh of relief.

"Roscoe. What are you doing here?"

"I heard you on the radio this morning."

"But I said we weren't coming."

"Something told me you'd be here, so I drove all day to get here." The old man eyed the young man standing next to Grandy. "Who's this with you, Grandy? Hope it ain't your new boyfriend." He chuckled at his own humor.

"This is my son, you idiot."

"Of course, Grandy. I was just playing with ya. Hi, I'm Roscoe. Nice to meet ya. I met your mother and her friend in Algona, Iowa. It was their first night out on the road."

Dakota extended his hand for a shake. "I'm Dakota."

"Say Grandy, I sure like your tattoo. Where'd you get it?"

"Some mall in L.A." Grandy unbuttoned one more button on her green, paisley blouse and proudly threw back her shoulders to stretch the printing on her chest. While Roscoe was admiring the tattoo, a woman about 50 years old, wearing a silver crepe dress tapped his shoulder and said, "Who are our guests tonight, Roscoe?"

"This is Grandy and her son, Dakota."

"Oh, Grandy! I'm so glad you came! I think you and your son will thoroughly enjoy our meeting tonight!" The lady's high energy nearly knocked Grandy and Dakota over.

"Grandy, I'd like you to meet the secretary-treasurer of the Dark Chapter of ISAET, Sassy Saucer."

"Thanks for the invite."

"We're so glad you've shared your adventures and love for aliens with the rest of the country. You are such an inspiration. Let's talk more after the meeting. It's about to get started." With a quick flurry, she shook Grandy's hand then was gone. In a nano-second, Sassy was standing next to the president of the club, who was about to open the meeting for business.

"Welcome, everyone. Let's get started. There's a buzz going around that we have some special guests tonight. Sassy, would you like to do the honors?"

"I'd love to, Vern! Please extend a warm welcome to our visitors, Grandy from the Chet Baxter Show and her son, Dakota."

The room broke into loud applause and whistles. Roscoe tried to act like part of the honored guests by putting his arm around Grandy. Faster than the speed of sound, it was slapped away and left dangling at his side.

* * *

221

Back at the Fleetwood, Bernice had made a mangled mess of her first attempt at disposable diapers. The formula had become too hot when she cooked it for three minutes in the microwave. Finally mastering the art of high-tech babysitting, she rocked little Rain to sleep and laid him on the bed. She shut the door to keep Ditch out.

As Bernice was returning to the living area, she noticed a car pull into the parking lot. Whereas most of the vehicles in the lot were all older pickups and SUV's, this was a new black Mercedes. It immediately didn't feel right and Bernice tucked herself out of view. She watched as two men got out of the car and look in the direction of the motor home. The frightened grandmother remembered Grandy's shotgun, but soon realized that even if it did work, she didn't know how to use it. The middle-aged man and elderly gent were almost to her door and Bernice began to panic even more. She quietly scooped up Ditch and went into the bedroom.

"Ssssh, Good Dog. Now don't bark, please!" She whispered firmly. She looked over at Rain sleeping peacefully. Silently Bernice began to pray, "What do I do, Lord? Please help me."

A knock on the door had Bernice on the verge of peeing her pants.

Chapter 64

The voices outside the motor home convinced Bernice that it was Avis and Lester snooping around.

"This is the only motor home in the parking lot, must be Mother's."

"Bet I can hot wire it. See if you can break the lock on the door, Son."

"That's not the way to handle this, Dad. Let's go inside and talk to Ma. Don't forget she has her roommate traveling with her. We can't leave either one of them stranded in this joke of a town."

Lester pounded on the Fleetwood door a second time and then replied in a short, gruff tone, "Fine. Let's get this over with."

Bernice held her breath while she waited for the men to move away from the vehicle. When she felt they were gone, she took a peek out the window. Grandy's relatives were on their way towards the front of the lodge. It was then she knew she had to act quickly. She looked in on Rain and said a silent prayer of thanks that he was still in a peaceful, deep sleep. She softly warned Ditch not to bark and wake the baby. With a feeling of false bravado, the frightened roommate tiptoed outside and made her way to the back door of the Moose Lodge. Just as she grabbed the door handle, it flew open, she yelped, dropped her cane, and nearly fell over.

"Oh! I'm so sorry," a surprised, young Trekkie said. "Are you okay?"

A barely composed Bernice replied, "Yes, I think so. Please excuse me, I must get a message to my friend inside."

Without another word, the nervous grandmother hobbled down the hallway, glancing inside each room until she found the one she was looking for. She frantically surveyed the mass of people dressed in costumes of every imaginable combination as well as hairdos that even outdid Grandy's bizarre taste. She saw her friend sitting in the front row, so she started to head up the aisle. A man she could tell was past fifty gently asked if she needed help.

"No, I'm not staying, I just need to get a message to my friend."

The man listened as she described her red-haired friend.

"Oh, you mean Grandy?"

"Yeah, that's her. I need to talk to her right away. It's an emergency."

The gentleman escorted Bernice up the aisle until they reached Grandy. Puzzled looks were thrown their direction and he said, "Sorry for the interruption folks, she says it's an emergency."

"This better be good." Grandy snapped as Bernice leaned down to give her the message.

"Avis and Lester are here." Bernice said in an anguished voice.

"What!? Are you sure?" Grandy's words were a mixture of surprise and anger.

"Yes."

"Where are they?"

"They're on their way to the front door. They should be here any second."

"Come on." Grandy stood up. "We have to get out of here."

Dakota placed his hand on his mother's arm and asked, "What's wrong? Something happen to Rain?"

"No, Son, your father and brother found us. We need to leave now!"

"I'll go talk to them, Ma, don't worry."

"Sorry, Son, but I don't think they'll listen to you. And if you aren't careful, they might try to commit you, too."

The small commotion had stopped the meeting and gained the attention of the entire room.

"Is there a problem, Grandy?" asked the president of the club.

"Yeah, there's a problem. My no-good ex-husband and leach-sucking son are trying to kidnap me and lock me away in some lousy old fogy's home. They're on their way inside right now!"

A huge murmur swept through the meeting room.

"What can we do to help, Grandy?" said a concerned Roscoe.

"Find some way to delay them so Bernie and I can get away."

"Be happy to, Darlin'," Roscoe put his arm around Grandy and gave her a squeeze. "Everything is goin' to be just fine. I'll meet you over at Area 51 when this is all over."

Grandy peeled Roscoe's hand from her waist. "I ain't your darlin.'"

"We wanna help too," a few of the group said in unison.

"I've got an idea," Roscoe announced. "A couple of you come with me."

"Did you see what they were driving, Bernice?"

"A dark-colored Mercedes. It's the only one in the parking lot. You can't miss it."

"Okay, Guys, let's get that Mercedes ready for a trip to the moon."

"How can you do that without them seeing you?" asked Grandy.

"I can distract them," announced Dakota," I've got a bone to pick with both of them."

"I told you, Son, they'll – "

Dakota gave his mother a big hug, "Ma, relax, I'll be fine. You and Bernice get out of here. The handsome man's smile was enough to convince Grandy that perhaps it would all work out.

"Alright, Dakota. You straighten' em out, but if either one of them gives you grief, come and get me. Maybe it's time I knock the crap out of both of them."

Dakota chuckled then said, "I'm sure you could, Ma, but for now, you and Bernice go back to the motor home, let the rest of us handle this, okay?"

"Come on Bernie, let's get outta here."

Chapter 65

Avis and Lester entered the Moose Lodge, quickly making their own search through the rooms for the retirement home escapees. As soon as they entered where the ISAET group was meeting, several peculiar-looking characters surrounded them. They included a set of middle-aged female twins dressed in outfits of glow-in-the-dark material and blue-tinted hair sculptured into a pyramid, a 12-year-old boy in a dirty, Star Trek uniform wearing eyeglasses so thick they barely stayed on the bridge of his nose; and two adult men sporting T-shirts with the ISAET name printed in silver sequins.

"Can we help you?"

"Excuse me," Avis said as he tried to look past the collection of oddballs. "I'm looking for my mother."

"Yeah, and I'm looking for my wife," Lester said in a distracted voice, as his eyes jerked themselves back and forth between the set of twin peaks belonging to the women.

A stern voice asked, "What does she look like?"

"She has hair the color of a poinsettia plant," replied Avis, making an attempt to maneuver his way past the group. "I think I see her over – "

"Well, there's a couple of people here with that description. Can you be more specific?"

Lester and his son glanced around the room and noticed more than one head of flaming red hair. After a brief process of elimination because of gender and age, their eyes locked on the back of Grandy's head. The two men pushed themselves out of the circle and headed up the aisle towards her and Bernice.

Grandy's ankle seemed to have miraculously healed itself and Bernice also showed signs of being more agile than ever. The silver cane barely touched the ground as they practically ran from their pursuers.

"Get out of my way!" Avis snapped. "I'll press charges against all of you if you don't let us through!"

Bodies began to step back and, just when Avis and Lester thought they could catch up with Grandy and Bernice, a tall figure stepped in front of them.

"Get – " Avis did a double-take. "Dakota?"

"How's it goin', Brother?" He said calmly but with a firm determination in his voice.

"What are you doing here?"

"What do you think I'm doing here? You and Dad need to leave Ma alone. She's not hurting anyone."

"Stay out of this, you know nothing of the situation. Now get out of the way!"

"I know more than you think I do."

"Boy, do as your older brother says, let us through," Lester had sidled up next to Avis, puffing his chest out like a rooster on the prowl.

"You leave her alone too, Lester. You haven't been her husband for a long time. This is none of your business."

"Lester? Since when do you call me Lester?"

"Since you haven't acted like a father in over 20 years."

A moment of silence passed over the old man's face before he continued talking about the previous conversation. "You twit. Your mother and I are still legally married, and that makes that motor home half mine."

"Figures you're only here to steal from her. If it's the last thing I do, I'm going to make sure your grubby fingers never touch one penny of Ma's money."

"Careful, Boy, what you say. Especially about the distance you're willing to go for your Mama." Lester's words were soaked in a threatening tone.

Avis stepped between his brother and father, then gave Dakota a hard stare. "Let us by Dakota. I have as much right to see Ma as you do. Come on, Dad, or we'll miss her."

The middle son didn't try to stop them because he knew his brief interference was still enough to give Grandy and Bernice a very good head start. Besides, with the plans that Roscoe was cooking up, Dakota was sure his mother would have a clean getaway.

* * *

Due to their age and limited mobility factors, Avis was confident he could catch up with the two senior citizens. But to his amazement, Grandy and her cohort had already reached the motor home door as he approached the end of the building. He ran at breakneck speed and grabbed the doorknob of the coach and pulled as Grandy yanked from her end. Bernice instinctively popped Avis on the head with her cane, while Grandy struggled to close the door.

"Let go of the door, Avis, before I spank the tar out of you!"

"Ma, I just want to talk to you. Let me come in, please."

"Talk, huh? Then how come you've got your no good, sleazy father with you?"

"It wasn't my idea for him to come along, he just showed up."

"Bull honky. You wanna talk? Call my cell phone."

"I do call, but you never answer or return my messages."

"Guess that means I don't want to talk to you then. Now git!"

"Ma – "

As Bernice raised her cane to pop Avis another one, his hands instinctively went up to protect his head. Grandy used this opportunity to shut and lock the door. She then quickly slid into the driver's seat, started up the Fleetwood and peeled out of the parking lot on two wheels.

226

Avis stood there, momentarily speechless, as he watched the coach speed down the highway. He then turned and headed for the car. Lester met up with him halfway across the parking lot.

Lester commented, "Why'd you let them go?"

"Where were you when I was trying to stop them?"

"I decided it would be better not to confront the old bat face to face. She'd jerk my eyeballs out and use them for earrings. I'm only here for my half of the motor home. You're young and strong, how come you couldn't stop them?"

The look Avis gave Lester was deadly and his short comment was seething. "Let's get the car. I know they can't possibly out distance us."

* * *

Roscoe approached Dakota. "We better leave before they realize they aren't going anywhere."

"Oh, yeah. Right. Did Ma get away okay?"

"Yeah, they're gone. Where you headed?"

"I'll be heading back up north before it gets too hot for Rain. Rain! Oh, my God!"

"Rain?"

"I forgot him."

"Him?"

"My son. He's with my mother. Do you know which way they went?"

"Not really. Hope they're going to Area 51 'cause that's where I'm headed."

"Thanks for your help Roscoe," Dakota shook his hand with vigor. "If you'll excuse me, I need to call my ma and find out where she is." Panic nearly suffocated Dakota as he dialed her cell phone number. The phone immediately went to a recording.

"Ma, its Dakota. Call me as soon as you get this message. You've got Rain! I'm going to try to catch up with you as soon as possible. Call me!"

* * *

"Are you sure you put gas in this thing?" Lester asked.

"It's not out of gas, Dad. Somebody messed with it. And when I find out who, I'm going to sue them for everything they've got."

"Well, let's just take a look. Pop the hood." Lester got out of the car and opened the hood. "You're right, Son. All the electrical wires have been cut."

"Damn." Avis kicked the tire and dialed 911 on his cell phone.

* * *

"Dispatch. This is Karen."

"Hi, Karen, this is Lori. I work over here at the Moose Lodge."

227

"Hi, Lori, what can we do for you tonight."

"Well, there's these two creepy guys outside. I just saw one of them try and break into a motor home and attack two crippled, old ladies."

"Are the ladies okay?"

"Yeah, I think they got away."

"Where are the men right now?"

"They're in front of the Lodge sitting in a black Mercedes. Hurry, please!"

"I've got officers on the way."

"Okay, thanks."

* * *

"Nice job, Bernie. I didn't know you had it in you."

"I didn't either. Do you think they saw which way we went?"

"Don't matter. They won't be going anywhere any time soon." Grandy laughed. "Guess we showed them, huh, Grandma."

"Yeah." Bernice gave Grandy a high-five. Ditch jumped up in Bernice's lap and this time she didn't mind. All was well with their little world until...

"What's that noise?" asked Grandy.

"What noise?"

"Listen. Didn't you hear that?"

"Oh my gosh, Grandy! It's Rain! We forgot to give Rain back to Dakota!"

"I didn't forget. You did. You're the babysitter."

"What are we going to do? We have to turn around and bring him back."

"Are you daft? We can't turn around. I'll give Dakota a call after we've gotten down the road and I'm sure nobody is following us. Now go back there and do your job. Feed him, change him, burp him, or whatever you need to do. Just take good care of my grandson." Grandy turned her attention back to the task of getting away.

Bernice sighed as she headed towards the bedroom, thinking that the adventures she had experienced so far were just a tiny morsel compared to what she and her roommate were about to encounter.

* * *

ACKNOWLEDGMENTS

First and foremost, we would like to thank our Lord, Jesus Christ, for bringing us together and keeping our friendship strong through all of life's peaks and valleys; for the joy and laughter we shared while "working" on this book; and for our great anticipation of the sequel.

Of course, Tami thanks her husband David for his immeasurable patience, support, and love. He has given her inspiration and renewed her enthusiasm for writing. Most of all, he taught her how to laugh again.

Dona thanks her husband, Bob, for choosing her to be his Queen for life and for his never ending love and support.

Tami would like to thank Becky and Justin Carter, her children; her heart; as well as her parents, Bonnie and David Krinke, for a lifetime of humor. Whatever talent she has she knows it comes from them and God. She also thanks Janet and Mike Riedeman for their son, for proofreading the manuscript, and for loving the animal grand babies.

Thank you, Tony Kilgallin, for your guidance through the process, and for your kind words.

Thank you, Leonore Wilson, for sharing your priceless knowledge, editorial expertise and encouraging words.

To Neil Magnuson, we appreciate your honesty and input; it helped keep us on track.

Lauana Nelson, we thank you for capturing our imagination through your artwork.

Thank you to all of our friends and family, too numerous to mention here by name, who shared their ideas along the journey.

And to Bob Barker for 35 years of entertaining the world on *The Price is Right,* Happy Retirement!